THE APOSTROPHE
THIEF

THE APOSTROPHE THIEF

A Mystery with Marian Larch

Barbara Paul

Charles Scribner's Sons
New York

Maxwell Macmillan Canada
Toronto

Maxwell Macmillan International
New York   Oxford   Singapore   Sydney

Charles Scribner's Sons   Maxwell Macmillan Canada, Inc.
Macmillan Publishing Company   1200 Eglinton Avenue East
866 Third Avenue   Suite 200
New York, NY 10022   Don Mills, Ontario M3C 3N1

Macmillan Publishing Company is part of the Maxwell Communication Group of
Companies.

Library of Congress Cataloging-in-Publication Data
Paul, Barbara.
    The apostrophe thief/Barbara Paul.
        p.   cm.
    ISBN 0-684-19553-4
    I. Title.
    PS3566.A82615A85   1993
    813'.54—dc20   93-16109

Macmillan books are available at special discounts for bulk purchases for sales promotions, premiums, fund-raising, or educational use. For details, contact:

                        Special Sales Director
                        Macmillan Publishing Company
                        866 Third Avenue
                        New York, NY 10022

10 9 8 7 6 5 4 3 2 1

Printed in the United States of America

THE APOSTROPHE
THIEF

1

When she woke up the next morning, Holland was gone. Breathing a sigh of relief, she padded barefoot through her apartment, praying he hadn't left her *a little note* somewhere.

He hadn't.

The shower head was turned to its strongest massage setting and the hot water pounded at her. She stood motionless under the barrage, wondering at the sheer animal need that had overtaken the two of them last night. He might as well have been a stranger; she'd never gotten inside his head, didn't truly know him. She didn't always like him, even. Holland was a curious man, very private, thought highly of himself, downright condescending at times. A cutting, sarcastic sense of humor, if humor was what it was.

The two of them had been thrown together almost against their wills—working allies, the FBI and the NYPD, joined by necessity, until last night when it had all come to a head. They'd turned to each other for . . . reassurance? Validation? For confirmation of some treasured cliché such as *Life goes on*? They'd needed something, and they'd needed it desperately.

Because he had killed a man, and she'd helped him do it.

A quick shampoo and she stepped out of the shower. The ventilator wasn't working properly and steam had fogged up the mirror; she rubbed a clear place with her fist and stared at her reflection. By no stretch of the imagination could she be called pretty; "plain" was the kindest adjective that came to mind. Always that same undistinguished face staring back at her. Plain yesterday, plain today, plain tomorrow. "But so was Jane Eyre," she said aloud. And *she* had ended up with Mr. Rochester.

Yes, Jane and her Mr. Rochester had lived happily ever after. *But only after he had been symbolically castrated.* Not your standard romantic ending.

The man she'd spent the night with had his own kind of trouble. The killing had been self-defense . . . but no one would ever believe that, not in a million years. He and the man he'd killed openly hated each other, had done so for years. No one who knew the two of them would ever think that the shooting had been in the line of duty—which it was. She'd been there, she'd seen. She'd helped Holland get hold of the gun that got them both out of there alive. But even with her testimony to back him up, he had too long a history of doing things outside the limits of the strictly legal to escape arrest and trial. And because of that, she was going to live with a lie for the rest of her life.

So, live with it, she told herself as she toweled her hair. When the time for accounting came, she had taken the credit/blame for shooting the criminal they'd tracked down together; no one would suspect *her* of eliminating a personal enemy. It all boiled down to one thing: she could take the heat, he couldn't. And take it she would; he'd saved her life last night.

She dressed hastily and strapped on her service revolver, completing the picture of who she was: Sergeant Marian Larch, NYPD detective. For a little while longer, at any rate.

It was nine o'clock and she was already an hour late. No sweat; no one was going to be yelling at her today. For a while, at least, she'd be the fair-haired girl of the Ninth Precinct. Marian figured she had about a week before the memory of last night's spectacular shoot-out began to fade, and by then she'd be gone. This was her last week as a cop. She had had it, she was fed up, she was *through*.

She was through working with a partner whose incompetence had endangered her more than once. No more spending the productive part of her life in a profession that had turned so sour that even its ablest practitioners no longer felt they could make a difference—a *practical* difference, not the idealistic, save-the-world, rookie-cop kind of difference. And no more putting her ass on the line to make some double-dealing bureaucrat of a precinct captain look good to his superiors.

Enough.

Marian wanted to walk in that very morning and announce her resignation, but too many loose ends were trailing about. Her hair still damp, she pulled on a raincoat and ran to her car; a gray, icy drizzle more suited to November than September was coming down. And it was Monday; oh yes, it was *very* Monday. On the drive to East Fifth Street she rehearsed her story. Tell the truth about everything that happened except who actually pulled the trigger. Lie about that. Lie like crazy.

She'd have to face down Internal Affairs. And the FBI would want a debriefing, since it had been a joint Bureau–Ninth Precinct investigation. She could handle that, presumably; but facing the precinct captain was another story. Somehow she'd have to find a way to keep herself from tearing his eyes out. How could *he* face *her?* He would, though; the man had no shame. Ambition, and industrial-strength self-interest, and a cunning ability to turn every situation to his personal advantage. But no shame.

The icy drizzle hadn't stopped when she pulled into the parking lot across the street from the Ninth Precinct stationhouse. It was the same lot where only a short time ago Marian and Captain DiFalco had gotten into a shouting match, where he'd threatened her with career death if she didn't fall into line. If Marian hadn't already made up her mind she was finished being a cop, that little scene would have convinced her.

Inside, a solicitous greeting from the desk sergeant, sympathetic murmurs or overhearty hellos from a few uniformed officers. Up the stairs to the Police Detective Unit room, queries of *Are you all right?* and a friendly hand or two on her shoulder. They all knew she had killed a man the night before, or thought they knew. They also "knew" it was her first—always traumatic, sometimes insurmountably so. Marian didn't know what it felt like to kill a man, but she did know what it felt like to be a hypocrite, garnering so much undeserved sympathy.

"How you doin'?" Detective Gloria Sanchez stood before her, concern written on her face.

"I'm doing just fine, Gloria," Marian said. "Don't you worry about me." *Please* don't worry about me.

"I wish you'd let me go home with you last night. You shouldn't have been alone."

I wasn't alone. "It's all right. I'm sorry it ended in a killing," but I'm not lacerating myself about it."

"That's cool. That's real cool. It had to end the way it did—you didn't have no choice."

"No."

Marian sat down at her desk, aware that her partner at the next desk was watching her out of the corner of his eye. "So you got him," Foley said low so only she could hear. "You must be feeling pleased with yourself." Resentful.

"Yes, to both."

He let his anger show and he forgot about keeping his voice

down. "You couldn't call me, could you? It'd really burn your ass to call me! You just had to keep the kill all to yourself."

Marian didn't expect understanding from her partner, but he was being even more stupid than usual. "That's sick, Foley! I didn't know I was going to have to shoot him." *Nor that anybody would.* "He was trying to kill us."

"Us? Oh yeah, you and your FBI buddy—how could I forget? You doin' all your work with the FBI now, Larch? Ninth Precinct not good enough for you anymore?" He pointed a crooked finger at her. "You should have called me, you fucking glory hog."

Marian stared at her partner. Foley was symptomatic of all the things that were so wrong in her job that she simply couldn't stomach it any longer. Ineptitude, laziness, bad attitude, lack of concern—they were all spelled *Foley.* "Why should I call you?" she asked him in a reasonable tone of voice. "You've already put me in jeopardy a couple of times by failing to back me up when you should have. You whine and you bellyache and you don't do a lick of work you don't have to do. You jump to conclusions and never check things out unless you're made to. You're never where you're supposed to be when you're supposed to be there. You're a menace to anybody you're partnered with, and you've always got an excuse. You're a bad cop, Foley, and you're never going to be any better than you are right now. That's why I didn't call you."

The room had fallen dead silent. No cop ever told another cop he was bad at his job, at least not in front of other cops; Marian herself would never have said what she did if she'd been planning to stay on. The faces of the other detectives in the room reflected a mixture of shock and reluctant agreement with her assessment of Foley's abilities. Pleasurable scandal. *Great* way to start the week.

Foley's face went dark purple. "Who the hell do you think you're talking to, you bitch? You sleep your way to that sergeant's badge and you come in here and—"

"Knock it off, Foley," someone said.

"Yeah, Foley, watch it," Sanchez added. "Remember what she's been through."

Marian sighed. "Thanks for riding to my defense, Gloria, but don't make excuses for me. Let it stand. I meant every word." Change the subject. "Is Captain DiFalco in?"

"Yep, making important phone calls, he sez. Do Not Disturb."

But Foley wasn't that easy to shut up. "You think you're riding high, don't you? But you're gonna get your ass kicked, Larch, that's what's gonna happen. You acted against orders and DiFalco's not gonna let that pass. You may even lose your badge."

"She stopped a killer, for Christ's sake," Sanchez said. "She's gonna get a citation!"

He muttered an obscenity and turned his back on them. Marian didn't give a damn what Foley thought; a few more days and she'd never have to look at his sneering face again. She winked at Sanchez as she rolled some forms into the old mechanical typewriter and started making out the report on how *she* had shot a wanted felon in self-defense. Marian was halfway through when her phone rang; Captain DiFalco wanted her in his office.

She was calm and distantly curious as she got up from her desk, wondering how DiFalco was going to handle it. He'd ordered her to lay off the investigation and she'd gone on with it, drawing in others to help her whose services she had no authority to commandeer. And in doing so she'd committed the worst offense possible: she'd proved herself right and her superior wrong. Captains didn't like being shown up by sergeants.

Last night when the shooting was over, DiFalco had gone before the TV cameras and taken credit for the resolution of the case, claiming Marian had been acting under his orders all along. Was that to be the deal—DiFalco would take no punitive action if she kept her mouth shut? Or would he follow through with his threats to make sure her career was at a dead end? Not that it mattered either way; Marian would listen, and nod, and hand in her resignation in a few days' time. And then she'd send registered letters to the Zone Commander, the Borough Commander, and the Chief of Operations, all of them aimed at exposing DiFalco's lies.

Whoa. That would sound as if she'd resigned in a fit of pique because DiFalco stole her thunder; whatever she said would be dismissed as sour grapes. This needed more thought.

Captain DiFalco was on the phone when she stepped into his office. He pointed to a chair, finished his conversation, and hung up. "Glad you're here—shooflies are on their way over. I didn't expect you before noon."

"Loose ends need tying up."

"Yah." He thought a minute. "The thing is not to get angry," he said. "They'll try to provoke you, bug you into blurting out something or contradicting yourself." He stared up at the ceiling. "It's IA's job to try to trip you up."

"I know," she answered. "I've had a brush with Internal Affairs before. A detective at Police Headquarters was being investigated." Where she'd worked before being transferred to the Ninth Precinct.

"Investigated for what?"

"For accepting bribes. There was nothing to it—some dealer he'd arrested tried to get a little payback by accusing him of being on the take. Still, IA made everybody connected feel like dirty corrupt sleazescum not worth wiping their feet on . . . even those of us who were just witnesses."

DiFalco was nodding, his eyes unfocused. "That's Internal Affairs, all right. Look, they'll be talking to you in Baxter's office. Just tell it straight, answer their questions as briefly as possible, and don't volunteer anything."

"All right. I thought Lieutenant Baxter was getting back from vacation today."

"He's back. But IA asked for a private room and that's it. After they finish with you, they're going to talk to Holland. I sure as hell hope your stories jibe."

"They will." Unreasonably, she resented the casual way the captain tossed off the name.

"Then you've got no problem. It was a righteous kill, Larch. They have to investigate, but they got nothing." A pause. "You holding up all right?"

Marian was bemused by this new solicitous attitude on the captain's part. Was this the way he was going to play it—they just weren't going to *mention* anything wrong between them? They were going to pretend she hadn't acted against orders and he hadn't grabbed the credit for her work? DiFalco hadn't looked her straight in the eye once since she'd come in.

Marian told him she was holding up as well as could be expected. "Where is Holland? Is he here?"

"Coming in at eleven. The FBI wants to talk to you too. They're going to keep you and Holland separated until you've made your statements." Still not looking her in the eye. "Are you sure the two of you are telling the same story?"

"I'm sure."

"Good. There's one more thing. You're going to have to see the police psychiatrist"

"Captain—"

"It's mandatory, Larch, you know that. You're involved in a shooting, you see the psychiatrist. You have to convince him you're fit to return to duty. Can you do that?"

"Oh, I suppose. I'm not suicidal, if that's what he's looking for."

"I don't know what the hell he's looking for. Play it by ear. But make him see you're handling it. You've got a three o'clock appointment—the FBI should be finished with you by then."

Marian wasn't thinking about the psychiatrist or the FBI as much as she was about DiFalco. The conversation seemed to be over, so she got up and left. DiFalco was playing for time, most likely, waiting to see whether she was going to make waves or not. Ha! She'd show him waves. Get a life*jacket*, Captain.

Foley got up and left his desk when he saw her coming back. Marian sank down in her chair dispiritedly. Her so-called partner and her two-faced captain—the two people who should be her closest allies, and both were enemies. DiFalco was interested only in making the right career moves, and Foley . . . Foley wasn't interested in anything. Neither of them should be a cop. Yet they were staying and she was leaving.

Marian found a note on her desk in Gloria Sanchez's handwriting: *Kelly called.* Marian frowned. She should have phoned her friend, early, before Kelly had time to see the news. Yet she was reluctant to call even now. Marian didn't mind lying to her police superiors, since they weren't going to be her superiors much longer. But lying to Kelly . . . that was hard.

"Sanchez!" said a new voice. "You and Roberts—in my office." The speaker was a stocky, hoarse-voiced man doing his best to look and sound tough; the results were spectacularly unsuccessful, especially as he was wearing a necktie decorated with mermaids.

Sanchez groaned. "I was thinking of taking some personal time."

"Take it tomorrow," said the hoarse growl. "Smash-and-grab on Tenth Street, an electronics store. Same MO as the others, but this time a bystander was hurt."

"I worked late last night!"

"Unauthorized overtime, the way I hear it." He looked down at Marian. "And you've been busy, too, Larch. Congratulations on a good shoot."

"Hello, Lieutenant," Marian said. "Enjoy your vacation?"

"I never enjoy my vacations," Lieutenant Baxter replied, "because I know every time I go away something is going to happen here. It never fails! I take even one day off, something happens."

Marian was tempted to say something happened there *every* day, whether he was there or not. "Hazard of the profession."

"Got your report on last night made out?"

"Working on it now."

"Don't leave anything out, Larch. That report's going to both Internal Affairs and the FBI, and they'll be looking for mistakes. Be *very* careful."

"I always am, Lieutenant."

"Good." Baxter looked around. "Where's Roberts?"

"Right here," Gloria Sanchez's partner said from behind him.

"Let's go." The lieutenant chugged off toward his office, the two detectives trailing behind.

Sanchez looked back over her shoulder. "Don't forget to call Kelly."

Marian nodded, but decided to finish her report first. When she was done, she read it through three times, searching for mistakes or omissions. It looked okay to her. She signed and dated it and turned it in.

Foley still hadn't come back. Just as well; she didn't want

him listening in on a private conversation, especially one in which she was going to lie to her closest friend. Marian squared her shoulders and tapped out Kelly Ingram's number. Kelly picked up the receiver on the first ring. "Before you say a word," Marian spoke hastily, "I'm all right. I wasn't hurt, and I'm not wallowing in guilt. Do you hear me, Kelly? I'm *all right.*"

A big sigh floated over the line. "You really truly honestly *are* all right?"

"Really truly honestly."

"Maybe it hasn't hit you yet?"

"Oh, it's hit me, no mistake about that." Marian took a deep breath and elaborated on the lie. "Kelly, it's something I've always known could happen sooner or later, and I was as prepared for it as anyone reasonably could be. I knew last night would be dangerous, and I braced myself for it going in." Her mouth tasted sour.

The seconds ticked off silently. It was the calm before the storm: *"You could have been killed!"* Kelly shouted. "He could have shot you! He could have shot you and Holland and anybody else he felt like shooting! How *dare* you take this so calmly! Why aren't you a basket case? Why aren't you screaming and hollering and pounding your fists on your desk? And what do you mean, you *prepared* yourself? How can you prepare yourself for killing someone? This whole thing is *unnatural,* and aren't you glad I called to cheer you up?"

Marian laughed in spite of herself. "I called *you.*"

"I called first. Marian, why did *you* have to go after him? Of all the cops there are in this city, why did it have to be *you?*" Her voice broke. "You could have been killed."

Aw. "Hey, Kel, listen. It's over. Put it out of your mind."

"Easier said than done." A sound something like a snuffle came over the line. "Can you get free for lunch? Or dinner?"

"Dinner. What time do you have to be at the theater?"

"No performance tonight—Monday, remember? The director's called us in this afternoon to smooth out a few rough spots, but we should be finished by six. Seven at the latest. How about seven-thirty at Sonderman's?"

"I'll be there. And Kelly, don't feel bad. There's no need, I promise you. Hold on a sec." Her thorn-in-the-side partner had come up to her desk and was grinning evilly at her. "What, Foley?"

"Shooflies want you. In the lieutenant's office."

Marian's stomach knotted; she wasn't as ready for this as she thought. "Gotta go, Kelly. See you at seven-thirty."

When she'd hung up, Marian took a moment to compose herself. She hoped Holland appreciated what she was going through to keep his neck off the block. Hold it . . . not fair. It had been her idea to take the responsibility for the shooting; Holland had been ready to face the music when she stepped in, diverting official attention from him toward herself. *It was your choice; now get yourself together.*

Temporarily kicked out of his own quarters, Lieutenant Baxter was busying himself at a file cabinet and sneaking looks at her out of the corner of his eye. Marian stood up and walked purposively toward Baxter's office, steeling herself for her confrontation with Internal Affairs.

2

Her interrogation by Internal Affairs was indeed high-sweat, but not the devastating ordeal she'd expected. It was a given that cops had the right to kill to save their own lives; the two men from IA were interested only in nailing down the fact of self-defense. Marian was one of their own and if she had indeed been threatened, no censure would result.

The two IA men, named Connelly and Reed, had her go over her account of the previous night's events again and again, giving her every opportunity to contradict herself or slip up in some other way. They asked questions, they wanted details of things she hadn't even noticed, they made her relive the scene minute by painful minute. But Marian stuck to her story, which was truthful except for that one minor matter of who actually did the shooting.

There was one sticky moment. Marian told them she'd been acting independently, that Captain DiFalco had, in fact, pulled her off the case. "He thought he had it solved, you see," she explained. It was only when she'd proved him wrong that he stepped forward and claimed Marian had been following his orders all along.

The Internal Affairs men were interested, in an unofficial way; Connelly even appeared amused. "DiFalco lied?"

"He lied." No elaboration necessary.

Connelly barked a laugh. "Doesn't surprise me. DiFalco could get something for himself out of an earthquake."

But Reed didn't find it amusing. "Sergeant, did somebody hear him order you off the case? Was anyone else around?"

Marian thought back. "No, we were alone."

"Any paperwork? Anything in writing to show he pulled you off?"

"Nothing."

"Then it's the word of a sergeant against the word of a captain?" Reed spread his hands. "Not good, Larch, not good. Better be careful what you say."

Marian felt like a fool. In anticipating the pleasure of exposing DiFalco, she'd never considered the possibility that she might not be believed. Reed was right; the word of a captain would be taken over that of one of his subordinates. She shook her head angrily. Too much trauma in the last twenty-four hours; she wasn't thinking straight.

But Internal Affairs wasn't probing into Ninth Precinct politics and the two men had Marian go over her story one more time. Eventually they were satisfied and told her she could go. "All we need is Holland's corroboration and it'll go down as a righteous kill," Connelly said. "We ought to be able to wrap this thing up today." He gave her an encouraging smile. "That was good shooting, Sergeant."

So it was over. As she got up to leave Lieutenant Baxter's office, it occurred to Marian that the interrogation would have gone even more smoothly without the complicating presence of the FBI. They would be checking into what happened every bit as thoroughly as Internal Affairs. It was the joint police–FBI investigation that had thrown Holland and her together in the first place. Holland was an FBI agent—correction: *yesterday* Holland was an FBI agent, as dissatisfied with his job as Marian was with hers. Today he was . . . what? A free man? Unemployed? While Marian had only thought about resigning, he had actually done it.

So it was with her thoughts full of Holland that she opened the door and found herself face-to-face with the man himself. Two other men were with him—FBI, of course. A tired-looking Holland stared at her with eyes like dark bruises, and she felt a quick surge of that same craving that had propelled them toward each other the night before. Marian caught her breath and pushed the feeling down. Holland was pressing his lips together . . . doing the same thing?

But before either one of them could speak, one of the other men said, "Sergeant Larch? I'm Agent Greer, and I must inform you there's to be no communication between you and former agent Holland until this inquiry is completed. Do you understand?"

Irritated, she said, "Of course I understand."

"Then I must ask you to come back to Bureau headquarters with me. I've cleared it with your captain."

"Now?"

"Yes, please." So polite.

Holland gave her a wry half-smile and stepped into Lieutenant Baxter's office for his turn with Internal Affairs. The other FBI man followed him in.

"Do you have a raincoat?" Agent Greer asked. "Nasty out."

Marian collected her raincoat and handbag and followed him down to the parking lot. The cold drizzle hadn't let up; Marian shivered inside her coat. How could it turn cold that quickly? Yesterday had still been late summer.

Greer drove her to Federal Plaza and escorted her to an upstairs room of the FBI building. There he made a quick round of introductions and discreetly disappeared.

The room was larger than Lieutenant Baxter's office, and cleaner. Marian sat at a small conference table and calmly looked around at the not-new, not-old furniture, the flag in the corner, the President's picture on the wall. She felt detached from it all and even from herself, somehow not involved with this person who had come here to lie to the FBI.

This time her interrogators numbered four instead of two, but the procedure they followed was the same as the one she'd just been through. Tell the story, tell it again, now tell it a third time. Answer the questions, provide details, go over it once more. The only real difference from her session with Internal Affairs was that this time she did not mention she'd been acting on her own.

When it was over, the man who seemed to be in charge told her that her story corroborated Holland's. "We're satisfied that you did the shooting, and it was clearly self-defense." Unexpectedly, he snorted. "It's just that we had trouble believing Holland didn't execute an old enemy when he had the chance—I think he's capable of it. Between you and me, Sergeant, I'm glad Holland has resigned. He didn't really belong in the FBI."

Amen to that. "Then you're closing the case?"

"We'll need to consult with your Internal Affairs Division, but I see no reason to keep it open. As far as I'm concerned, this one is history. Agent Greer will drive you back. Thanks for your help, Sergeant. I'm sending a letter to your captain expressing appreciation for your cooperation—never hurts to have a few of those in your permanent file, hm?"

I get a cookie because I was good. Outside in the hallway, Greer was waiting to escort her downstairs to the car. On the way back to the Ninth Precinct Marian realized it was almost two and she'd missed lunch. The cold drizzle had stopped, but she still wanted something hot in her stomach. She asked

Greer to drop her at a small restaurant near the stationhouse. He waved a cheery goodbye and was gone.

Inside, Marian ordered a large bowl of chili and dug in. The place was crowded, so she had to share her table with a Texan—who, like all Texans, felt compelled to announce, "Real chili don't have beans." Marian finished her late lunch and left to keep her appointment with the police psychiatrist.

It was a strange session. The psychiatrist kept probing for guilt feelings, for signs of self-recrimination. Marian kept expressing regret over the shooting while being careful never to blame herself for creating the circumstances that made the shooting necessary. "It came down to him or me," she said, "which one of us was going to walk out of there alive. I wasn't about to let myself be killed when I had the means of stopping him."

Evidently that was the right thing to say; the psychiatrist gave her a clean bill of health and told her to call him if ever she felt the need to talk. She thanked him for his understanding, feeling more like a hypocrite than ever, and headed back to the stationhouse.

Captain DiFalco was not in his office. Just as well, since protocol required her to report to the lieutenant first, though what she was doing worrying about protocol at this stage of the game was beyond her. Lieutenant Baxter's door was open; he motioned her in. "So? How did it go?"

"Okay—not as bad as I thought it'd be." She sank down into the chair at the side of his desk. "The FBI's satisfied it was self-defense, but they were more interested in making sure I was the one who did the shooting than anything else. But they want to consult with Internal Affairs before they close the case."

"Then your problems are over," Baxter said, "because I just got a call from IA. They're calling it a righteous kill. It's official."

She let out a breath she hadn't known she was holding. The lie had been accepted. "Hallelujah."

"Yeah—big relief, huh? Congratulations. You did good, Larch."

"Lieutenant, I want to take some personal time tomorrow. The whole day."

Baxter was interrupted by the phone before he could answer. Marian tuned out the one-sided conversation. She wanted some time off just to think. DiFalco had outmaneuvered her, every step of the way. She'd had some vaguely formed vision of solving her last case as a cop (by acting against orders), then flinging the results at DiFalco's obtuse head and marching out in a blaze of glory. But the good captain had hopped on her glory train before she'd even noticed, and the IA man, Reed, had made her see that simply accusing DiFalco of being a liar and a fraud wasn't enough. She knew she should just walk away . . . forget DiFalco and her useless partner Foley and everything else that was wrong, forget the entire Ninth Precinct. But it galled her, like leaving a case unsolved.

Marian was distracted from her musing by the sight of Baxter prissily patting the curls on the top of his head. It was a mannerism that everyone in the station had laughed at, one time or another. Gloria Sanchez said he did it to reassure himself his hair was still there. Baxter was a pencil pusher, a paper-shuffler, a maker of lists. Nothing gave the lieutenant so much pleasure as the keeping of records. And he kept good records, Marian had to give him that; his obsession with written data had saved the Detective Unit a lot of grief. No perp arrested in the Ninth ever walked because of fouled-up paperwork, and that was Baxter's doing.

The lieutenant hung up the phone and turned back to Marian. "You were saying . . . ?"

"Personal time. Tomorrow."

"Oh yeah. Sure. Take a week if you want—as much time as you need."

Marian raised an eyebrow.

Baxter grinned. "Instructions from Captain DiFalco. 'Give her whatever she wants,' he said. You could probably ask for the moon right now and get it."

She sighed. "Well, maybe two days. I'll call in tomorrow."

He cocked his head at her. "Are you all right? I mean, are you all *right?*"

"Just tired, mostly. But I do need some time to myself."

"Then take it. Take whatever you need to get yourself back together. A screwed-up cop is no use to anybody."

Gee, thanks, Lieutenant. Marian thought that an appropriate note to leave on. She went back into the Detective Unit room and sat down at her desk. For a long moment she stared at the typewriter, wondering what she was doing there. It wasn't four yet, the end of her shift; but she couldn't think of any reason to hang around. The only one there she'd care to talk to was Gloria Sanchez, and Gloria was out on a case. So was Foley, thank god. Marian gathered up her things; but before leaving the building, she wanted another look into DiFalco's office. This time, he was there.

She stepped inside and closed the door behind her. "We need to talk."

"Did Baxter tell you IA's calling it a clean shoot?" he said hurriedly. "They didn't even—"

"Captain. Let's stop this pussyfooting around and get it out in the open. You pulled me off the case and I went ahead with it anyway. Then when I wrapped it up, you stepped in and pretended I was acting under your orders. That makes me disobedient and you a fake."

"What are you talking about? I never pulled you off the case."

Marian stared at him with her mouth open. "Are you telling me you don't remember that shouting match we had in the parking lot? When you threatened me with every little dirty job that came along if I didn't fall into line?"

DiFalco waved a hand dismissively. "Oh, that. Look, we were both angry and saying things we didn't mean—"

"I meant it."

"All right, I lost my cool, I admit it—Jesus, didn't that ever happen to you? But you were never off the case. God, if I knew that's what you were thinking—"

"I see." Marian let her disgust show. "You didn't really mean it."

"Yah, that's right—I thought you understood that." DiFalco didn't look the least uncomfortable at telling such a whopper. He knew she knew he was lying, she knew he knew she knew . . . "Hey, I'm sorry for this little misunderstanding, but everything worked out okay, didn't it?"

Little misunderstanding. "No, Captain. Everything is not okay. I have no intention of working under these conditions—"

"Hold it. Whatever you're going to say—don't. You look and sound composed, but I know you can't be. Killing a man . . . that screws you up inside. I know, happened to me once. Go home, unbend. Take a vacation. Do something physical, work it off."

"Don't you patronize me!" she snapped. "We'd be having this conversation whether I shot a man or not, and I'll not have you pretending it's because I'm 'screwed up' inside. *You're* the one that's screwed up."

"Wait a minute. I'm going to overlook that, because I know you're under stress. Let me show you something." He pawed through the papers on his desk and came up with a carbon of a letter. "Read this."

She took the carbon copy, still standard at the uncomputerized Ninth. It was a letter to the Commissioner in which DiFalco endorsed Marian for a commendation. He gave full credit to her; he said she organized and directed the investigation and brought the case to a satisfactory conclusion even at risk to her own life. Unstated but still implied was that all these wonderful things were done under the ever-watchful eye of Captain DiFalco himself.

Marian wadded the flimsy paper into a tiny ball and flicked it lazily toward DiFalco. "You insult me, Captain," she said, "to think you can buy me off that cheaply."

That didn't come out exactly the way she meant it, implying as it did that she could be bought off at a higher price. But it made as good an exit line as any. She left.

Marian and Holland watched each other warily across the tiny table in Sonderman's bar. He'd shown up at her apartment just as she was leaving to meet Kelly Ingram for dinner and proceeded to invite himself along for drinks. Marian could have told him no, but didn't.

Holland asked, "Do you feel as if you've been x-rayed, CAT-scanned, fluoroscoped, spectroscoped, blood-tested, Geiger-counted, and mind-read? Your Internal Affairs was even more thorough than the Bureau's boys. I wish you hadn't had to go through that."

Marian shrugged. "It's over now, and everyone's satisfied. It could have been worse."

"Still." He took a swallow of his drink; the table was so small that his knees were pressed against hers.

"All day long people have been asking me if I'm all right," she said, "but I doubt that anyone has asked you. Are you?"

He made an ambiguous sound. "I'll live."

There was something she had to know. "Is this the first time you've had to shoot someone?"

His eyes flickered. "No." A short silence followed. Then: "I will find some way to repay you. Somehow."

"It's not necessary."

"Yes, it is. I don't like owing people."

"I'm not *people*, Holland. And you can repay me by not letting it bother you."

He nodded in acknowledgment of her point, and then gave her a sardonic smile. "No. You are definitely not *people*."

They had quickly reached a point where their talk could veer into either intimacy or distance; Marian chose distance. "What are you going to do, now that you're out of the FBI?"

"I haven't decided yet. What are you going to do when you resign from the police force?"

She stared at him in astonishment. "How did you know I was going to resign? The only one I told was Kelly!"

"It's written all over you. Do you have anything planned?"

She shook her head. "I'm taking a couple of days off, just to think." She made a face. "Right now I'm looking for a way to thumb my nose at Captain DiFalco when I walk."

"Ah, yes. Go out with a bang, not a whimper. But after you've made your nose-thumbing gesture, you might consider going into business with me."

That surprised her. "Doing what?"

He raised a hand. "Private investigation. It's what we're best suited for."

She was surprised again; surely he didn't think . . . "You can't just open an office and declare yourself a private investigator. Your FBI time could fill the three-year apprenticeship requirement, but you still have to take the exam. . . ." She stopped when Holland waved a hand dismissively.

"I already took care of that," he said, "years ago." When she looked skeptical, he pulled out his billfold.

Marian examined a current New York private investigator's license in the name of Curt Holland. "That's legit, all right.

You kept your private license up-to-date all the time you were in the FBI?"

Wry smile. "You never know what might come in handy. So, what do you think about opening an office together? I can handle the computer fraud cases, and you can do the hard work."

She smiled. "Tell me how that's an improvement."

"We choose our own clients. We charge a great deal of money. We control our working environment. And if you find me impossible to work with—well, we'll orchestrate something we both can live with. Just tell me you'll think about it."

"All right, I'll think about it." She looked at her watch. "What time is Kelly supposed to be here?"

"Right now. She's usually prompt."

Holland finished his drink. "Want another? No? How long have you and Kelly known each other?"

"A little over three years, but it seems longer."

His eyes narrowed. "How much does she know about last night?"

Marian looked at those narrowed eyes, the defensive body posture. "I told her nothing. She knows nothing about either of the two things that happened last night."

Holland's face relaxed. "I'm sorry. I should have known without asking." He moved one foot under the table, closer to hers.

"It was the hardest thing I had to do all day, lying to Kelly. Internal Affairs and the FBI were a piece of cake compared to that."

He nodded. "And you say I don't owe you."

Feeling perverse, she said, "I may just tell her you spent the night."

He smiled his mocking smile. "I think the usual response is, 'Are you bragging or complaining?'"

Marian wasn't about to touch that one. "Relax. Kelly and I don't gossip about men."

"Hm. What does a Broadway star gossip about? I know very few show people."

"The business, most of the time. Show biz people, backstage stuff."

"What's the name of her play again?"

"The Apostrophe Thief."

"Right. You know, they say the depth of performers' insecurities can be measured by the size of their entourages. The more people they keep around them, the more precarious they feel their position to be—ah, here's your friend now."

Kelly had come alone.

Marian waved an arm to catch her attention. The bar was crowded, but, as usual, the crowds parted to let Kelly Ingram pass—a trick that always left Marian open-mouthed. Kelly didn't say a word but wrapped both arms around Marian in a big hug. It should have been awkward, with hugger standing and huggee seated, but Kelly brought it off with her usual grace. "You *are* all right, aren't you?" Kelly asked. "I can tell."

"Of course I am," Marian said. "I told you not to worry."

"Sit here," Holland said, offering Kelly his seat. "I'll find another chair." He went off in search of one.

"Whoo, these tables are little," Kelly said as she sat down. "You and Holland must have been playing kneesies. Is he having dinner with us?"

"No, he just came for a drink."

Kelly reached out and took Marian's hands. "When you first told me you were through being a cop, I thought you were out of your mind. But now I think it's a damned good idea. Quit. Right now."

Marian had to smile. "This is my last week."

"You can get killed in a week."

"Nothing's going to happen—I'll not be taking any new cases. Kelly, the danger . . . that was always part of the job."

"Yeah, and you're so cool and above it all you make me ill. Knowing about the danger and seeing it so close to home are two different things. I don't understand how anyone can live with so much tension all the time!"

"Oh, I got used to that long—"

"I'm not talking about you, noodnik, I'm talking about me! *I'm* the one who can't stand the pressure!"

Marian was laughing when Holland came back with a chair. "Well, you made her laugh," he said to Kelly. "That's more than I was able to do." He sat sideways at the small table.

A young couple came up to the table and asked Kelly for her autograph. When they'd left, Kelly turned to Holland. "So, Holland," she said, "how are you holding up?"

"Tolerably well."

"Tolerably, huh? No nightmares about what would have happened last night if Marian had missed? No shakes, no tremors?"

"None."

"No regrets?"

"Thousands."

Kelly obviously took his recalcitrance as a challenge; the two had known each other only a short while, and Kelly didn't yet realize that his speech patterns were not like other people's. "Holland, I don't know your first name. What is it?"

"Curt."

Marian watched Kelly biting back the obvious retort. "Okay, I'll call you Curt. And you can call me Your Majesty. I've always wanted somebody to call me Your Majesty."

He smiled at that. "Then I beg Your Majesty for leave to withdraw. Your dinner undoubtedly awaits."

"Permission granted. Although you're perfectly welcome to join us."

"Not this time." His eyes locked on to Marian's for a second, and then he was gone.

"Strange man," Kelly said. "And good-looking."

Marian's eyebrows rose. "Good-looking?"

Kelly's eyebrows did the same. "You don't think so?"

Marian shook her head. "I think he might have been good-looking some years back."

Kelly considered. "No, some years back he'd have been *pretty*. Now he's good-looking."

"Ah, me. And I just told him you and I never gossip about men."

"Then let's not. I'm starving! Is our table ready?"

It was.

3

Marian spent the night at Kelly's place, glad of the strange bed devoid of all emotional connection. She didn't know if Holland had tried to reach her late last night at her own apartment, and she didn't want to know. If he had, he was likely to take her absence as a rejection. She wasn't sure she meant it as such—but then she wasn't sure she didn't.

Both she and Kelly slept late, and it was close to noon by the time Marian got back to her own apartment. The first thing she did was change the bed sheets. The second thing she did was start a pot of coffee. She couldn't think without coffee.

As it turned out, she couldn't think *with* coffee, either. It seemed to her that somehow within the past twenty-four hours, her disgust with the entire law enforcement system had degenerated into a petty desire to get even with Captain DiFalco. Marian knew how that would go, if past experience was any indicator: that petty desire would dwindle even more and shame her by its very smallness, until the whole thing would slip away with nothing done about it.

Not good enough! She wanted the whole damned bureaucracy to understand *why* she was leaving . . . as if that would make any difference. The NYPD was not exactly waiting with bated breath to hear what Sergeant Marian Larch was going to do next. DiFalco's superiors were probably every bit as self-serving as he was, and they sure as hell weren't going to take action against him on her say-so. But something should be done about a man in a position of police authority whose interest in stopping crime could be measured by the degree it generated more of that authority for himself. A man who would ignore or deliberately misinterpret evidence if the results made him look good.

But maybe the entire hierarchy of police officialdom from the level of captain on up was populated by just such men as DiFalco. Career cops, not openly corrupt, but loving their power, jockeying for position among themselves. And she was going to change all that by pointing her finger at her captain when she left?

"God, what a child," Marian said to herself.

There, it had started already. The slipping-away.

She decided she needed a distraction, something unrelated to her problem that would demand her full concentration for a while. A play? Tuesday afternoon; no matinee. She went to a movie.

The film was advertised as a "psychological chiller"; what Marian was hoping for was an intricate plot with lots of complicated dialogue that would force her to pay attention. What she got was a succession of mood visuals, constantly flickering shadows, close-ups of nontalking heads, lingering shots of emblematic (and enigmatic) images—a dripping faucet, a horse's flaring nostrils, a withered flower stuck into a pencil sharpener. Marian left.

She stopped in a deli. The place was noisy; she tried eavesdropping on the other customers' conversations while she ate but quickly got bored. After a bit the noise began to bother her. She paid her bill and started walking aimlessly through the streets, even though the weather was chilly and a bit damp. After a block or so she stopped fighting it and let her mind wander.

But it wasn't Captain DiFalco who forced his way into her thoughts; it was Curt Holland. Marian relived their brief time in bed with a pleasure that astonished her; she still didn't understand why she was so attracted to a man about whom she knew so little. Yes, she did understand: it was glands calling to glands, nothing else.

Holland was what used to be called a computer "whiz"; at one time he'd used his considerable talents to collect otherwise uncollectable debts, on commission, by manipulating the electronic transfer of funds. The money he'd collected was all legitimately owed, but his manner of collecting was anything but legitimate. He could get into any bank record in the world; he could have stolen the country blind if he'd wanted to. The fact that he had not meant more to Marian than his strong-arm methods of collection. But that didn't quite eradicate her anger at knowing every bit of information about her on record—credit history, information about social security, her driving record, tax returns, purchases she'd made, anything at all—it was all there for the viewing, available to anyone with enough knowhow to access it.

The FBI had eventually caught on to Holland's lucrative-but-illicit debt-collection business. But instead of prosecuting, they'd pretty much shanghaied him into joining their ranks—because they'd needed his expertise. But now Holland was free of the Bureau and too smart to go back to his old line of work. He was thinking of setting up as a private investigator? Marian didn't know if he was serious about that, or even about his asking her to join him. He probably was; Holland wasn't given to joking around. They had worked well together on the case they'd just finished, in spite of some initial dislike and distrust—not all of which was totally dispelled.

But that was all she knew about the man. She didn't know where he was born, or when. She didn't know where he lived, or how to reach him. And she had no idea of what he'd done with his life before the FBI got interested in his sub rosa collection enterprise. He appeared to be in his early- to mid-forties but was probably younger; his was a face that looked aged by experience. But most of his life was a blank to her. Her instincts told her he was basically a decent man. But Marian was not as trusting of her instincts as once she'd been, especially when it came to choosing men. She'd made a couple of bad mistakes, and that still rankled. Now she was gun-shy.

She sniggered at her own double entendre. *Or maybe I'm finally learning from experience—yep, that's more like it!* "Gunshy, hell!" she said out loud.

"You tell 'em, *bébé!*" a Milli Vanilli look-alike said with a grin.

Startled, Marian laughed and lifted a hand in acknowledgment as he passed. Talking to herself now. And where the hell was she? She stopped walking and looked around to get her bearings. Bloomingdale's was across the street; she'd no idea she'd walked so far. A cold drizzle had started coming down; time to catch a bus and go home.

Back in her apartment, she checked her answering machine for messages. There was one. Holland's voice spoke the seven digits of a telephone number, which he followed with exactly four words: "If you want me."

Well, well. So now she did have a way to reach him. Marian wrote the number down on a Rolodex card.

If you want me.

A book she'd been meaning to read didn't do the trick, and Marian had nodded off. At 6:30 the phone woke her. "Wha'?"

"Marian, it's me," said Kelly's excited voice. "We've been robbed! All sorts of stuff is gone! Can you come? Right now?"

"Wait a minute." Marian wasn't fully awake. "Who's been robbed? Where?"

"All of us! Here at the theater! Come on, Marian—hurry!"

"I'll be right there."

She splashed water on her face and made a few passes at her hair with a brush. Then she shrugged into a raincoat and struggled with the buttons on the way down in the elevator.

No drizzle, praise be. Marian took the subway to Times Square and hurried along West Forty-fourth to the Broadhurst Theatre, where the marquee proclaimed that Broadway's newest hit, *The Apostrophe Thief*, was now playing. Marian flashed her badge at the ticket-taker and went inside.

The stage curtains were closed, but she could hear voices, many voices, all of them angry. She made her way behind the curtains to find pandemonium in full swing. The entire company seemed to be assembled on the stage; they were all talking at the tops of their voices, no one listening to anyone else. And no one paid the least attention to the presence of Sergeant Marian Larch among them.

Marian cleared her throat. "Could I have your attention, please?" A few people stopped talking and looked at her.

"Marian!" Kelly came running out from the opposite wing. "I'm so glad you're here! You've got to find him and make him give them back!"

"Give what back?"

"The scripts! Every single one of them has been taken! And my Bernhardt jacket! And—"

"The play scripts? All of them?"

"All of them! Mine and Ian's and Leo's and—"

"Whoa. When did you notice they were missing?"

"Just now, when we all got here. The scripts were here last night."

"Anything else taken?"

A male voice said, "My antique shaving mug."

"*All* my make-up," someone else contributed.

"Most of the stage props."

"And the costumes—they're gone! What are we going to *wear* tonight!"

"Hold it," Marian said in a commanding voice. "Is someone in charge here?"

"Leo Gunn, the stage manager," Kelly told her. "But he's on the phone right now calling costuming companies. If he can't get anything over here fast, we're going to have to go on in our street clothes."

"Where is he?" Marian looked where Kelly pointed, just long enough to know Leo Gunn the next time she saw him. "Where were the scripts kept?"

The cast members all kept their script copies in their dressing rooms, which were locked each night. Marian inspected one of the dressing room doors; it had been pried open with a crowbar. Not one of the more subtle burglars in town, then.

"Kelly, why are those scripts so important?" Marian asked. "You know all your lines—"

"Ah, well, you know. You might forget. And Abby might want to change something later."

"Even if I didn't," said a new voice, "there's the question of piracy."

Marian turned to see Abigail James approaching; *The Apostrophe Thief* was her play. Marian had met her once, briefly. "What about piracy?"

"Pirated copies circulate," the playwright said, "and other companies mount productions without paying royalties. Not a great deal of money is involved, but it's just another form of theft."

"Someone mentioned an antique shaving mug."

"That was Ian's. It belonged to his grandfather."

Ian Cavanaugh, she meant, the play's leading man. "Sounds more like souvenir-hunters to me," Marian said. "A star's personal possession? Just the sort of thing a fan would want. And didn't someone say that stage props were taken?"

"Mm, you may be right." Abigail James looked carefully around the stage. "The place is filled with expensive lighting equipment, but none of that was touched."

"But why *all* the scripts?" Marian mused.

"Leo had the master script," Kelly said, "the one with *all* the blocking written in—"

"Blocking?"

"Stage movement. And it had the lighting cues and things like that as well. Leo kept it chained to his desk, so nobody would wander off with it. But they took that one too. Cut right through the chain."

"Abby!" Ian Cavanaugh called from across the stage.

The playwright excused herself and left them. Marian said, "Kelly, you did call the police, didn't you?"

Her friend stared at her. "I called *you*. Oh lord, you didn't resign today, did you? I thought you were staying out the week!"

"No, it's not that. But this isn't my precinct. The Broadhurst is in Midtown South's jurisdiction. They're the ones who'll handle the investigation."

"But, but I thought *you* . . . "

Marian shook her head. "Where's a phone?"

"In my dressing room. Oh, hell. Look, I'll make the call. You go on and see how much you can find out. Midtown South, you say?"

"Just dial nine-one-one."

Muttering under her breath, Kelly headed toward her dressing room. Marian went in search of the stage manager. His desk was in fact a wide podium; a middle-aged woman was using his phone. Leo Gunn was talking to two young men she supposed were stagehands.

"Each of you take half the prop list," Gunn was saying, giving each man a sheet of paper; disturbingly, Gunn had a two-pronged hook in place of a right hand. "Don't waste time looking for exact matches. Like, if they don't have a black address book, get a brown one. Hell, get an orange one if that's all they have in stock. But get something, and get it fast. Go!" The two young men hurried away.

Marian stepped forward and identified herself. "Mr. Gunn, was anything of real monetary value taken?"

"Monetary value? Well, the costumes run high, but other than that . . . no, I guess not. But my copy of the script was invaluable to me—to the play, too. Now I've got to sit down and try to remember all the light and sound cues, or tonight's going to be a shambles." He scratched his neck with his mechanical hook. "Curtain's going to be late."

"Depending on when the stagehands get back with the props?"

"Stagehands? Oh—Mort and Pete. They're my assistants." Gunn grinned sourly. "Stagehands don't run errands. They don't do anything unless the union says so."

The woman on the phone hung up and said to the stage manager, "Essex says they can fit Ian Cavanaugh—they're sending over half a dozen suits right now. He's the only real problem. Shoulders are too big." She looked at Marian. "Who are you?"

Marian showed her badge and asked the same question, learning that the woman was the wardrobe mistress. Marian said, "Would you make me a list of the costumes that were stolen and their cost? Shoes, accessories, everything."

"Glad to. The biggest loss is the Bernhardt jacket . . . that's irreplaceable. I just hope those blasted thieves know what they got."

"Kelly mentioned a Bernhardt jacket," Marian said. "What is it exactly?"

"It's an ornamented jacket that once belonged to Sarah Bernhardt," the wardrobe mistress explained. "Our producer bought it at an auction in Paris. He was letting Kelly wear it for a little while, but eventually it'd go to a museum."

"Oh, what a shame. About that list . . . ?"

"I'll do it now, before those off-the-rack replacements start getting here." She hurried off.

"And I'd like a list of the missing props from you, Mr. Gunn."

He groaned. "The first night the properties master calls in sick. I just made out a list for my assistants—okay, I'll do it again."

"And I'd appreciate it if you could have everyone else gather on the stage for a moment. Which one is the director?"

"He isn't here yet. Anything else?"

Marian smiled sympathetically. "No, nothing else. I won't bother you any more."

That sour grin again. "Good. You know, short of planting a bomb in the theater, there's no better way of shutting down a show than by stealing all its small necessaries." He hurried away.

A *third possible motive?* Marian mused. Play piracy, or souvenir-hunting, or the intent to close *The Apostrophe Thief* before the natural end of its run? Which?

Leo Gunn didn't waste any time. In less than two minutes the cast, the playwright, and the stagehands were all assembled on the stage.

Marian moved to a spot where she was facing most of them and called for attention. "I'd like each of you to write down exactly what was taken from you—script, personal belongings, anything at all that's missing. List the dollar value if you know it. Then sign the list and give it to me. Please do it now, before the replacement costumes arrive."

"We're getting costumes?" someone asked.

"So I understand. Please go make out your lists now."

They all moved away purposefully. Giving them something to do might help settle them down a little, although Marian's real purpose was to save time for the detectives from Midtown South when they got there. Speaking of which . . .

She went to Kelly's dressing room. "You did call nine-one-one, didn't you?"

"Sure did," Kelly answered. "They said they'd get someone here as soon as they could." She signed her name with a flourish. "Here's my list."

Marian read it. "Script, hairbrush, lotion . . . a pair of old sneakers?"

"Very old. But comfortable as all get-out. I wore them during rehearsals a lot." A sigh. "But now they're gone." Kelly had listed their value as twenty-nine cents.

Why would a burglar take a worthless pair of sneakers? Marian went back out to the stage, where Abigail James handed her a sheet of paper with only her name written on it. "You lost nothing?"

"I keep nothing here." A wry smile. "The playwright doesn't merit a dressing room or an office."

"There are offices backstage?"

"One. The director uses it. Sergeant, we've met before, haven't we?"

"We have indeed. At the opening night party."

"Ah, I remember. You're the one who asked me about the meaning of the title." *The Apostrophe Thief,* she meant. "The only one to ask."

"Still?"

"Still."

Right then Ian Cavanaugh came up with his list. *Shoulders are too big,* the wardrobe mistress had said; they looked just fine to Marian. "Here you are, Sergeant. Truthfully, now, is there any chance of getting these things back?"

"Truthfully, not much," Marian admitted, reading his list. "Most of the items taken seem to be of negligible value, but maybe some of them will turn up. Antiques dealers can be notified about your shaving mug—uh, it's worth five thousand dollars?"

Abigail James laughed softly. "Oh, Ian."

"It's worth that to me," he said blandly. "Would it help if I offered a reward?"

"Doubtful," Marian told him. "The burglars took it not because of its intrinsic value, whatever that might be, but simply because it was there. They'll dispose of it the same way—casually."

The actor groaned. "That's what I was afraid you'd say. You know, something like this happened once before. Remember, Abby? That piece John directed a couple of years ago, the one that called itself a circus-drama?"

The playwright remembered. "You're right—I hadn't thought about that. It was Gerald Hemley's last play, ah, *Three Rings*, it was called." She frowned. "But only the scripts were taken then, I think John said."

"Who's John?" Marian asked.

"John Reddick, our director. He could tell you about *Three Rings*."

"Is there a Sergeant Larch here?" The voice that spoke belonged to a young black uniformed officer. He was followed by another officer, a jowly white man who seemed content to let his partner do the talking.

Marian identified herself. "Are you from Midtown South? Where's the detective in charge?"

The young black officer grinned at her. "Yeah, we're from Midtown South . . . and *you* are the detective in charge."

"What? I can't be—I'm Ninth Precinct."

"We're not fussy. What we are is a little short of manpower tonight, and the captain said as long as you're already on the scene—"

"Whoa—how did he know I was here? I don't even *know* your captain."

The officer's grin got bigger. "Well, it seems that the star of this here show called it in, and she made it *purr*-fectly clear that you have the sitcheation well in hand. Captain Murtaugh says tell you he'll clear it with your captain tomorrow. Now, what do you want us to do?"

Kelly.

Marian turned just in time to see her friend darting back to the safety of her dressing room. "You can arrest that woman," she growled.

4

The following morning found Marian once again sitting in Captain DiFalco's office. The captain was making a bad job of hiding how delighted he was with the current turn of events. *Wants me out of his hair until I cool down,* Marian thought. DiFalco kept up a steady line of talk aimed at keeping her from saying anything.

"Sorry about breaking in on your personal time like this," he said, looking anything but sorry, "but we didn't call you, Kelly Ingram did. Still, there's something to be said about getting back on the horse."

And you had to say it.

"The job at Midtown South won't last long. The theft of some playscripts and a few baubles isn't a high-priority crime. Go through the motions, do what you can. But don't sweat it."

I don't intend to.

"You'll report to Captain Murtaugh or his lieutenant—shit, what's his name? O'Bannion, O'Casey . . . another Mick, something starting with 'O.' But see Murtaugh, he'll give you your instructions. This is the first time Midtown South has borrowed one of our people . . . make us look good, Larch! Murtaugh won't keep you on it more'n two, three days. But the change'll be good for you."

And for you.

"Keep your eyes open while you're there, see what you can pick up. One thing I'm sure you've thought of." He actually winked at her, *us conspirators against the rest of them.* "You won't have to work with Foley."

Marian finally spoke. "I'll never work with Foley again."

"Hell, never say never. We'll work out something. I'm going to have a good talk with Foley while you're gone, straighten him out, make him see where he's falling short—"

Marian got up and walked out.

His voice followed her. "Hold it right there, Larch! You don't walk out on *me!*"

She kept on walking, right into the Police Detective Unit room. Foley was at his desk, ignoring her; fine. Marian had brought a cardboard box with her that morning; she set about clearing out her desk.

"Hey, mon, you movin' or somethin'?" Gloria Sanchez's Latina lilt floated across the room, more Sanchez today than Gloria. "The cap'n tol' us you'd be gone only a few days."

"I'm going for good, Gloria. I won't be back." She put a travel alarm, toothbrush and toothpaste, and a variety of headache medications into the cardboard box.

"What?" Foley's voice rasped, his attention now fully on Marian. "You're quitting?"

"No, wait a minute," Gloria said, her Hispanic persona forgotten in an instant. "It's a transfer, right? You've been assigned to Midtown South permanently?"

Marian shook her head. "It's just that I'm never going to work for that man"—she waved an arm toward DiFalco's office—"or *with* this man"—she looked at Foley—"again. Ever."

Gloria gasped. Foley barked, "Too rough for you, huh?" and sniggered.

Marian didn't answer him. "Don't ask questions, Gloria. I'll call you later and explain." Coffee mug, notebooks, Kleenex, two nail files, a small carton of Wash'n Dri towelettes—into the box.

The other woman looked dubious, amazed, even a little alarmed. "Okay, if you say so. I hope you know what you're doing."

"So do I," Marian muttered. She packed the Rolodex and picked up the cardboard box.

"Hey!" Foley objected. "You can't take the Rolodex!"

"I paid for it, I'm taking it," Marian snapped. "Gloria, I'll call you tonight or tomorrow morning. Don't fret—please."

Still looking dubious, Gloria nodded, reluctantly granting Marian permission to go ahead with whatever noodlenut plan she had.

The truth was, Marian had no plan. But sitting in the captain's office and listening to oily-politician DiFalco trying to con her into accepting the status quo, she'd only become more determined to clean out her desk and be rid of the place. It did occur to her that if she simply refused to work with DiFalco without having officially resigned, she'd be subject to disciplinary action and might lose certain benefits when she did leave. So she would put in her final days among strangers at Midtown South; she ought to be able to keep out of office politics for that long. Too many DiFalcos and Foleys in law enforcement, not enough Gloria Sanchezes. But Gloria certainly wasn't the only good cop in town; Marian felt a little like a deserter.

But saving the world was going to have to be somebody else's job; she just wasn't up to it. She'd do what she could about what she thought of as Kelly's minor problem at the Broadhurst and then get out. She'd explain why, in great detail, to anyone who'd listen, and then she'd go. If she could open somebody's eyes to the type of cop Captain DiFalco was—great. If she couldn't, too bad. But she wasn't going to waste one more minute of her life agonizing over the problem. It wasn't worth it.

She carried her box down the stairs to the first floor of the stationhouse, where she was surprised to see Kelly Ingram, wearing a visitor's badge and sitting disconsolately on a wooden chair. The Ninth Precinct didn't get a lot of celebrity visitors; every cop in the place seemed to find an excuse to walk by. "Kelly," Marian said, "why didn't you come upstairs?"

"I didn't want to disturb you." Kelly looked up and saw the box in Marian's arms; her eyes grew wide. "Does that mean what I think it means?"

"You didn't want to *disturb* me? I can't believe you said that. Come with me while I put this stuff in the car."

Kelly caught on that Marian didn't want to talk in front of the other cops. She returned her visitor's badge and held the door open for Marian, and they trooped across to the other side of East Fifth to the stationhouse parking lot. There were shadows under Kelly's eyes; she'd gotten up too early. Kelly's workday began at about the time other people were thinking of dinner.

Marian stowed the box of belongings in her car and said to Kelly, "I haven't resigned yet—I'm just not going back there again, thank god. I've been temporarily assigned to Midtown South. To check into your missing scripts et cetera. I'll do what I can there, before I quit."

Kelly groaned. "That's why I came—to apologize."

"For what?"

"I tell you in no uncertain terms that I want you to resign *right now*—and the first thing that goes wrong, I scream for you to come make it right. I just didn't think about the resigning business, Marian, not until you were already on your way. The minute I saw we'd been burglarized, the only thing I could think was *Call Marian.*" She paused. "You must think I'm terribly two-faced."

Marian smiled. "No, I think you were scared. A stranger invades your private space and helps himself to your things . . . that scares everybody."

Kelly made a face. "Do you have to be so damned understanding? I'd feel much better if you'd yell at me a little."

"No way, kiddo—you gave me a perfect excuse for walking out of that place. Without those scripts to go looking for, I'd be over there telling people off and getting into all sorts of hot water."

Kelly glanced across the street at the stationhouse. "And you're really never going back?"

"Really never. How'd you get here, by taxi? Get in—I'll drop you off."

They climbed in the car and Marian pulled out of the parking lot. Kelly said that new costumes were being made, and all the missing props would be replaced in time for that evening's performance. "Do you want to see the play again?" she asked Marian.

"You bet! You said you'd let me know when a few remaining rough spots got ironed out."

"Well, we're pretty close to that now. By Saturday we ought to have everything right. Is Saturday night okay?"

"Saturday's fine—thanks, Kel."

Kelly hesitated. "How many tickets?"

Marian thought a moment. "Make it two."

"Terrif. Who're you bringing? Whom."

"Oh, I'll find somebody."

Marian dropped Kelly off at her building, and then headed for the Midtown Precinct South stationhouse on West Thirty-fifth Street.

*   *   *

Captain James Timothy Murtaugh had a lived-in face and graying temples; he sat behind his desk like Authority Incarnate, a man who'd long ago stopped being surprised by what he saw. The captain looked as if he didn't smile often, but his manner of speaking was friendly enough. "I thought the first thing I'd say to you would be an apology for the high-handed way I preempted your services last night." He paused. "But now that doesn't seem like enough. Last night I didn't know you'd taken down a perp Sunday and were on personal time. If you're not ready to come back, say so. I'll get somebody else to take the Broadhurst case."

Marian shook her head. "Not necessary, Captain. I don't need any more time off."

He leaned back in his chair. "Internal Affairs says it was a clean shoot. You saved your own life and that of an FBI agent who was working with you in what was an unusually messy situation. You harboring any guilt feelings?"

So he'd been checking up on her. "Regrets, but not guilt," Marian said. "I wish there'd been another way of handling it, but I know there wasn't. It was him or us. No, I don't feel guilty." *Since I didn't shoot anybody.*

Murtaugh nodded. "That's good enough for me." He sat up straight. "I'll tell you, Sergeant, we wouldn't bother investigating the theft of a few playscripts, but the value of the costumes puts last night's little bit of chicanery into the category of grand larceny. Then there's a couple of paintings taken from the dressing room walls, an antique shaving mug—"

"Ah, I think some of those dollar-value estimates are a mite inflated," Marian murmured.

"Probably. But we have to check them out just the same. Go see Lieutenant Overbrook—you'll be reporting to him. And Sergeant . . . glad to have you with us."

"Thank you, Captain."

After a little searching, Marian found Lieutenant Overbrook's office. The lieutenant was almost a stereotype of the grizzled old cop—sloppy, overweight, overworked, and losing his gray hair; Marian thought he must be near retirement. DiFalco's voice suddenly spoke in her head: *Another Mick, something starting with 'O.'* Asshole. Overbrook surprised her by shaking her hand and then waved her to a seat.

"Glad you're taking this on, Larch," he said, picking up the lists of missing property she'd collected the night before. "We're godawful squeezed for manpower here. Any idea what's behind this?"

"Three possibilities," Marian said, getting down to business. "Number one, Abigail James—the playwright—thinks it's play piracy. Steal copies of a play before it's published and skip paying the royalties."

"Um. Number two?"

"Souvenir-hunting, plain and simple. As for number three, the stage manager hinted this kind of petty theft was a good way to sabotage a play."

"Did it?"

"No, they went on last night with hastily rented costumes and improvised props. It could be nuisance sabotage, somebody with a grudge against the play who just wants to make a little trouble."

"What's your choice?"

"We can rule out number one," Marian said. "I can see a thief coming in to steal the scripts and then picking up a souvenir or two as an afterthought. But all the doors had been pried open with a crowbar and the dressing rooms systematically looted. Whoever did it—and there had to be more than one of them—came prepared to carry away a lot of stuff."

Overbrook nodded. "Sounds right. That leaves possibilities two and three." He leaned forward over the desk, his weight on his forearms. "What does it *smell* like?"

Marian grinned. "It smells like souvenir-hunting."

"Then start with that. See if there's a market for things like"—he looked at one of the lists—"Kelly Ingram's old sneakers." He raised two shaggy eyebrows.

"There probably is. Do I get any help?"

"Sporadically, when it's available. I can let you have Perlmutter for the rest of the morning, but he's due in court at two o'clock." Lieutenant Overbrook heaved his considerable bulk up from the desk and stepped over to the office door. "Perlmutter! In here."

Marian looked at her watch: after ten. An undernourished-looking man in his thirties with a nimbus of wiry black hair appeared in the doorway. Overbrook introduced him as Detective Perlmutter, no first name, and brought him up to date. "Sergeant Larch is in charge of the case. You help her whenever you can squeeze out a spare minute."

Perlmutter nodded noncommittally at Marian. "What do you want me to do?"

"I want you to find out how the thieves got into the theater. They used crowbars to break into the dressing rooms but all the outside doors are intact. Check watchmen, people in the box office, whoever."

"Okay. Where'll you be?"

"I want to talk to the play's director. Another play he once worked on had all its scripts stolen."

Lieutenant Overbrook raised his hands, palms up. "Have fun."

Marian and Detective Perlmutter set out to walk the nine short blocks uptown to the Broadhurst Theatre. If the director of *The Apostrophe Thief* wasn't there, somebody would have his home address.

"Where'd you transfer from?" Perlmutter asked.

"Ninth Precinct, but I'm here for just this one case."

Perlmutter made a sound of surprise. "For stolen play-scripts? That's all?"

"Costumes, too. And personal belongings."

"Still not big enough to import a sergeant for. I don't get it."

"I was on the scene last night," Marian explained, "and Captain Murtaugh pretty much shanghaied me into taking it on."

The other detective laughed. "That sounds like Murtaugh. At least he bucked the case down to Lieutenant Overbrook instead of running it himself."

Marian shot him a look. "That's an advantage? What's wrong with Murtaugh?"

"Nothing, really. He's a good cop, good to work for. But he does have a reputation for being kind of hard on his sergeants." Perlmutter paused.

Marian knew a cue when she heard one. "In what way?"

"Well, a sergeant he was working a case with once took a shotgun blast meant for Murtaugh."

"Good god. Did he live?"

"Yeah, if you call spending the next forty or fifty years in a wheelchair 'living.' The blast guaranteed he'd never be a poppa, and a fragment got all the way through to nip the spinal cord. Can't walk, can't screw. Can't bloody do anything. Of course, that was back when Murtaugh was still a lieutenant." As if that made a difference.

Marian was silent a moment and then slid her eyes sideways toward her companion. "Is that the story you scare all the new kids with?"

Perlmutter grinned. "Yeah, but it's true just the same. Just thought you ought to know, you bein' a sergeant and all." His tone changed. "Look, I can give you only a few hours today—I have to be in court by two."

"The lieutenant told me."

At the Broadhurst, one of the two people in the box office said that John Reddick, the play's director, was backstage. Perlmutter lingered to interview the box office crew while Marian made her way through the auditorium. The curtain was open; the stage set loomed dim and shadowy under the minimum-wattage work lights. The place was utterly silent.

Reddick's office was a windowless cubicle next to the prop room. The director was on the phone when Marian stepped into the doorway, in the midst of trying to soothe whoever was on the other end of the line. "Relax, Gene, it's under control. Most of the new costumes have been promised for four o'clock—that leaves time for fittings and whatever small adjustments have to be made. And the rest of the costumes will be ready by tomorrow. It's all taken care of." He held the receiver away from his ears and rolled his eyes; a man's voice chattered unheeded from the receiver.

Marian cleared her throat and held up her badge.

Reddick's reaction was one she'd never run into before; he positively beamed at her. "Gene, I've got to go—the police are here. Catch you later." He hung up with a sigh of relief. "Producer," he said to Marian with a scowl. "He's supposed to take care of this kind of thing, but I end up doing it and he bugs *me* about it." Reddick tried to peer around Marian. "Should I have said the police *is* here?"

"My partner's out front. I'm Sergeant Larch, and I want to ask you about a play called *Three Rings*."

"Ah, somebody told you about that. Have a seat, Sergeant. Yeah, those scripts were stolen too, but that's all. No costumes or anything."

"Did you ever get them back?"

"Nope."

The only other chair in the office was piled high with

bound papers; she picked them up and put them on the corner of Reddick's desk—and then realized what they were. "New copies of the script?"

"They just came in. Some actors get panicky if they don't have scripts, even after a play's opened. Security blanket."

Marian sat down. "Why were the originals stolen, do you think?"

"Oh, they'll be worth a few bucks on the black market. People will steal anything—hell, people will *buy* anything, anything at all connected with show biz."

"Even though they're so easily replaced?"

Reddick shifted his weight. "Well, you see, the originals are all marked up. A script with Ian Cavanaugh's stage directions written throughout in his own hand has value to collectors of stuff like that." He gestured toward the new scripts on the corner of his desk. "Now those, without anything written on them, aren't worth anything." He grinned. "Don't tell Abby James I said that. I meant they wouldn't bring anything on the collectors' market."

"And that was why the personal stuff was taken too?"

"Absolutely. That old shaving mug of Ian's wouldn't be worth two cents if it belonged to Joe Blow."

Marian thought back. "You didn't lose anything, did you?"

"No, they didn't even bother breaking in here." He laughed. "I feel insulted—they didn't think I was worth stealing from."

A small, elderly safe was sitting in one corner of the room, doing double duty as a table. Marian pointed to it. "What about that?"

"Empty," Reddick said. "Besides, I can't even get into the damned thing. Our producer is the only one who ever thought to write down the combination. That old safe has been here so long I doubt if even the theater owners remember how to open it."

When Marian asked who actually dealt with stolen theater

memorabilia, Reddick couldn't help her. He pointed out that the legally owned material was sold through legitimate auction houses. Sotheby's, for instance, wouldn't touch one of the stolen copies of *The Apostrophe Thief*.

"And none of the old copies of *Three Rings* has surfaced?" she asked.

"Not that I know of. But it's been only a couple of years. Someone's probably sitting on them, to increase the value a little more."

Just then Perlmutter stuck his head in through the door. "Sergeant?"

Marian thanked John Reddick for his help and stepped out of his office. "Something?"

"They came in with the cleaning crew," Perlmutter said. "Three of them. The crew thought they were stagehands—one was carrying a tool box and the other two were pushing a laundry cart, one of those big ones like they use in hotels. That's how they got the stuff out."

"And the stage doorkeeper didn't notice anything funny?"

"He wasn't on duty yet. They all came in the front way—the guy getting ready to open the box office thought they were stagehands too."

"What time was this?"

"Around nine, in the ay em."

"Description?"

"One middle-aged man and two younger ones. The older man was short, stocky, and wheezed when he talked. One of the younger men was tall, dark hair worn in a ponytail, didn't talk much."

"And the other?"

Perlmutter grinned. "'A hunk,' unquote."

"Okay, it's a start," Marian said. "We'll have to get the cleaning crew to look at mug shots—you can start picking out possibles. Mind if I use your phone while you're in court this afternoon?"

"Help yourself."

They stopped for greaseburgers and coffee before going back to the station. Then Marian spent the afternoon calling auction houses as well as all the listings under "Collectibles" in the yellow pages. No one had ever seen a *Three Rings* script offered for sale, and no one could (or would) give her a name of someone even remotely associated with the black market in souvenirs; most of those she spoke to got huffy when she asked. A touchy subject, evidently. Shortly after four she called it a day.

When she got home, Marian tapped out the number Holland had given her. It turned out to be a voice-mail service; she left a message saying there was a play she wanted him to see Saturday night.

5

The next day Marian went to an auction.

An auction house in Sheridan Square was advertising a collection of "cinema and stage treasures"; the *pièce de résistance* was to be one of Madonna's girdles. Marian took the subway and arrived just as the doors were opening.

Inside, she paid a fee and received a printed program listing the items to be auctioned. Marian had decided not to flash her badge; she'd probably get a better reception if she posed as a collector. But she didn't see any playscripts listed and wondered if she was wasting her time.

Rows of padded folding chairs were set up facing the auctioneer's desk, currently unattended. Marian sat down near two not particularly well-dressed women. The woman closest to her had a beaked nose and bulging eyes, giving her an avaricious look. "What's your field?" the woman asked unexpectedly.

"Uh, playscripts. I'm looking for a copy of *Three Rings*."

"Huh. You won't find it here."

The other woman, a plump blonde, leaned around the beak-nosed one and said, "What do you want that one for? *Three Rings* flopped, didn't it?"

"Actually, it's the director's copy I'm looking for," Marian improvised. "I collect John Reddick."

That made sense to the two women; specialists were commonplace. "Scripts run high," the woman with the nose said. "Personally, I don't bother with paper."

"Paper?"

"Scripts, posters, play programs, autographs . . . you know, *paper*. I think personal items are so much nicer. The last thing I got was Tyne Daly's travel alarm clock. From when she was touring *Gypsy*? I just loved her in *Cagney and Lacey*."

"I collect stage props," the blonde said happily. "Last month I got the original spear Raul Julia carried in *Man of La Mancha*."

"It's a repro," the first woman muttered.

"It is *not*. I wish you'd stop saying that."

Feeling the conversation slipping away from her, Marian interposed, "You know what I'd like to get my hands on? John Reddick's copy of *The Apostrophe Thief*."

"Oh yeah? Well, that won't be around yet. The play just opened last week, didn't it?"

"You haven't heard?" Marian leaned forward in her best conspiratorial manner. "Someone got into the Broadhurst and took all the scripts!"

"No!" Both women looked shocked/delighted. "Did they get anything else?" the blonde wanted to know.

"Costumes, some props, *and* personal items as well. Kelly Ingram's hairbrush, Ian Cavanaugh's shaving mug—"

"How do you know all this?" the first woman asked suspiciously.

"I know a cop who works out of Midtown South," Marian said blandly. "What bugs me is that a friend of mine ran into a fellow who said he had a line on the scripts—but she didn't get his name! I could kill her."

"She say what he looks like?"

Marian put on a trying-to-remember face. "Short, middle-aged, wheezes when he talks."

"That sounds like Harley Wingfield," the blonde said, "but he collects Elvis."

"A shaving mug belonging to Ian Cavanaugh," the hook-nosed woman said dreamily. "God, I'd leave my husband for that man! No electric razor—a real, live shaving mug. And he used it before every performance, I bet."

The blonde had been thinking. "Lenora, what about that guy who's allergic to stage dust? Has some sort of attack every time he goes backstage. *He's* short and middle-aged."

Lenora came back from dreaming about the shaving mug and said, "Oh, yeah, I know who you mean. What's his name?" Neither one of them could think of it.

"Is he a collector?" Marian asked. "Or a dealer?"

"Both," the blonde said. "Deals out of his apartment, I think. Most of them do."

"And you can't remember his name?"

Lenora jabbed Marian's arm with a long bony finger. "There's somebody who can tell you. See the guy in the yellow shirt? He knows him."

"That's right, Augie knows him," the blonde echoed.

"Augie, huh?" The fellow they'd indicated was in his late twenties, stoop-shouldered, wearing glasses. Marian stood up. "I'll give him a try. Thanks a lot."

"Good luck," they called after her.

The folding chairs were filling up fast. Marian walked down a few rows and found a seat behind Augie; she tapped him on his yellow shoulder. "Augie? My name's Marian. Lenora says you can help me find someone I'm looking for."

Augie turned a bespectacled face toward her and smiled, lots of teeth. "Hel-*lo*, Marian. Delighted to help, if I can. Whom seek ye?" His speech was pure Bronx, nasal and loud.

"I don't know his name." Once again she described the man seen by the cleaning crew at the Broadhurst.

"Harley Wingfield," Augie said promptly. "You're into Elvis?"

"Not Harley Wingfield, and I'm looking for playscripts. This man I'm trying to find, he's supposed to be allergic to stage dust and—"

"Oh, you must mean Ernie Nordstrom. Stage dust does make him wheeze when he talks. Ernie deals everything he can lay his hands on, not just playscripts."

"Nordstrom, huh? Is he here?"

"I haven't seen him . . . oh good! They're ready to start."

"Where can I reach him?"

But Augie just said *Shh* and gave his full attention to the auctioneer. Marian waited impatiently until the first item was sold, a pair of somewhat tattered tragedy masks from an Off-Off Broadway production of the *Oresteia*. Then she leaned over Augie's shoulder and repeated her question.

He turned around and looked at her. "Marian, you seem like a nice lady, so I'm going to tell you straight. You don't want to deal with Ernie Nordstrom. He's not too particular about authenticating his stuff, you know what I mean? I don't think he actually manufactures fakes, but you can't take his word about what he's got." Augie sighed. "Sometimes he latches on to a genuine piece, but I've heard too many people grumbling about Ernie to put much trust in him."

"He's the only lead I've got," Marian persisted. "Where can I find him? Do you know?"

"I don't know where he lives, but you could always try the Zingones."

Marian blinked. "What are Zingones?"

Augie gave her his big-toothed smile. "You're new at this, aren't you?"

"Brand new. I need all the help I can get."

"Buy me lunch and I'll take you there."

"You're on."

But they couldn't leave yet. Augie had come to bid on a costume from A *Chorus Line* and wouldn't budge until it came up to the auctioneer's desk. Unfortunately, he had to drop out of the bidding; the costume went to a mustachioed man who'd seemed willing to pay any amount to walk away with the glittery outfit.

"I'm sorry you didn't get your costume," Marian said as they left.

"Oh, I didn't want it. The seller is a friend, and I was just bidding the price up. Collectors help each other out when we can."

They went to a place called Alpha House, one of those thousands of Manhattan restaurants that will never play host to the dining critic of the New York *Times*. Augie's last name was Silver, and he worked as a tailor for a theatrical costuming company. "Mostly we do rentals," he said around a mouthful of salad that seemed to be mostly iceberg lettuce. "Amateur productions, low-budget Off-Broadway, like that. Costume parties. We get a lot of out-of-town business—high schools and universities."

"Then you weren't one of the companies *The Apostrophe Thief* called on for help Tuesday night?" When he didn't know what she was talking about, Marian explained about the thefts from the Broadhurst. "Not just costumes, but scripts and personal belongings as well. Somebody made a real haul."

Augie had the same shocked/delighted look on his face that Lenora and her friend had had. "They took all the costumes?"

"All of them."

"And that's the script you're after? *The Apostrophe Thief?*"

Marian smiled ruefully. "I don't think I have much chance of finding that one—although I'd give ten years of my life for the director's copy. No, what I'm looking for is *Three Rings*. Remember it?"

"Sure, but it didn't run very long. Why do you want that one?"

Marian thought it was time to elaborate on her story. "I'm writing a book about John Reddick—the director? So, I want to get my hands on every script of his I can." When Augie looked suitably impressed, she added, "He's being very cooperative, but a few of his scripts are missing. *Three Rings* is one of them."

"And now *The Apostrophe Thief* is another." Augie nodded. "I see. So you're in the market for *The Apostrophe Thief* as well, then?"

Marian raised her eyebrows. "Damn right. But the thief won't just advertise what he's . . . Augie, do you know something?"

He shook his head vigorously. "I just like to keep track of what people are looking for. For the finder's fee?"

She pretended to think it over. "I'd be willing to pay a finder's fee. What's usual?"

"Ten percent."

"That seems high."

Augie shrugged. "A dealer would charge you twenty."

Marian groaned. "Okay, ten percent. Do you think you can get a line on Reddick's copy?"

"I have no idea. But I can put the word out, and we'll start with the Zingones." He wiped his mouth with a paper napkin. "Do you want me to leave the tip?"

Marian took care of it, and they left the restaurant to head up Seventh. "This Ernie Nordstrom," she said as they walked, "does he have a partner? Younger, tall, wears his dark hair in a ponytail, doesn't talk much?"

"No-o-o-o," Augie said. "Can't say I ever heard of one. Ernie tends to work alone."

"What about another younger fellow, hunk-type?"

"No. Where are you getting these descriptions?"

"Friend of mine. The one time she talked to this Ernie Nordstrom, if it's the same man, these other two guys were with him."

"Here we are," Augie said. "Upstairs. It's a sort of unofficial clearing house for show biz collectibles. They know everything that goes on." He pushed a bell; after a moment something unintelligible squawked over the intercom. "Augie Silver," he said back. The steel door buzzed open. "What's your last name?" he asked as they climbed the stairs.

"Larch."

The Zingones turned out to be four siblings—Matthew, Mark, Luke, and Janet. Their place of business was jammed full up to the ceiling with props, stacks of souvenir programs, posters, rack after rack of costumes, shelves filled with books, trinkets, photographs, gewgaws, memorabilia of all sorts. There was a beer tray decorated with one of the Marilyn Monroe calendar nude photos. And a Charlie McCarthy bank; the dummy's mouth opened to receive the coin. Another oral knickknack: a Geraldo ashtray, with a widely gaping mouth as the place to put the butts. There was even an Antoinette Perry Award statuette locked away in a showcase.

"Whose Tony?" Marian asked.

One of the Zingones pronounced a name she didn't recognize. "It's for scene design."

Augie made the introductions, stressing that Marian was a writer and not a collector, and that he was acting as her agent. Marian translated that as: *This is my pigeon; you want in, you'll have to deal through me.*

"Not a collector." All four Zingones immediately lost interest—not exactly dismissing her, but not eager to get acquainted, either.

Marian made a point of looking around her with an awe

that was not totally affected. "No, I'm not a collector—but I'm beginning to think I'm missing something. Look at all this great stuff! This . . . staff, is it?" She bent over a locked display case and read an index card. "Did James Earl Jones really carry this in *King Lear?*"

"He really did," Matthew Zingone said with a smile. He was the only one of the four who wore glasses and was thus easy to distinguish from his two brothers. "The Delacorte in Central Park. That one was used in only the first two performances—it was too heavy. They made Jones a lighter one."

"You didn't have to tell her *that*," Janet said with a laugh.

"Everyone knows about it," drawled either Mark or Luke; all three brothers looked so much alike they could pass for triplets. "As long as we're on a truth kick today, Jones stopped using a staff altogether before the end of the run. But the two are remahrkably alike," he continued in his affected drawl. "You have to scrutize them quite closely to tell them apart."

Scrutize? Marian looked at a white silk muffler that the index card said may have been worn by Edward Woodward in *The Equalizer.* "*May* have been?"

"It was," Janet declared firmly.

"We're pretty sure it was," Matthew said. "Production companies aren't always careful about labeling things."

"Is that how this stuff gets on the market? The production companies sell it?"

"Unless the stagehands or the properties crews or the costume people steal it first," the drawly one said. "But production companies have to get rid of the stuff. Storage costs in this town are *unreal*. We have that problem, too. We had to pass up a backdrop curtain from *Rosenstern and Guildencrantz Are Dead* because we don't have room for it."

Rosenstern . . . ? Marian looked at him to see if he was joking, but he wasn't. Then something glittery caught Marian's eye. "Are those . . . Dorothy's ruby slippers? From *The Wizard of Oz?* I thought they—"

"They're copies," Augie interposed in a bored tone. "The originals went at an MGM auction back in 1970, thereabouts."

In spite of herself, Marian was tempted. "How much?"

"Six thousand," a Zingone said.

She gulped. "Dollars? Oh, I get it—these are famous counterfeits somebody tried to—"

"Nope, they're *advertised* as copies."

Marian was appalled. "And they still bring six thousand dollars?"

Four heads nodded in unison.

"Only five hundred pairs were made," Janet explained. "And the original shoemaker's last from the movie was used, so they're all Judy Garland's size six. They initially sold for five thousand, but we had to pay more than that to get this pair. And they'll appreciate even more."

"It's a good investment," Matthew said, fiddling with his glasses. "Especially if you're just starting a collection."

Marian was saved from having to refuse when Augie decided it was time to get down to business. "That's not what she's looking for, Matthew." He explained about the missing Reddick scripts, but none of the Zingones looked surprised when he said the Broadhurst had been raided.

"Tuesday, wasn't it?" Matthew said. "We heard."

"They hear everything," Augie said with a sigh.

Mark or Luke asked, "Do they have any idea who did it?"

"I don't know," Marian replied innocently. "But if the director's script happens to come your way—"

"They'll get in touch with me," Augie interrupted. "Right now, however, what we're looking for is the director's copy of *Three Rings.*"

"Don't have it," Janet said. "Those scripts were stolen, too, weren't they? None of them came through here."

"Well, then, have you seen Ernie Nordstrom lately?" Augie asked.

At that moment they were interrupted by the doorbell. Luke or Mark buzzed in a couple of customers and moved away to take care of them. The newcomers were both women in their thirties, and one of them asked, "Do you have any Bernadette Peters personal items? Clothing, jewelry, letters, anything?"

Her friend laughed, gently. "An old toothbrush, a pencil stub . . . "

The first woman said, unnecessarily, "I collect Bernadette Peters."

"You do?" the Zingone brother said, but then made a quick recovery. "We did have a fringed shawl of hers, but it may have been sold. Let's go take a look." He led the two women to the back of the shop.

"Ernie Nordstrom?" Augie prompted.

Matthew said, "We haven't seen him in a couple of months."

"Hurray, hurray," Janet muttered.

Matthew grinned. "Janet doesn't like Ernie."

"He always was a little bit strange," Janet said. "But after the *Lucy* thing he turned downright weird."

"What Lucy thing?" Marian asked.

"The *I Love Lucy* pilot episode," Mark or Luke drawled. "Ernie Nordstrom spent nearly twenty years of his life looking for it—it was the only one of all the *Lucy* episodes that was missing. Then somebody's wife finds a copy she didn't know she had, and they casually show it on television for anybody to copy who wanted to. Twenty years Ernie had been looking . . . and he ends up out on a limb without a paddle! That would turn anyone sour."

"Oh, yes," Marian said, thinking back. "I believe I watched that. Pretty bad, as I recall."

Augie laughed shortly. "It was dreadful. But that's not the point. The point is it was one of a kind and nobody could find it. Ernie Nordstrom had just about made a career of looking for *Lucy* . . . and suddenly all these VCRs are whirring away, taping the thing straight off television." He laughed again. "Jesus."

Marian asked, "Do you have an address for him?"

The Zingones shook their heads. "Ernie doesn't want people to know where he lives," Mark/Luke said. "He deals out of his apartment, so he keeps a lot of valuable stuff there. He's just being careful."

"Do you know of any partners he might have?" Marian asked. "Younger—one's dark and quiet, wears his hair in a ponytail, and the other's a hunk?" She got more head shakes, this time accompanied by looks of incipient suspicion that she hastened to squelch. "I got a tip that some man who had two younger buddies with him knew something about the *Three Rings* scripts. Augie's pretty sure the one I'm looking for is Ernie Nordstrom, but I'd hate to spend a lot of time tracking down the wrong guy. All I have to go on is a description—short and stocky, wheezes a lot, middle-aged."

"That could be Harley Wingfield," Janet said, "but unless it has 'Elvis' written on it, Harley's not interested."

"So that leaves Ernie Nordstrom," Augie said with an air of finality. "If he's got a line on the *Three Rings* director's script, I'd like to let him know a customer's waiting to do business." He cleared his throat. "So if anybody who knows him comes in . . . "

"We'll take care of it," Luke/Mark promised. "That'll be our number-one agenda on things to do. We'd like to know what happened to the Broadhurst haul too."

Janet spoke up. "Wait a minute. You said one of the younger guys is dark-haired and quiet?"

Marian looked at her quickly. "That's right."

"Not a partner, but . . . " She turned to her brothers. "Didn't Ernie use to hire some Latino whenever he had heavy lifting to do, or a whole bunch of stuff he needed to move—"

"You're right," Matthew said. "Uh, what's his name . . . Vasquez?"

"Uh-huh, Vasquez, that's it. He barely speaks English, I remember."

"First name?" Marian asked. Nobody knew that, or where he could be reached.

The bell rang again; more customers. Augie looked at his watch and said, "I've got to get to work."

Marian thanked the Zingones and followed her "agent" out. Back down on the street, she and Augie exchanged phone numbers. "You'll get in touch the minute you hear anything?" Marian asked.

"Count on it," Augie said with his big-toothed smile, and waved goodbye.

Lieutenant Overbrook looked amused. "Matthew, Mark, Luke . . . and Janet?"

"Best-laid plans," Marian said with a grin. "But these two possibles look pretty good—they fit the descriptions. Vasquez is just muscles-for-hire, and I'm guessing the hunk is too. Ernie Nordstrom is the one we want. Shady dealer, small-time."

"APB?"

"Not yet, it might spook him. Let's give Augie and the Zingones a chance first. And now that I've got a name, I can do some more hunting myself."

Overbrook was frowning. "Vasquez . . . the cleaning crew didn't mention one of the men was Hispanic. Perlmutter would have said so."

"Maybe they were too busy ogling the hunk. Janet Zingone

said Vasquez didn't speak much English. If he didn't talk at all in front of the cleaning crew, they might not have realized he was Hispanic. Depends on his coloring."

"Possible. How's this Augie Silver going to get in touch with you?"

"I gave him my home phone number," Marian said. "He thinks I'm a writer researching John Reddick—Reddick's the director of *The Apostrophe Thief.* I'm pretending to be looking for the script of an earlier play he directed . . . which was also stolen."

"Same thief?"

"No reason to think so—it just gave me an excuse to go looking for someone fitting the description we got. If Ernie Nordstrom is the one who raided the Broadhurst dressing rooms Tuesday, he's not going to sell a copy of *The Apostrophe Thief* to the first person who comes along looking for one. So, I'm supposed to be trying to track down this earlier play. *Three Rings*, it's called."

"Good, good," Overbrook said, nodding. "And I like your cover story. Everybody's used to running into writers—they're all over the place these days. Okay, writer, go write up what you've got so far. You can use Korobovsky's typewriter."

Marian went out into the squadroom and asked Perlmutter which desk belonged to Korobovsky, whoever he or she was. When she'd finished typing up her report, she spent the rest of the workday trying to get an address for Ernie Nordstrom. He had no police record, not even a traffic citation. The two E. Nordstroms in the NYNEX white pages were both women, and the phone company said he didn't have an unlisted number. The gas and electric companies had no record of him, and he didn't subscribe to cable TV. Nor did he own a car. He wasn't registered to vote, and he didn't carry any plastic;

Marian tried the major banks and credit bureaus but they'd never heard of him. He didn't even have a checking account that she could find. Social Security had over a hundred Ernest Nordstroms on its rolls, but not one of them lived in New York.

Yet nobody could be that anonymous; it was beginning to look as if "Ernie Nordstrom" wasn't his real name. Marian put through a routine request for information to the FBI, but she didn't hope for much there. Nordstrom was small cheese, maybe a little bent and maybe not, but clearly not a big-time criminal. Still, he'd certainly made sure no one could find him in a hurry. Marian kept at it until her shift ended before finally giving up and going home.

To find Curt Holland lounging against the door of her apartment. "This play you want me to see Saturday night," he said casually, "it wouldn't happen to be *The Apostrophe Thief*, would it?"

6

Marian and Holland sat across from each other at her kitchen table, eating the Thai food they'd sent out for. They dug into the cardboard cartons, chewed thoughtfully, and watched each other. Holland still had shadows under his eyes, but the pinched, strained look was gone from his face. The trauma of the shooting was fading, for both of them; they were recovering, in their different ways.

A certain formality hung in the air; they were both treading cautiously, as if fearing traps lying in wait, tiptoeing around the question of whether there would—or could—be more between them. Marian was wondering if she *wanted* more. No, that wasn't true; she did want more. But. There were too many things about this man she didn't like . . . or perhaps didn't understand. Still, she wasn't about to yield to impulse; she'd been burned before, doing just that.

"What did you do today?" she asked around a mouthful of Evil Jungle Princess Chicken.

"I looked at office space."

"See anything you liked?"

"Not really." He offered no details. "What about you? Are you still on personal time?"

"Lord, no. I'm in up to my ears." She told him about the burglary at the Broadhurst Theatre and her subsequent temporary assignment to Midtown South. She described the auction, Augie Silver, and the Zingones. "You should see the stuff they have there. A silk fan Helen Hayes carried in some play, hotel bills from a Beatles tour, a couple of *Star Trek* uniforms—the ones really used, not just copies . . . you name it, it's there. And the prices! I can't believe what people are willing to pay for what are really nothing more than souvenirs."

"I can," Holland said. "Who collects these castoffs? Sad ineffectual nonentities with no lives of their own, out of touch with quotidian reality and hoping for a little reflected glory from the mere fact of owning something once handled by a celebrity. Riding in the wake of others because they're unable to make waves of their own. Sheer voyeurism."

There it was, that damned arrogance of his. "Holland, do you have any idea how condescending that sounds?"

"Does that make it any the less true?"

"But collecting's a harmless form of self-indulgence. It hurts no one and it makes the collectors feel good. Who wouldn't buy a little happiness if they could?"

"It hurts the collectors themselves," he said in the overly precise manner that he affected whenever involved in a disagreement. "It feeds a sick illusion that they're a part of That Great Big World Out There and not just lookers-on. Besides, celebrity-worship has reached epidemic proportions in this country, and 'epidemic' is the right word because it's an illness . . . or more properly a symptom of one. The illness is empty lives."

"You're being too harsh. The people I met today *love* what they're doing . . . they're excited by it. You can't dismiss that kind of commitment out of hand."

Holland leaned back in his chair and gave her his sardonic smile. "You had fun today, didn't you?"

Startled, Marian stopped to think. "Well, yes, I guess I did."

"You like being back in harness. You enjoy the hunt. What happened to that high-minded cop who was going to resign in a blaze of hellfire and damnation?"

"She's still going to resign, but I've pretty much given up on the hellfire and damnation part." Marian paused for a sip of tea. "I plan to spend another day or two trying to track down the scripts and other things missing from the Broadhurst—I wouldn't even be doing that if it weren't for Kelly. But then I'm gone. I'll write a letter detailing Captain DiFalco's shoddy police work the best I can. If they want to do something about it, fine. If they don't, too bad. But after this week, it's no longer my problem."

"In that case, perhaps you'd like to go office-hunting with me."

She laughed. "Perhaps. But one thing at a time."

He leaned toward her. "The time is now. Forget these doo-dads stolen from the Broadhurst and walk away, or you'll spend the rest of your life taking orders from incompetents and fools. And you'll go on watching men who are less able and less intelligent than you being promoted over you. The NYPD doesn't want you in a lieutenant's office—not someone who had the effrontery to get herself born a woman. But with me, there'll be no limits. None."

That struck home. Getting passed over had not been an easy pill to swallow; despite her high score on the rarely given lieutenants exam, Marian had watched the only opening go to a man with an equivalent score but fewer years served on the force. It was an inequity that rankled all the more because she was powerless to do anything about it; she didn't need reminding. "Don't pressure me, Holland. I've got a job to finish up, and then I'll decide. It's only a matter of days. Ease off."

Holland nodded, willing to wait . . . for the time being. They exchanged a long look, and then they both smiled—easily, naturally. The wall of formality separating them had disappeared; nothing like a good friendly squabble for breaking down barriers.

The moment was spoiled by a ringing telephone. Marian sighed and picked up the receiver. "Yes?"

"The hunk! The hunk!"

"What?"

"I got him! I got the hunk! He—"

"Augie?"

"Yeah, it's Augie. This guy showed up at the Zingones' place asking if they wanted to buy Kelly Ingram's hairbrush." His Bronx-accented words were coming fast. "The Zingones told him no, but they could put him on to somebody who would. Matthew called me and put the hunk on the phone and the two of us arranged to meet. . . . I figured he could tell us where Ernie Nordstrom lives. I said I represented someone who was interested in anything belonging to Kelly Ingram. Was that all right?"

"That was downright brilliant. Where's the meeting place?"

"A bar called Huey's, in half an hour. Remember the Alpha House, where we had lunch? Huey's is right across the street, down a few doors. But you'll have to hurry. Uh, Marian, there's no way to be sure it really is Kelly Ingram's hairbrush—unless it has a monogram?"

"I doubt it."

"Right. So how'd he know it was hers unless he took it? That wasn't in the papers, was it?"

"No, it wasn't. You'd make a good detective, Augie. What's this guy's name?"

"He wouldn't say. Look, can you hurry? I don't know if I'll be able to stall him. He sounded jumpy on the phone."

"I'm on my way."

Marian hung up and ran for her raincoat and handbag. "Are you finished eating?"

"We're going somewhere, I take it?" Holland asked casually.

She grabbed his arm and dragged him out of the apartment. "We're going to Huey's to meet the hunk. Come on!"

"Aha. A nice play title, that—*Meeting Hunks at Huey's*."

"Come *on*."

They snagged a cab that was just letting out a passenger, and Marian told the driver to take them to Seventh Avenue and Tenth Street. "I hope this guy doesn't get spooked and leave," she said to Holland. "Augie said he sounded jumpy."

"Does he have a name?"

"Not yet."

"And all you want from Nameless Hunk is an address, correct? Ernie Nordstrom's address?"

"Right."

"So who am I?"

"Mm. You're my husband."

"No rings."

"All right, POSSLQ, then. Significant Other."

Holland nodded, and then said to the obviously interested cab driver, "How does that sound to you?"

The driver nodded his head. "Jake with me."

When they got out on Tenth Street, Marian told Holland it might help if he acted as if he found her interest in collecting a bit foolish. "If we all seem too eager, he might suspect something. So toss in a discouraging word now and then."

"That shouldn't prove too difficult," Holland said dryly.

Huey's turned out to be a bar that Marian couldn't get a quick fix on—not working class, not artsy, not singles or gay, not yuppie. The lights were dimmed about as low as they could go without being off altogether, either to create a mood of secrecy or to hide dirt, Marian didn't know which. But no music was blaring, no big-screen TV dominated the room; they could talk there.

When her eyes had adjusted, Marian could see Augie Silver waving frantically from a booth. Across from him was sitting an extraordinarily good-looking man in his mid-twenties, a bodybuilder who wore the sleeves of his tee rolled up to show off his biceps. Whoever he was, he'd made working-out a religion.

"Marian!" Augie said in relief as they approached the booth. "I want you to meet . . . um, ah, huh."

Marian established eye contact with the stranger as well as she could in the dim light. Then she took hold of Holland's hand with both of her own in a way so intimate that the other two couldn't help but notice. "This is Holland."

The two in the booth nodded, accepting him. Marian slid in next to the hunk while Holland sat next to Augie. "What do we call you?" Marian asked the young man next to her.

He favored her with a practiced smile. "Anything you like."

"Well, that's agreeable of you. We'll call you Rocky." As she'd hoped, that pleased him. "Rocky, I hear you have something I might be interested in."

"I dunno. What are you interested in?"

"Anything of Kelly Ingram's."

"Then I might have something. But wouldn't you like a drink first?" Again the practiced smile, which did not extend to his eyes. Playing it cautious, delaying.

Two empty Bud Light bottles stood on the table. "Beer," Marian said.

"I'll get it." Holland stood up. "Augie? Rocky?"

They both said yes and Holland headed for the bar. Marian had to struggle to keep from laughing. The rendezvous in the dark mysterious bar, the man with no name, the high-stakes bargaining yet to come. And for what? A hairbrush. She decided to try a little flattery. "So, Rocky—what line are you in?"

"Why do you want to know?"

"Because I feel I've seen you before. You're a model, aren't you?"

This time the smile reached his eyes. "I'm an actor."

"Ha!" Marian said so loudly that Augie jumped. "I knew I'd seen you! You've got a face people don't forget. What have you done?"

He shifted his weight so he was facing her. "Remember the Vitalo Sunscreen commercial, the two couples on a sailboat? It ran on CBS all summer."

She didn't remember it. "Sure. You were in that?"

"I was the guy who climbed the mast."

Marian put on a comes-the-dawn expression. "Of course! You went right up the—that *was* you! Oh, that's terrific! Augie, you know the commercial, don't you?"

"I think so," he said dubiously.

Back to Rocky. "So you're an actor. Did Augie tell you I'm a writer? Maybe we could work out an interview—what it takes to break in these days, you know, like that."

"I won't say no to that." Then he seemed to remember why they were meeting. "Uh, on second thought, could we put that on hold for a while?"

None too swift, Marian thought. "I suppose."

Holland came back, carrying four bottles of beer and two glasses with his fingers alone, a little bit of showing off Marian suspected might have been for Rocky's benefit. "Here we are." He sat back down and started filling his glass.

Marian took a swallow of beer and got down to business. "Okay, Rocky, about this hairbrush—how do I know it's Kelly Ingram's?"

Augie choked on his beer.

But Rocky didn't see anything unusual about her approach. "Oh, it's hers, all right. I can vouch for that."

"Yes, but you see, I don't know you," Marian pointed out. "And you've got to establish the authenticity of the brush before we can start talking price."

Rocky frowned, and then thought of something. "It has her hair in the bristles!"

Holland laughed shortly. "You could put a strand of your mother's hair in a brush and claim it was the Queen of England's. Come on, Marian, let's go—this ninety-seven-pound weakling doesn't have anything."

"Hey," said Rocky.

"Wait a minute, wait a minute!" Marian turned back to Rocky. "There might be a way. Is the hairbrush part of a whaddayacallit, a collection, a—"

"A lot," Augie said helpfully, seeing she was floundering. "Is it part of an auction lot, a selection of various items?"

"Yes, a lot," Marian said, mentally blowing Augie a kiss. "A lot that has some other item that might verify the rest?"

"Just one moment," Holland said sharply. "Marian, you're not thinking of buying the entire lot? We don't have *room* for any more of these ostensibly priceless castoffs you insist upon accumulating against all dictates of common sense. The place looks like a warehouse now."

"We'll make room," she said earnestly, "or we'll find a bigger place. Rocky, is there anything at all that might establish ownership? A letter, a diary, anything like that? I know her handwriting."

He shook his head. "No letters or diaries. You want more than the hairbrush?"

"No," Holland said adamantly.

"Yes," Marian said loudly. "Don't listen to him. If it's authentic, I want it. But there has to be *something* with writing on it."

Rocky was frowning in concentration. "I don't think so."

"A shopping list, a Post-it note?" Marian took a deep breath. "Maybe notes she took, notes on instructions her director gave her?"

Finally he thought of it. "How about a script? Her copy of the playscript, that'd have her handwriting in it."

Marian let her eyebrows climb. "Her playscript? Yes, that would do—that would do very nicely."

"How much money we talking about here?"

"For the lot, or just the hairbrush and the script?"

Rocky struggled with that one for a moment. "Just the brush and the script," he said reluctantly.

Marian shot a look at Augie, who picked up his cue. "The hairbrush, fifty bucks at most. The script, maybe as high as a thousand, depending on its condition."

Holland exploded. "A thousand dollars!"

"I was hoping for more," Rocky said.

"You'll *get* more, if you sell the lot," Augie interposed, getting into the swing of it. "But once you break up a lot, the price drops considerably. You can't sell items individually for as much as you can sell the lot."

"Why not?" Belligerently.

Augie shrugged. "That's the way the market works. Look, say we go to twelve hundred for the script. That plus the hairbrush, and you'll still net less than thirteen hundred dollars. If you sold the lot, you could end up with ten times that, maybe even twenty thou. Depending on what else you've got."

Rocky looked at Marian. "You got that kind of money?"

"I can get it."

"This is absurd," Holland snarled. "Now you're talking about throwing away twenty thousand dollars as if it were pocket change! And for what? You don't even know what you're buying!"

"I'm not buying anything until I see the goods!" she snapped back. "Do you think I'm stupid? Rocky, I want to see the script before we go any further. If it's genuine, then we'll talk money. How about it?"

Rocky began to look uneasy. "Uh, well, I don't exactly *have* the script—"

"What!"

"Now, don't get excited—this guy I know has it, that's all."

"Then what's the problem? Take us to him."

He shook his head. "No, no . . . I can't do that. He wouldn't, uh, no, I can't." Rocky thought it over. "In fact, he wouldn't like it . . . if he found out I'd said anything, I'd be in deep shit." He thought some more. "Look, that was a mistake. Forget I said anything about the script. I can't help you."

Marian studied him, evaluating. "What if I sweetened the pot a little? How would you like an introduction to a big Broadway director? A private introduction, no other people around."

He was openly skeptical. "How big a director? Who?"

"John Reddick."

He laughed scornfully. "You know John Reddick? Sure you do."

"She does know him," Augie said with a grin. "She's writing a book about him."

That stopped the laugh. Rocky looked at Marian uncertainly.

"I told you I was a writer," she purred. "And what I'm writing right now is an authorized biography of John Reddick. That's *authorized*, Rocky. He's cooperating. Put me in touch with your friend who has the script, and I'll take you to the Broadhurst and introduce you to Reddick in his own office."

Rocky was torn; he licked his lips and shifted his weight. Finally, self-interest won over caution. "All right, I'll try. But this guy . . . he's kind of peculiar. Let me talk to him, see what he says."

"Well . . . okay. But how do I get in touch with you?"

That required a moment's thought. "Meet me here tomorrow. And I'll want to see a bankbook or something. To prove you can pay." Rocky looked pleased with himself for having thought of that.

"Fine. Say, four o'clock?"

"Uh, make it six. I work out Friday afternoons."

"Work," Holland said, "out. Are you an athlete?"

"Yeah." Smug. "I'm an athlete."

"Gold medal in Velcro jumping?"

"Six o'clock," Marian said hurriedly. "What if you can't get the script? Will you still show up?"

"Yeah, yeah—I'll show. Now, let me out, willya? I gotta get moving."

Marian slid from the booth to let him get out. He walked away without another word.

Holland watched the younger man's departure with a frown. "You're letting him go?"

Marian sat back down. "Loose rein for a while, I think." She grinned. "Besides, while you were getting the beer, he told me his name and address."

"He did?" Augie said.

"What about you, Augie? Can you make it tomorrow?"

"Sure." He cleared his throat. "You know those prices I quoted are off the wall, don't you? I thought you'd want some bargaining room."

"I was wondering about that," Marian said. "Thanks for thinking of it."

Augie looked from Marian to Holland and back again. "Are you sure you're a writer? The way you led that guy to right where you wanted him . . ."

Holland laughed. "Isn't that what all writers do? Or try to." He stood up. "We seem to be finished here—shall we go?"

Marian nodded and said, "Six o'clock."

"I'll be here," Augie promised.

Friday morning Marian called CBS to find out which advertising agency had made the Vitalo Sunscreen commercial. Then she called the agency to get the name of the actor who'd shinnied up the mast of the sailboat. The agency had a name but no address for him; they'd gotten him through a talent agency.

Marian went to the talent agency in person, and the display of her badge got her the address. She asked for and was given one of Rocky's publicity photos. Her next stop was the Broadhurst Theatre, where she caught the cleaning crew just as they were getting ready to leave. Every one of them enthusiastically identified Rocky as the hunk they'd seen in the Broadhurst Tuesday morning.

"His name's Kevin Kirby," Marian told Lieutenant Overbrook, "or at least that's the name he's using for his career. He shares an apartment with two other Mel Gibson wannabes at 1066 Hastings Street. He doesn't have a record—I checked. Evidently he's been living on residuals from a commercial he made and is just looking to pick up a little change wherever he can until another acting job comes along."

"Like helping to burglarize the Broadhurst," Overbrook said.

"Yep. I got a positive ID from the cleaning crew—Kirby was one of them, all right. And I'd say that makes it a dead certainty that Ernie Nordstrom and Vasquez, first name unknown, were the other two. Kirby is going to be contacting Nordstrom today." She told him about the meeting in the bar and everything that was said there. "We're meeting again at six."

"And he'll be bringing the script then?"

Marian hesitated. "I'd say no. Kirby's none too bright, but that doesn't mean Ernie Nordstrom is equally slow on the uptake. Look how cautious he is about keeping his place of residence hidden. I'd guess that today we'll either be told the deal is off or that Nordstrom wants a meeting. *If* Kirby shows up. But we won't be winding it up today," she finished apologetically.

Lieutenant Overbrook laughed. "I forgive you. Frankly, Sergeant, when you first came in here I didn't think you had a chance in hell of getting a line on these boys. But Captain Murtaugh's going to be pleased to hear how far you've gotten. What are the chances of getting the costumes back?"

"Pretty good, I'd say. My guess is that Ernie Nordstrom hasn't disposed of them yet—too risky, for one thing. For another, they'll appreciate in value the longer he holds on to them. All we're missing to nail this thing down is his address."

"Okay, so what do you need?"

"I'll need a bankbook in my name showing over twenty thousand dollars—to convince Kevin Kirby I'm serious about buying what he has for sale. Make it twenty-three thousand."

"You got it. What else?"

"Lieutenant, I'd like to pay Augie Silver a consultant's fee. He thinks he's in this for a percentage, and it was his connections that led me to Kirby in the first place."

"How much?"

"Couple of hundred should do it."

"Make out the requisition and I'll sign it. Anything else?"

"Can't think of anything."

Overbrook loosened his tie and ran a finger around inside his collar. "Your meeting's at six? That's after your shift, so you'll be on overtime—and carrying your weapon. I know, Kirby has no history of violence, but what if he shows up with Ernie Nordstrom, hm? That guy is a b-i-i-i-g question mark. I don't want you taking any chances."

"All right, Lieutenant, but it's a low-risk situation. I rather doubt the secretive Mr. Nordstrom is going to put in an appearance at this point."

They'd said all there was to say, so Marian got up and left. She was rather surprised at the time and attention Midtown South was giving to such a low-priority crime; in the Ninth

Precinct, it would have been recorded and forgotten. Of course, Midtown had a "free" investigator—her. But Lieutenant Overbrook was giving her all the support she asked for, and she didn't even have to fight to get it.

What a *pleasant* change.

7

Holland had said he might drop by Huey's, just for kicks; but he wasn't there when Marian showed up at six on the dot. Neither was Kevin Kirby, a.k.a. Rocky the Bodybuilder. Augie Silver was in the same booth they'd occupied the night before . . . and one of the Zingone brothers was sitting across from him.

"Where's the iceberg?" Augie greeted her.

It took her a second to realize he meant Holland. "He's coming later." Marian sat down next to him. "Or not."

Augie gave her a querulous look. "You two fighting?"

"No." She didn't elaborate. The Zingone brother across from her wasn't wearing glasses; not Matthew, then. "Mark?"

"Luke. I hope you don't mind," he drawled, "but we thought that if this muscle man you're calling Rocky does have a pipeline to the Broadhurst loot, one of us ought to check it out. I won't queer your deal, I promise."

Marian glanced at Augie, who ducked his head. So he'd worked out something with the Zingones; deals within deals. "I get first claim on the scripts—any and all of them," she insisted, mostly because Luke seemed to be waiting for her to say something.

"Okay," Luke agreed. "Ernie Nordstrom knows us. I can ease the way a little."

"Good."

Augie cleared his throat. "You really going to buy all that Kelly Ingram stuff? Just to get to Ernie?"

"I'm hoping I won't have to," Marian said. "If Rocky can put me in touch with Nordstrom, maybe I can cut through the bullshit and tell him what I really want." *Which is a nice, clean collar.*

Augie made a face. "Seems awfully roundabout."

But Luke was nodding knowingly. "Any hook in a storm."

Oh, *that* Zingone. Luke's presence made it clear that he and his siblings were none too particular about how their items-for-sale came to be for sale in the first place. No telling how much of their inventory was bootleg. Marian wondered just how big a business the collectibles racket was; obviously more was going on than she'd suspected.

Marian found she was expected to buy the beer. No waiters appeared to be in evidence, so she went to the bar. Still no sign of Holland. The bartender gave her a tray to carry everything back to the booth.

When they'd all had their first swallow, Marian took out the two hundred dollars Lieutenant Overbrook had approved for payment to Augie as a "consultant" fee. She pushed the money toward him and said, "Augie, I want to put you on retainer."

His eyebrows shot up. "Why?"

"You know your way around the collectibles game and I don't. I need a guide. And if I'm going to take up your time, I want to pay for it."

"Well, all right!" He scooped up the money and grinned.

Luke looked annoyed, probably thinking he or one of the other Zingones should have been the one she retained. To distract him, she said, "Luke, that Tony statuette you have in your shop—where'd you get that?"

"Pawnshop on the East Side," he said. "We check 'em out regularly—you can find all sorts of things in those places. I just picked up an Elvis wall clock for Harley Wingfield today."

Marian groaned. "Harley Wingfield again! Who *is* this guy?"

"Oh, Harley's a good old boy from Tennessee," Luke said. "When he's not at home, he's in Vegas or Hollywood—digging up roots, you know? He doesn't come to New York more than a couple of times a year, but everybody knows Harley."

"Is he an 'Elvis lives!' freak?"

Augie snorted. "Those are the ones he *sells* to."

Suddenly Kevin Kirby was standing by the booth, startling Marian with his noiseless approach; she hadn't even seen him come in. The new arrival stared at Luke. "You're one of those four in that shop, the Zingone place. What are you doing here?"

"I'm Luke," Luke said pleasantly. "I'm always on the q.t. for theater items, so I thought I'd come along with Augie . . . in case you have anything more than a hairbrush for sale. Do you mind? I'll leave, if you want. I don't believe in pushing in where you're not wanted."

Kirby was silent a moment, probably trying to figure out what Luke meant, but then said, "Naw, that's all right." He sat down and looked pointedly at an unopened bottle of beer Marian had bought. She pushed it toward him and watched as he twisted off the top.

Augie cleared his throat. "So, Rocky. Have you seen Vasquez lately?"

Marian clenched her teeth and wished she'd never told Augie he'd make a good detective. Kirby hesitated, and then asked, "You tight with Vasquez?"

"Barely know the dude," Augie answered breezily. "Friend of mine is looking for him and I said I'd ask around."

Kirby frowned. "I haven't seen him for coupla days. But he has a gig at The Esophagus next week."

Luke made a noise of surprise. "Vasquez is a musician?"

"Isn't everybody?" Augie asked dryly.

Kirby said, "He's with some new shock-rock group—can't remember their name."

"Shock rock?" Marian asked.

"Yeah, you know. A more pissed-off sound than even speed metal. Wholly salient."

Salient, huh? "Sounds, ah, cool."

"Yeah."

So Vasquez was connected to the rock scene; Marian would have liked to know more but was afraid of making Kirby suspicious. She took out the faked bankbook Lieutenant Overbrook had gotten her and opened it so Kirby could read the balance. "Don't you have something to tell me about a playscript?"

He glanced at the bankbook balance but then looked uncomfortable. "There's gonna be a slight delay."

"What do you mean, a slight delay? What's wrong?"

"Nothing's wrong—it's just that this guy, the one who has the script? He's gone to California."

The other three sighed heavily. "When's he coming back?" Augie asked.

"Don't know. Depends on how long it takes him to, uh, to do what he went to California to do."

Marian smiled. "And what's that? Or is it a secret?"

"Naw, no secret. He just got a line on the hairy-spider scene from *King Kong*."

Both Augie and Luke hooted. Kevin Kirby grinned and shrugged. Marian stared at the three of them. "What hairy-spider scene? I don't remember any hairy spider in *King Kong*."

"Because there never was one," Augie said.

"Yes, there was," Luke contradicted. "But the print was destroyed years ago. It'd be worth a mint—anything to do with *Kong* means money. An original lobby poster sold for fifty-seven thou a couple years back. But the spider scene was shot."

"Bull," said Augie.

"What are you talking about?" Marian demanded.

Luke explained. "Remember the part on Skull Island where Kong has just taken Fay Wray . . . and the men from the ship are following them through the jungle? They come to this gorge or gullet or something, and the only way across is this huge old dead tree that's fallen over the opening. Do you know what I'm talking about?"

"I'm with you—go on."

"Well, the men start across, but then Kong comes back. The hero gets away . . . what's his name?"

"Bruce Cabot," said Augie.

"Right. Bruce Cabot makes it to the other side, but the rest of the men are still crawling across when Kong picks up one end of the tree and starts rotorating it, back and forth, back and forth."

"And the men all fall off," Marian said in an attempt to hurry him along.

"That's a great scene," Kirby announced feelingly.

"*But,*" Luke went on, his eyes gleaming, "that's the point where Cooper shot another scene. Merian Cooper, he directed. The scene showed that one of the men survives the fall, for all the good it does him. Because down at the bottom of the gorge is this hugemongous hairy spider, big as a two-story building—and the spider has the survivor for lunch. But Cooper himself cut the scene from the final version. Claimed it was too frightening."

"Wow," Marian said appreciatively.

Augie gave a sarcastic little laugh. "Yeah, it makes a good story. But it never happened."

"Yes, it did, Augie," Luke said testily. "It's been documentaried. The only print was thrown away back in thirty-two, thirty-three, whenever the hell it was. But it's been documentaried."

"Docum*ent*ed, not documentaried," Augie snapped, getting a little testy himself.

"Whatever. But you can check it out."

"The point is," Augie said to Marian, "that no print exists *now*. Ernie's a dreamer. Chasing off to California after a nonexistent scene? Sheesh."

Marian kept a poker face and prayed that Kevin Kirby hadn't caught it. But while he was slow, he wasn't that slow. "Ernie?" He looked from Augie to Luke to Marian and back to Augie again. "Who said anything about Ernie?"

The color drained out of Augie's face when he realized his gaffe. "Why, uh, you did, Rocky. You said somebody named Ernie had a line on the hairy-spider scene and—"

Kirby's handsome face had tightened. "I did not. I didn't mention any names at all. What the hell's going on here?"

Marian made an attempt to save the situation. "Yes, you did say 'Ernie'—I heard you. Didn't you hear him, Luke?"

Kirby jumped up. "First Vasquez, and now Ernie! What the hell?" He jerked away from the booth and hurried out of the bar.

Luke sighed. "Nice going, Augie."

Aaarrrrrghh! Marian screamed mentally. But she said nothing; it was a risk you ran when you worked with civilians.

"Oh jeez, I'm sorry!" Augie whacked his forehead with the palm of his hand. "Stupid, stupid, stupid!"

Luke nodded solemnly. "You should have been more precautious."

"Me and my big mouth! Marian, I'm sorry. Look, let me out—maybe I can catch him."

Marian slid out of the booth and let Augie go, knowing Kevin Kirby was already out of reach. Luke mumbled something about helping Augie and followed him. When they were both gone, she sat back down and stared disconsolately at the empty beer bottles.

"Well, that was an invigorating exercise in futility," said a familiar voice. "One Augie Silver needs a few lessons in discretionary interrogation techniques, wouldn't you say?"

Marian leaned around the end of her seat to look into the next booth. "Oh, that's cute. What did you think you could learn by eavesdropping that you couldn't hear sitting with us?"

"Nothing." Holland got up and joined Marian in her booth. "But maintaining my role of naysayer while you were moving in for the kill would have put undue strain on the negotiations. By the way, where did your friend Luke learn to speak English—Albania? Too bad Rocky got away. I assume you have his real name and address?"

Marian said yes. "But there's no point in bringing him in— we couldn't hold him. And I can't even take him in for questioning. He'd get spooked and warn the other two."

"And Ernie Nordstrom's off in California looking for hairy spiders." A mocking laugh. "You were right. These people *do* love what they're doing. And they're thoroughly convinced of its importance. Shock rock, ancient movies, and Elvis. God bless America."

Marian grinned at him. "Oh, I don't know. I'd kind of like to see that hairy-spider scene myself."

"Sometimes you worry me. What are you going to do now?"

"Well, I lost the hunk, so I guess I'll go after the ponytail. At The Esophagus next week, whatever The Esophagus is."

"Probably an East Village rat hole," Holland said. "Does this mean you'll be taking the weekend off, just like normal people?"

"Looks like it." She smiled at the thought. "Like normal people."

The Saturday night audience in the Broadhurst Theatre was utterly, pin-drop silent for about ten seconds—and then came an explosion of applause and cheering that rocked the rafters. It went on and on, as if the members of the audience couldn't say loudly enough how much they liked the play. The same thing had happened the other time Marian saw *The Apostrophe Thief*, on opening night. It had been exciting then; it was exciting now.

Even poker-faced Holland was clapping his hands. When the curtain calls were over and the hubbub began to die down, he turned to Marian and said, "I want to meet Abigail James."

Not a word about Kelly. "If she's here," Marian said. "Let's go backstage and see."

The play had been running only a little more than a week, so there was no noticeable lessening in the crowd of well-wishers backstage; the only difference was that camera crews no longer prowled about looking for celebrities. Kelly's dressing room was packed, as was Ian Cavanaugh's. Abigail James was there, standing off to the side and talking to two earnest interviewers, both of whom were thrusting microphones into her face.

". . . he was partially right," the playwright was saying. "It's when we allow the *minutiae* of life to be stolen from us—and what could be more minute than an apostrophe?—that we lose control over the quality of life in general. But I meant the title in a literal sense as well . . . in the area of language, that is. The degeneration of language is typically a good indicator of the erosion of standards in other areas of life. For example, the word 'Halloween' used to have an apostrophe in it. What happened to that apostrophe? Where did it go? Carelessness concerning the use of apostrophes just happened to be the example I fixed on, but it could be anything."

"Would you say the degeneration of language is an omen of erosion to come in the rest of life?"

Abigail James appeared to think. "No, I would say it follows. The erosion has already begun."

"Can we stop this degeneration of language?"

"I doubt it. All we can do is warn each other. I know no way to enforce linguistic vigilance."

"But if there were a way, would the effect be retroactive? Could restoring linguistic standards lead to the restoration of other, unrelated life-quality standards?"

The playwright's eyes glazed over. Then she turned and looked directly at Marian. "Sergeant Larch! How delightful you could come!" To the interviewers: "You'll have to excuse me. An old friend." The two turned off their tape recorders, murmured their thanks, and went hunting for other game. Abigail James looked at Marian contritely. "Please forgive me for using you to end that farce, Sergeant. I don't know how much longer I could have kept a straight face."

Marian shook her head in mock disapproval. "Is this the same Abigail James who once told me she paired the words 'apostrophe' and 'thief' for the sole reason that she liked the way they sounded together? That the title of the play has absolutely no meaning at all?"

The other woman laughed, and even looked a little embarrassed. "Did you happen to see the Friday *Times*? Some idiot wrote a piece about how the apostrophe is the most microcosmic of microcosms, and 'thief' is a metaphor for anything or anyone who destroys by means of attrition. The piece was pompous and pretentious and utterly nuts. I thought it was hilarious. But all day today I've had people like those two *seriously* questioning me about it. And no matter what nonsense I spout, they tape it or write it down as if it were Holy Writ."

Holland spoke up. "And some earnest theater student in west Texas will read those very words . . . and make them the basis of a graduate thesis."

"Alas. And that's my contribution to knowledge."

"No. That's your contribution to *education*."

"Ah. They aren't the same, are they? Sergeant, introduce me to this man."

Marian did; soon Holland and the playwright were deep in a discussion of the latter's use of minor characters to "shadow" the major conflict of the play. Marian left them to it and tried working her way toward Kelly's dressing room. She got as far as the door but had to stop; no room inside.

She turned away and resigned herself to waiting. After a moment she caught a glimpse of Leo Gunn doing whatever it was stage managers did after a performance. Marian amused herself for a while watching the postperformance performance being given by a young woman who played Kelly's kid sister in the play. She was putting on quite a show—flirting, laughing gaily, playing the sweet young innocent to the hilt. She had an odd first name . . . Xandria, that was it. And young Xandria was having the time of her life, holding court backstage at the Broadhurst Theatre. *Well, why not?* Marian thought. She was young, pretty, and in a hit Broadway play—why not show off a little?

Suddenly Marian found herself caught in wall-to-wall people; evidently Kelly and Ian Cavanaugh both had shooed the rest of their visitors out at the same time. The last one out of

Kelly's dressing room was John Reddick. He came out laughing and shaking his head. "I should have known she'd rope you into coming along," he said to the man right ahead of him. "One dancing partner isn't enough! Where does she get her energy? She gave two performances today, she has one tomorrow—and she wants to go dancing!"

The other man said simply, "Be thankful."

"Oh, I am, I am!" Then Reddick spotted Marian. "Well, hello, Sergeant. Gene, this is the police detective investigating our burglary, Sergeant, er, Birch."

"Larch."

An exaggerated sigh. "I knew it was something arboreal. Sergeant Larch, this is our producer, Gene Ramsay."

Ramsay was monochromatic: tan suit, tan hair, almost the exact shade as his face. Even the irises of his eyes looked tan. They both muttered *Gladtameetcha*, and Marian said, "You're going dancing? Kelly loves to dance."

"But I don't," Ramsay said. "John, if you were a better dancer, I wouldn't have to do this."

The director placed one hand flat on his chest. "I try. God knows I try. Is it my fault I was born with two left feet? Besides, it's the producer's job to keep his star happy. Oh— there's Leo. Excuse me, folks, I have to see him about something." He hurried off after the stage manager.

Marian smiled. "Seems to me he's not exactly lacking in energy either."

Gene Ramsay grunted. "John's been rejuvenated. He used to wear the rest of us out, he was so go-go-go all the time. But then he got a little older, as we all did, and everyone breathed a sigh of relief when John started slowing down. But now—" He laughed.

"But now?"

"Now he's back to go-go-go again, worse than ever."

"Hm. Is he sharing the mystery of his newfound youth or is he keeping it to himself?"

"Oh, no mystery. John's not the first director to fall in love with his star, and he won't be the last. Nothing like it to get the old juices flowing again."

"What?" Marian wasn't sure she'd heard right. "What did you say?"

But before he could answer, Marian heard her name being sung out in bell-like tones. Ian Cavanaugh stood posed in the doorway of his dressing room, drawing the eyes of everyone backstage. "Sergeant, did you come to tell me you've recovered my shaving mug?"

Marian saw Abigail James laugh and turn back to her conversation with Holland. "Not yet," Marian said. "But we do have a line on the thieves."

"You do?" Gene Ramsay said.

Cavanaugh dropped his pose and came over to her. "You mean there's a real chance of getting our things back? Frankly, I never expected to hear that."

"Frankly, I never expected to say it. I don't want to get your hopes up, but we do have a shot at recovering your things— including the scripts."

The actor waved a hand. "They're no longer urgent—we have our new scripts marked now. Of course, Abby always worries about play piracy. But I'll be glad to see that old shaving mug again." He raised his voice slightly. "Abby—I'll be ready to leave in about ten minutes." She waved acknowledgment.

When Cavanaugh went back to his dressing room, Marian turned to ask Gene Ramsay what he'd meant, but the producer was no longer there. John Reddick in love with Kelly? She went over and knocked on Kelly's door. "It's me."

Kelly said to come in; Marian spent the next few minutes telling her friend how great her performance had been that evening, with Kelly encouraging her every step of the way. Both women were laughing—and it hit Marian with a shock that she felt happy. What had happened to her depression?

"Lock the door, will you?" Kelly asked. "I don't want someone walking in on me while I'm changing." She slipped out of the sparkly jacket she wore in the last scene and hung it up.

Marian went over for a closer look at the garment. "Is this a copy of the Sarah Bernhardt jacket?"

"Not an exact copy. The costumers had to come up with something fast, and they were working from photographs instead of designs. Gene Ramsay . . . our producer?"

"I just met him."

"Gene got the jacket at an auction in Paris. I think he meant it to go straight to the theater costume museum, that one on Fifth? But . . . do you remember that rough period I was going through during rehearsal? That time I was thinking I was just a television actor, that I'd ruin the play for everybody?"

"Ohhhhhh, yes!"

"Well, Gene brought me that jacket as a sort of confidence-booster. He gave me this little speech about how the jacket should be worn only by those worthy of it—me, brand new to the stage, wearing something that belonged to Bernhardt herself! Whoo! But I wore it, you betcha! And now it's gone."

"So wearing it was an honor?"

"Just slightly short of canonization. Is that the word I want? When somebody's made a saint?"

"That's the word. Was the jacket kept in the costume room along with everything else?"

"Yes, but Gene had new locks put on. It was *supposed* to be safe there."

"Safe . . . what about that safe in John Reddick's office? Why not keep it there?"

"That little old thing? You'd have to wad the jacket up into a ball to get it in *there*."

Marian ran her fingers over the imitation gemstones that were sewn on the front part of the jacket; the sleeves and back were an amber velvet. "Are you sure this is just glass? From the audience, they look like real jewels."

Kelly grinned. "That's the idea. They aren't cheap, you know. Good fakes cost money. And those are larger stones than the ones on Bernhardt's jacket. These show up a little better, I think." She'd finished changing. "Marian, you can do me a tremenjous favor. Come dancing tonight. I've already got two dancing partners lined up—"

"John Reddick and Gene Ramsay, I know. But I'm no dancer, Kel. Why don't you ask Ian Cavanaugh and Abigail James to go along?"

"Oh, *them*." Kelly dismissed the two with a wave of her hand. "Their idea of a good time is to go home and lock the doors and shut out the world. They *never* go to clubs like Column Left."

"That's the name of the place you're going?"

"That's the place *we're* going."

"Sounds like a marching order—about face, column left. Change of subject, Kelly. Gene Ramsay just told me that John Reddick is in love with you."

Kelly made a face. "Gene is a terrible gossip. John *thinks* he's in love with me. It's the Pygmalion thing," she said earnestly. "He took this raw television personality and created a real actor out of her—and then fell in love with what he'd created . . . isn't that the way the story's supposed to go? Well, that's how he looks at me. But he'll forget all about it when he starts work on a new play. I hope."

"Did he 'create' you?" Marian asked skeptically.

"He helped." Kelly was trying to be fair. "But I created

myself. God, that sounds extensional, uff, I mean existential. But I think John is giving himself too much credit." She laughed easily. "It's best not to take him too seriously."

"I'll remember."

"Now—you *are* coming dancing. No arguments!"

"Uh, I've got Holland here with me."

"Holland?" Kelly didn't try to hide her surprise. "Well. Imagine that." She mulled it over for a moment. "Curt Holland, huh?" Then the corners of her mouth lifted and she asked: "Does he dance?"

Marian laughed. "I have no idea."

Kelly's smile got even bigger. "Well, then—let's find out."

8

Holland didn't dance, or wouldn't. When Kelly invited him to come along to Column Left, he spun toward Marian and snapped out, "Is that what you want? Celebrity dancing? A whirl in the old spotlight? A little reflected glory for yourself?"

"Whoa!" Marian said, annoyed. "What's the matter? Is dancing against your religion?"

"I find it . . . exhibitionistic."

"Oh, thank you very much," Kelly said archly.

Marian found that an odd comment, coming from a man who at times displayed more than a touch of the exhibitionist himself. "It's just a way to unwind, Holland," she said mildly. "Don't make it into something else."

"You're determined to go?"

She hadn't been, until his surprisingly unreasonable response to such a simple invitation. "I'd like to go, yes."

He smiled his most cynical smile. "Then far be it from me to interfere with your pleasures." And with that, he walked out.

"What an *aggravating* man," Kelly growled, low in her throat.

Marian agreed. What had set him off like that? She was provoked with Holland, and with herself as well, for allowing his behavior to push her into something she'd only half made up her mind to do. But she went along to Column Left with Kelly and her two conscripted dancing partners, John Reddick and Gene Ramsay. And she went determined to put Holland out of her mind; every time she thought she was coming close to understanding him, he pulled some stunt like this one. But if the man was determined to remain an enigma, let him.

Column Left had a long line of customers waiting to get in. Gene Ramsay ran an eye over the crowd and said, "Remember those restaurants in China that were found to be putting opium pods in their dishes to addict customers to their food?"

"Nothing that sneaky here," Kelly said. "This is just one of the few places in town with a dance floor bigger than a postage stamp."

They were able to bypass the line once the doorman caught sight of Kelly; luminaries had priority there. The waiting customers hooted good-naturedly as the four of them were ushered in, perhaps thinking that soon they'd be on the same dance floor as the celebrated Kelly Ingram. Inside was about what Marian expected; jam-packed with customers, strobe lights playing over the dance floor, a band performing with ear-shattering intensity. The place had one nice touch: the tables were divided from the dance floor by a thick Plexiglas partition that muted the music enough to permit talking without having to shout. But the effect of that was to make stepping on to the dance floor something like entering an arena, an arrangement that intimidated Kelly Ingram not at all.

Marian spent the next hour sitting at a table and talking to whichever man was not trying to keep up with Kelly on the dance floor. John Reddick was drinking a lot, tossing it down while watching Kelly like a moonstruck schoolboy. Gene Ramsay was right; the director was besotted with his star. But Kelly was the same old Kelly—friendly but not encouraging, having fun but keeping her would-be lover at arm's length. At one point Kelly acquired *five* extra partners on the dance floor, men and women both, all of them strangers and all of them having a glorious time.

"Look at that, Larch-Tree," John Reddick said blurrily. "Everything rotates around her. She makes her own universe, wherever she goes!"

Oh dear. "How about some coffee, Mr. Reddick?"

"John. Call me John. Are you tryin' to get me undrunk?"

"Wouldn't be a bad idea."

"It would be a *terr'ble* idea. And why, you ask? No, you don't ask. But I'll tell you anyway. It would be a terr'ble idea because . . . because . . . I don't remember why because."

Marian asked the waiter to bring a pot of black coffee.

Gene Ramsay came back and sank into a chair, panting and laughing. "Kelly doesn't need me out there. Whoo! I'm too old for this."

"Sheesh really byooful, isn' she?" the director mumbled.

Ramsay winked at Marian. "Yes, John. She's really beautiful."

The waiter brought the pot of coffee. Marian poured a cup and pushed it across the table. "John—drink this."

He made a face but did as she said. "I'm makin' a fool of myself, arn eye?"

The producer laughed. "Not yet, but you're getting there. The coffee's a good idea, Marian. Do you mind if I call you Marian? 'Sergeant' and 'Mister' seem a little formal for this setting."

Marian didn't mind.

A young woman hiding behind a ton of make-up and wearing a short dress that looked made of aluminum foil came up to their table. "Excuse me—aren't you Gene Ramsay?"

He groaned. "Only during office hours, darling, only during office hours."

"Mr. Ramsay, I was wondering if you'd look at my portfolio? I know it's an imposition, but—"

"You take your portfolio dancing with you?"

"Oh, I don't have it *with* me, but I thought—"

"Drop it off at the office and someone'll take a look. Just don't bother me now."

"Really? You mean it? You promise?"

"Really, I mean it, I promise. Now run along."

"Oh, *thank* you, Mr. Ramsay, that's really wonderful, I really ap*prec*iate it . . . " She went on burbling until he turned and glowered at her; she backed away, still thanking him.

Marian was curious. "Will you look at it?"

"Someone on my staff will. I've got one person who does nothing but read portfolios and reviews and mail from the wannabes. Every third person in New York is an actor looking for work, which still beats California, where *everybody* is an actor. We'll look at this girl's portfolio—there's always a chance she has talent."

"How can you tell that from a portfolio?"

"Her credits. You don't get a lot of roles without *some* talent. But if all she's done is Marian the Librarian in her high school production of *The Music Man*, we'll pass."

"Ha!" said John. "*Marian* the Librarian."

Marian waved a hand. "Not me—I've never worked in a library."

Just then the band took a break; Kelly came back and sat down. "John, your turn next, when they come back."

He made an attempt to rise but sank back to his seat. "Larch-Tree, you dance with her. I tol' you I have two left feet."

"And I've got three," Marian said. "The music's stopped anyway. Here, have some more coffee."

Kelly realized John was a little tipsy and ordered him to

sober up immediately. "I have to talk to you about Xandria. Did you see what she did tonight? She tried to upstage me three different times."

"They learn fast," Gene murmured.

John was nodding. "I saw. I'll speak to her tomorrow. Can't have s'porting players upstaging the star."

"We can't have anybody upstaging *anybody*," Kelly insisted. "You said that yourself, the first week of rehearsal."

"I'll talk to her, I'll talk to her!"

"She's young, Kelly," Gene said. "Still trying to find out what she can get away with."

"Well, she can't get away with upstaging me. I'll nail her shoes to the floor."

"What's her last name?" Marian asked. "I don't remember."

"Priest," Kelly said. "Xandria-Holier-Than-Thou-Female-Priest."

"I'll remember *that*," Marian declared.

After a while the band came back from its break, and John valiantly struggled to his feet and followed Kelly out to the dance floor. Marian watched as he stood weaving in place and occasionally waving an arm in the air as Kelly danced around him. A for effort.

Gene Ramsay touched her arm. "I heard you telling Ian Cavanaugh you had a line on our burglar. Who is it, can you tell me?"

"I'd rather not say. What if I'm wrong? Besides, my suspect's not in custody yet."

"Why not?"

"Out of town. Let me ask you something. When did Sarah Bernhardt die?"

His eyebrows rose. "You're thinking of the jacket. Bernhardt died sometime in the twenties, I don't remember the exact year."

"So that jacket's at least seventy years old. And it was still wearable?"

"The seams had to be strengthened and the lining replaced. But the velvet wasn't faded—the jacket had been kept folded away in tissue paper all this time." He smiled. "You know, Bernhardt thought that jacket brought her luck. She called it her *veste à bonne chance*. Eventually it would have gone to the New York Museum of Theatrical Costuming—I'm on the board of directors. I only hope the thieving sonuvabitch who took it knows its true value." A sigh, and he changed the subject. "This music is starting to sound monotonous. Are you sure you don't want to dance?"

"Positive."

"Oh, *thank* you," he said with a laugh. "My feet hurt. I don't see how Kelly does it."

But after another fifteen or twenty minutes, even Kelly had had enough. Gene and his still-sobering director climbed into one cab while Marian and Kelly took another, the latter having decided that Marian was spending the night at her place. Marian was too sleepy to protest.

However, sleep was not what Kelly had in mind. She kept Marian up listening to her complaints about Xandria Priest. "She never just *talks* to people," Kelly said. "She *flirts*. Every sentence that comes out of her mouth is a flirt-sentence, even when she's talking to women. She can't even say 'It's raining' without making it sound like a come-on. That's the only way she *knows* to talk. She comes in wearing pink and does that cute, coy, poor-little-me act until I want to puke."

Marian yawned. "Notcher problem."

"The hell it isn't! I've got to watch her trying to seduce every man in the place with that innocent little girl act—do you know she even hit on Ian Cavanaugh while Abby was watching? And she knew they were living together."

"Mmnph."

"And every night she goes out of her way to flirt with Leo Gunn. Somebody told her Leo doesn't care for girls, but did that stop her? Not on your life."

"Mh."

"I know what this sounds like," Kelly said morosely. "It sounds like plain, old-fashioned jealousy, doesn't it? A woman can't say anything about another woman's behavior without being called catty. But damn it, Marian, that girl *embarrasses* me! She makes all women look bad! It's demeaning."

Finally she let Marian get to bed. Marian fuzzily wondered about Kelly's tirade; was she in fact jealous? No, Marian decided; jealousy was not part of Kelly's psychic make-up. She just didn't like Xandria Priest, that was all.

Well, she's entitled. Marian pulled the comforter up under her chin and sank happily into oblivion.

When Marian got home the next day, she found a message from Augie Silver on her answering machine. He said he'd heard some playscripts would be offered at the flea market held in St. Sebastian's Church on East Seventy-fourth all day Monday. He'd be there in the afternoon, if she wanted to meet him. Poor Augie, trying to make up for losing the hunk.

No message from Holland.

Marian spent the rest of Sunday doing laundry and making a pass at housecleaning, reading the *Times*, and dozing. She didn't envy Kelly, who was expected to give a brilliant performance in the middle of a Sunday afternoon; impossible task. Marian got her clothes ready for the next few days, thinking resignedly that she'd expected to be out of the policing business by now.

Monday morning she walked into a subdued and somber mood at Midtown South. "Lieutenant Overbrook had a coronary yesterday," Captain Murtaugh told her. "He's in Christ Hospital in Jersey City—he was visiting his daughter when it happened. Last word we had, he's resting comfortably."

"Oh, poor man!" Marian said feelingly. "I'm sorry."

"So am I. Overbrook's only six weeks from making his thirty-year retirement."

So close! "Is he going to lose the pension?"

"We're hoping not. The plan is for him to use all the personal time he's got coming before getting back to work. It'll be close, but he should have enough time to recover . . . unless there are complications. He's not a young man, and he's fifty pounds overweight." Murtaugh made a visible effort to shift mental gears. "So you're going to have to bring me up to date on your investigation. Friday, Overbrook told me you had a line on the burglars, is that right?"

"A pretty good line, I think." Marian filled him in on everything she'd found so far, up to and including Augie Silver's slip of the tongue that had scared off her most promising link to Ernie Nordstrom. "There's still Vasquez, though," she said. "He's performing with a rock group this week—we can catch him there. But I was told he speaks almost no English, so we'll need someone who knows Spanish."

"That might be a problem." Captain Murtaugh frowned. "Campos has gone to Miami to pick up a prisoner and Esposito's going to be tied up in court the next few days. I'm not going to request an interpreter for a low-priority crime like this one. Budget's too tight."

"Excuse me, Captain, but if you don't mind borrowing from the Ninth Precinct again, there's a detective there who speaks Spanish. Her name's Gloria Sanchez and I've worked with her before. She's half Puerto Rican and half black, and she changes ethnic identities as easily as you and I change clothes.

Gloria'd do a better job of approaching Vasquez than I could, since she wouldn't need to haul an interpreter along."

"When's this Ernie Nordstrom getting back from California?"

"Don't know. He might even be back now."

"Then we'd better move on it—I don't want to drag this thing out any longer. Captain DiFalco isn't going to be too happy about giving up another of his people, though . . . unless I offer him a substitute. I'll give him a call. Sergeant, since you don't have a desk here, use Lieutenant Overbrook's office until he gets back. It's open."

"Thanks, Captain." *Who said I'd never make it to a lieutenant's office?* Marian thought wryly. She went into Overbrook's cubicle and had a sudden flash: What if in six weeks when Overbrook retired . . . ? She shook her head, ashamed of her quickness to exploit a sick man's absence— and amazed at the stab of ambition still in her belly.

Marian pulled out the NYNEX yellow pages and started flipping through. The Esophagus turned out to be a club with an address on Bowery; Marian dialed the number and got a recording. A nasal voice informed her The Esophagus was closed on Mondays, but Tuesday night the feature attraction would be that hot new shock-rock group, Waltzing Brünnhilde. Two shows nightly, ten and midnight.

Then she started calling airlines. Forty-five minutes later she had what she wanted and went to knock on Captain Murtaugh's door. "Ernie Nordstrom's back in town—he took United's red-eye from Los Angeles last night. We can't move on Vasquez until tomorrow night, though, because Waltzing Brünnhilde doesn't open 'til then. They—"

"Waltzing . . . what?"

"Brünnhilde. That's the name of the rock group Vasquez is

with, Waltzing Brünnhilde. But The Esophagus is closed on Mondays."

The captain nodded. "Okay, I'll request Detective Sanchez for a briefing period tomorrow and we can work out the details then. That enough time?"

"Should be. It's not very complicated."

"No. I haven't been able to reach DiFalco yet, but there won't be a problem. Sergeant, I like the way you've handled this case. You've taken up a minimum of administrative time and you've gotten results. That's what I like to see."

"Thank you, Captain."

"What next?"

"Well, since I'm going to have some time, I thought I'd go to St. Sebastian's flea market this afternoon. I've heard there'll be playscripts there."

Murtaugh said that sounded like a good idea, in an absent sort of way; he was already thinking of another case. Marian went to the files and pulled out the list of items taken from the Broadhurst. She sat at Lieutenant Overbrook's desk and made up her own list, items she was guessing would be of most value to a dealer of collectibles. Costumes even more than scripts, especially the Bernhardt jacket. She left out things such as a six-pack that one of the stagehands claimed was taken; after a moment's hesitation she ruled out all of Kelly's personal items. Kevin Kirby must have lifted Kelly's hairbrush when Ernie Nordstrom wasn't looking; but Marian couldn't see that even in the artificial values of the world of collectibles a pair of old sneakers or a bottle of hand lotion would be worth much.

Primary on the list were the scripts and the costumes; they would bring money. Also included was Ian Cavanaugh's shaving mug, although he'd obviously inflated its antique value.

Marian's memory brought up a picture of the hawk-nosed woman named Lenora whom she'd met at the auction in Sheridan Square . . . and how she'd virtually drooled at the thought of owning the mug. It was worth something.

Two paintings had been taken from the walls of the dressing rooms. One belonged to Xandria Priest and the other to an actor named Mitchell Tobin. The names of the artists and the titles of the paintings meant nothing to Marian. She put them on the list.

Also taken from Xandria Priest's dressing room: a diary. Ah. Secrets? Gossip? Juicy stuff that would bring a tidy sum once young Xandria had passed from the ingenue stage to that of established performer? On the list it went.

But Mitchell Tobin was the one hardest hit. In addition to the painting, he lost a tape deck, a portable CD player, a clock radio, and a notebook computer—all electronic items that may have been taken for their easy disposability as much as for their souvenir value. Marian tried to remember which one Tobin was. Yes: he played Xandria's boyfriend in *The Apostrophe Thief*, acting a role ten years younger than his true age.

Other radios and clocks were stolen, as well as a six-inch television set; but larger, more cumbersome TVs were passed by. Also taken: several bottles of liquor and one of champagne. Plus a fountain pen, four flower vases, two small stuffed animals (both actor-owners claimed they were good-luck charms), a dressing gown. A framed, autographed photo of Geraldine Page. No cash, no jewelry; none had been kept in the dressing rooms.

All in all, it still made quite a list. Except for Mitchell Tobin's electronic toys, Marian had a real hope of recovering the missing items. If Ernie Nordstrom made a habit of storing his loot in his home, the police might just turn up a few other articles of interest as well. It all depended on Vasquez. One way or another, they'd have to get the address out of him.

Marian checked her watch. Time for an early lunch and then on to the flea market at St. Sebastian's.

9

Augie Silver was pacing back and forth before the entrance to St. Sebastian's Church, waiting for her. "I was afraid you wouldn't come," he greeted her, "after I scared off Rocky. I really am sorry, I didn't—"

"Forget it, Augie. It's done. And all is not lost. . . . There's still Vasquez."

"You don't want to kill me?"

Marian laughed. "Not today." She noticed he didn't offer to return her two hundred bucks. "Are you on your lunch hour?"

"I'm taking a couple of hours. And I'll work late to make up for it. My boss is real good about that. He doesn't care when we work, so long as the work gets done."

"Hold on to *that* job. So, what's this flea market here?"

Augie beamed. "Fun and games. A glorious mishmosh of show biz collectibles. There'll be people from all over—buying, selling, trading. A lot of the stuff is junk, but you can usually count on a few quality finds. Most of what's for sale is movie memorabilia, but there's always a fair assortment of theater goodies. And the prices are on the cheapish side—the high-priced stuff all goes to auction. Let's go in."

Marian followed him down to the basement of St. Sebastian's, into a babble of voices and an array of color and shapes that made her pause. Almost all the floor space was taken up by tables laden with various wares, with only the narrowest of aisles in between. The walls sported posters, hooks with costumes hanging from them, framed photographs, and a tattered American flag purporting to be the one used in *The Sands of Iwo Jima*. "Those are *not* Sonja Henie's skates!" an annoyed male voice proclaimed.

"This way," Augie said. "The theater people usually set up along the back wall."

He led her past tables separating collectors and dealers haggling over price. One loudly contested item was a black cowboy hat autographed by Cher. A Woolworth's writing pad with Hedy Lamarr's picture on the cover sold for eight dollars. Another dime store item was a card of bobby pins featuring a picture of Rita Hayworth. A matchbook cover advertised *The Thief of Bagdad*—the 1924 version with its eccentric spelling. Cary Grant grinned out from a cigarette card. Dixie Cup lids, sporting pictures of Clark Gable, Ginger Rogers, William Powell, Tom Mix—priced from fifty cents to six dollars. Marian smiled at a soap statue of Shirley Temple, but didn't quite know what to make of an empty cardboard container bearing the words "Valley Farm's Bing Crosby Vanilla."

"Philip, I've told you a dozen times," a cranky voice said, "I collect *John* Hurt, not William Hurt."

Augie stopped and pointed. "See the guy in the blue windbreaker? That's the Bogart man. Nobody knows his name, but he lives out of his van and travels all over the country hauling his Bogart lobby cards with him."

"Um," said Marian. They pushed on.

"It looks authentic, sure," a suspicious woman was saying. "But how do I know this is really Ronald Reagan's autograph? His mother signed most of his photographs for him."

"Here we are," Augie said. "Hiya, Wadsworth. Made any good scores lately?"

A mournful-looking man with no chin shook his head sadly. "I almost got the apron Joan Plowright wore in *The Entertainer*, but some woman from Cincinnati beat me to it."

"Aw, that's too bad. Marian, this is Wadsworth. Wadsworth, this is Marian. She collects John Reddick."

"Hello, Wadsworth," Marian said.

The gloomy man returned her greeting. "John Reddick, the director? I don't believe I've run into a Reddick collector before."

"I'm looking for his copies of playscripts. You wouldn't happen to have any, would you?"

Wadsworth looked as if he wanted to cry. "I was *this close* to a copy of *Foxfire*," he said, holding thumb and forefinger about half an inch apart, "but I was outbid."

"Er, I already have that one," she lied. "I'm looking for *Three Rings* . . . or maybe *The Apostrophe Thief?*"

His voice broke as he said, "I've never seen a copy of *Three Rings*, and it's too early yet for *The Apostrophe Thief*. What about play programs? I can get you his programs."

"No, thanks. Just scripts."

Wadsworth looked crushed.

Augie picked up a box from Wadsworth's table. It was a jigsaw puzzle called Broadway Stars; the illustration on the lid showed a caricature drawing of about a dozen people. "There's Tallulah," Augie said, "and Lunt and Fontanne. And I suppose that could be Helen Hayes. But I can't identify any of these others. This isn't a Hirschfield drawing, is it?"

The dealer sighed dolorously. "It's an imitation Hirschfield. Those are said to be even more rare than the originals."

"How much?"

"Forty dollars."

Augie put the box back on the table. "I don't think so."

Wadsworth's face was a tragic mask until he saw Marian

looking at a bedraggled ostrich plume on his table. "That's from the fan Mae West carried in *Diamond Lil.*"

"Ah. Where's the rest of the fan?"

"It went for six hundred dollars!" the dealer wailed. "I didn't have the cash!"

Both Marian and Augie hastily offered words of condolence until Wadsworth had regained some measure of self-control; then they slipped away. Augie leaned in close and said, "To hear Wadsworth tell it, he's forever getting *that close* to the find that'll set him up for life. He's always crying about the one that got away."

"Then how can he make a living from it?"

"Oh, Wadsworth just deals part-time. He's an aglet-maker from Passaic."

"A what?"

He gave her his big-toothed grin. "He makes aglets. And he's always crying about that, too. Says it's not the same, now they've switched from metal to plastic."

"But what's—ow!" An elbow in Marian's side.

"Sorry," a distracted woman said as she squeezed by.

"Is it always this crowded?" Marian asked.

"Not always," Augie said. "But sometimes it's worse."

Four or five rows of tables away, a short chubby man in a plaid jacket was waving his arm and calling out something that was lost in the general hum and babble of the room. Marian looked behind her to see whom he was calling to, but no one seemed to be paying any attention. She looked back; he waved again and grinned. Marian pointed to herself: *me?*

The man in the plaid jacket nodded vigorously and disappeared into the crowd. Now what was all that about?

Marian and Augie inched along the row of tables, asking about scripts, pausing to look at some piece of memorabilia that caught their eye. Several of the tables had playscripts for sale. Marian went through the motions of looking through them, mostly for Augie's benefit; but of course *The Apostrophe Thief* wasn't there. But scripts seemed to be of minor interest here; most of the buying and selling involved personal items that once belonged to celebrities. Augie himself bought a bow tie worn by Anthony Quayle in *Sleuth*. Marian stared incredulously at an old Kleenex with a touch of lipstick on it; the dealer claimed it was Jessica Tandy's, from the time she was doing *A Delicate Balance*. Suddenly, Holland's voice saying *Voyeurism* spoke in her head; musing that he just might be right, Marian moved away.

Sitting behind the second-to-last table was the one female member of the Zingone clan; she was accepting money from a beaming customer, a man in his forties dressed in tattletale gray who was clutching a yellowed play program encased in a plastic bag. The dealer glanced up and saw them. "Hiya Augie, and . . . Marian?"

"Right. And you're Janet."

She nodded. "People, I want you to meet Dudley. Dudley collects play programs." She seemed to be trying not to laugh. "But only programs for plays that start with the letter *H*."

Augie stared. "*Only* with *H*?"

"That's right," Dudley crooned happily. "And Janet just found me one I didn't have." He held up the program; the play was titled *Half a Widow*, and the date was 1927.

Janet grinned wickedly. "Why don't you tell them some of the plays you have, Dudley?"

"I got *Hair* and *The Hairy Ape*," he said happily. "I got *The Homecoming, Harvey, How to Succeed in Business without Really Trying, Hotel Universe, A Hatful of Rain, The Heiress, Hopalong Freud, The Happiest Millionaire, High Spirits, Huckleberry, Hellzapoppin, Hello Dolly*, and *Hello Solly*. I got fourteen *Hamlet*s and three *Hedda Gablers*."

"Uh, I think I see somebody who, um." Augie started edging away.

"I got *Here Be Dragons, A Hole in the Head, Hunter's Moon,*" Dudley went on. "*Hay Fever, The Humbug, Home, Hope Is the Thing with Feathers,* three *Henry IV*s, two *Henry V*s, *High Tor, How to Be a Jewish Mother, How a Nice Girl Named Janet Contracted Syphilis.*"

"Thanks a lot," Janet said dryly. Marian cast a longing glance after Augie, who by then had made his escape.

"I got a lot of 'House' programs. I got *House of Flowers, House of Bernarda Alba, House of Atreus, House of Rothschild, Heartbreak House, The Housekeeper, The House on Cristo Street, Houseboat on the Styx. . . .*"

Would this never end? Marian interrupted his spiel: "Well . . . Dudley. That's an impressive list, that is. Um, what do you plan on doing with all those programs?"

Dead silence. Dudley stared at her with a mixture of shock and scorn, and then said passionately, "What do I plan on *doing* with them? Is that what you said? I plan on *having* them, that's what I plan on *doing* with them! You think maybe I'm going to plaster the walls with them?" In a huff, he turned and shouldered his way through the crowd.

Janet was laughing. "That is the one question you never ask a collector. Not ever."

"Yeah, I guess so," Marian said. "Well. So, where are your brothers?"

"Oh, Luke's in Indiana, Mark's minding the store, and Matthew's cruising here, looking for bargains."

"What's Luke doing in Indiana?"

"Attending a private auction. Movie memorabilia." Janet looked thoughtful. "You know, the people who started collecting seriously back during Hollywood's Golden Age are all getting on in years now. And whenever one of them dies, the heirs almost always put the collection up for auction. A lot of good items are available now that have been out of circulation since the thirties. This man in Indiana—he specialized in horror movies. Bela Lugosi's cape, things like that." She smiled at the thought of the goodies Luke would be bringing back, but then shifted her attention to Marian. "Anything new on the *Apostrophe Thief* loot?"

"I had a line on it, but it didn't pan out."

Janet smiled sympathetically. "Luke told us what happened. About how Augie's big mouth spooked that guy, the one you were calling Rocky? I'm sorry you lost your lead."

"Well, I'm not sure he knew Ernie Nordstrom's address anyway," Marian said. "But Vasquez would know, wouldn't he?"

"Oh, sure." Janet's eyes narrowed. "They're a strange pair. Vasquez never talks and Ernie never shuts up. You think they're the ones who ripped off the Broadhurst?"

"Don't know. I think Luke thinks so."

"Luke is convinced of it. If you find Vasquez, how about giving us a call? One of my brothers or I would like to go along."

"The scripts are mine."

"Absolutely. But the other stuff—you're not interested in that, are you?"

"Nope."

"I didn't think so." Janet picked up a card from the table. "Here's our number. You let us in on it, we'll return the favor."

Marian took the card. "I don't mean to be naive, but aren't you afraid of getting into trouble? Receiving stolen goods, like that?"

The other woman pooh-poohed the notion. "The police have more important things to keep them occupied than what they see as just a bunch of souvenirs. If it doesn't have to do with drugs, they're not interested."

So that's how they see us, Marian thought. Just then she caught sight of an arm waving in the air; it was the chubby man in the plaid jacket again. More irritated than curious, Marian told Janet Zingone goodbye and moved away from her table; she didn't relish being stalked by either collector or dealer, whichever he was.

No sign of Augie. Marian briefly considered looking for him, but she'd never find him in that constantly moving mob of people. Maybe he was waiting outside. She started working her way toward the stairs.

"Hundred twenty-five is as high as I'll go," a man examining a woman's scarf was saying. "Come on, you're not going to do any better'n that . . . who collects Ann Rutherford?"

Marian climbed the stairs and glanced around; no Augie. She went outside the church and looked both ways along the sidewalk, but couldn't spot her erstwhile guide anywhere. Well, no matter; she was finished here anyway. She started off toward the nearest subway station.

"Marian!"

She turned and looked; it was Chubby Plaids.

"You are Marian, aren't you?"

Wondering, she nodded.

He puffed his way up to her, grinning happily. "You're a hard lady to catch," he wheezed, and stuck out a meaty hand. "I'm Harley Wingfield. I hear you're looking for Elvis?"

The next morning Marian stood outside of Captain Murtaugh's office, waiting until he finished giving instructions to two detectives investigating a jewelry store robbery. Murtaugh glanced up and saw her through the glass part of the door, and waved her away: This will take a while. Marian nodded and went back to Lieutenant Overbrook's office.

While she waited, she got to thinking about Wadsworth the

Aglet-Maker from Passaic. Overbrook had a dictionary on his shelves; it told her an aglet was the little sheath on the end of a shoelace. Marian half moaned, half laughed. This was a *profession*? And Wadsworth was moaning over the switch from metal to plastic? Shoelace tips! As the old song said, little things mean a lot.

The phone rang; it was Murtaugh summoning her to his office. As soon as she'd gone in and closed the door, he said, "Tell me what kind of man Captain DeFalco is."

"Political animal," Marian replied without hesitation. "Smart, but doesn't strain himself in the ethics department. More interested in hearing his name on the news than in nailing the right perp. Steals credit for work done by others. Selective memory. Lies to his own people, when it suits his immediate purpose." Marian sighed. "He's active—not afraid of confrontations or challenges, but he'd sell out his grandmother for a momentary advantage. He knows how to run a good investigation up to a point, but then he jumps to conclusions from the flimsiest of evidence. Also, he lies a lot."

Murtaugh was silent a moment. Then: "If all that's true, why do you stay in his command?"

Marian grinned ironically. "I thought I was in your command."

The captain thought that over. "You're not going back to the Ninth Precinct, are you? Have you put in for a transfer?"

"No."

Then he understood. "You're going to resign."

"Not until this business at the Broadhurst Theatre is cleared up," Marian told him. "I promised Kelly Ingram I'd see it through."

"But then you're going to quit? Because of one captain in one precinct?"

Marian shook her head. "DiFalco's just the final straw. This has been coming a long time, Captain. Why did you ask me about him?"

But Murtaugh wouldn't be diverted. "I don't know what brought you to this point, Sergeant, but I hope you'll reconsider. You know how to run an investigation, and you're a self-starter. If I had an opening here, I'd offer it to you. It couldn't have been easy for you, earning that gold badge you carry. Don't throw it away."

Marian remained silent.

Murtaugh nodded. "All right, you're not going to talk to me about it. I asked you about DiFalco because he wouldn't let me borrow Gloria Sanchez until I gave him my word his precinct would be credited for whatever collar you and she make."

Marian laughed shortly. "What did you tell him?"

"I told him he could have the collar—I just want to clear the case. He's sending Sanchez over for a briefing this morning, but she has to go back and work out the rest of the day for him. *And* we pick up her overtime, for tonight at The, ah, Esophagus."

Just then Perlmutter stuck his head in through the door, a look of wonder on his face. "Captain, you aren't going to believe this," he said in awestruck tones, "but Whoopi Goldberg's here to see you."

Marian sighed. "That's Gloria."

"Send her in," said Murtaugh.

Perlmutter went to get her, and then lingered when he'd shown her in. Gloria Sanchez was wearing what she called her cool duds, meaning she had on nothing that could be ordered from a catalog. She'd fixed her hair in tiny ringlets, hundreds of them that hung down around her ears and stuck up and out in a few places and even hid her eyes, almost. In an odd sort of way, she did look a little like Whoopi Goldberg. Gloria peered out from under her hair long enough to wink at Marian before she said, "Captain Murtaugh? I'm Detective Sanchez. Captain DiFalco says you got a job for me."

Murtaugh stood up to shake her hand and then pointed to a chair. "It'll mean overtime tonight. Any problem with that?"

"Noop." Gloria sat down next to Marian.

"Is this the Broadhurst thing?" Perlmutter asked. He'd brought the theater's cleaning crew in to look at mug shots, with no results, but it gave him a kind of stake in the case.

"You know about the burglary at the Broadhurst Theatre?" Murtaugh asked. Gloria nodded. The captain proceeded to summarize what Marian had learned, ending with, "This Vasquez is our best bet for finding out where Ernie Nordstrom lives. The trouble is, Vasquez speaks little or no English. And since he's bound to be on his guard, it'd be better if he were approached in a 'friendly' environment . . . and by another Hispanic."

Everyone looked at Whoopi Goldberg.

"Do you have any idea," Gloria said heavily, "how *long* it took me to fix my hair this way?"

Murtaugh's eyes crinkled into a smile. "We'll need some plausible reason for you to strike up an acquaintance with him."

"Why not just bring him in for questioning?" Perlmutter asked.

Marian said, "He may already have been warned." She told about losing Kevin Kirby, alias the hunk, and added, "If Kirby was that cautious, Vasquez will be even more so. We can't go at him straight on. We need something decidedly underhanded."

"So you sent for me," Gloria said wryly.

They tossed a few ideas back and forth, but nothing struck

anyone as particularly workable. "She can go in as a groupie," Perlmutter said, "that's easy enough. But what reason would a groupie have to ask for Ernie Nordstrom's address?"

"None," Murtaugh said. "But what if she's looking for something Vasquez knows Nordstrom has, some part of the Broadhurst haul?"

Marian pulled out her list of stolen items. "Scripts. Costumes. Small TV, notebook computer, radios and so forth. Two paintings."

"Paintings," said Murtaugh.

Marian read off the titles of the paintings and the names of the artists. "The cash value was probably inflated by the owners, but neither painting is in the Picasso class."

"All right, we'll leave those for now. What else?"

"Xandria Priest's diary."

"Ah," said three voices.

Marian nodded. "That's it. You *have* to get your hands on that diary before anyone else does, Gloria—that's your story."

"Forget the groupie pose," Murtaugh said. "Tell Vasquez you came looking for him because somebody tipped you he might know about the diary."

"What somebody?" Gloria asked.

"Kevin Kirby," Marian said quickly. "You, ah, worked with him on a commercial."

"Okay. But he's not going to lead me to the diary out of the kindness of his heart. I'll have to show him money."

"Right," Murtaugh said. "I'll arrange it. But he's not going to lead you to the diary in any event. If he buys your story, he'll probably want to set up a meet with Ernie Nordstrom, or just go get it from him—but don't let him put you off. You have to get that diary tonight. Make him think you're desperate."

"Why?" Perlmutter asked. "I mean, what if Vasquez asks her why she wants it?"

"I tell him I can't tell him," Gloria answered. "The story'll be more credible if I seem to be holding something back." She looked at Murtaugh. "I got a good desperate-woman act."

He raised an eyebrow. "Glad to hear it. All right, say he buys your story when you flash a wad of greenbacks at him. Then what? He tells you to meet him somewhere later and goes off alone to Ernie Nordstrom's place?"

The others nodded. "Seems reasonable," Marian said.

"At which point it turns into a tail job," the captain said. "And that's the part I don't like. It's got to be a two-tail. Larch is okay, but he'll know Sanchez. If he spots you—"

"Ah, Captain—" Perlmutter interrupted.

"No more overtime, Perlmutter," Murtaugh said. "They'll have to handle it alone. But I don't like it."

"No problem, Captain," Gloria said. "I'll wear something flashy when I talk to him, but I'll have something dark on underneath. I can do a quick change in the ladies' room."

They worked out a few more details until Murtaugh was finally satisfied. "That's it, then. Let's wrap this up tonight."

"Solid," Gloria said and waved goodbye.

Perlmutter followed her out. "Did anyone ever tell you you look like Whoopi Goldberg?"

Murtaugh watched them go. "Can she really make a convincing Hispanic?"

"Don't worry, Captain," Marian reassured him, "tonight she'll be Chita Rivera. Something else—is there time to get a warrant?"

"Already in the works. We'll have it by this afternoon. Sergeant . . . proceed with caution. This Vasquez is an unknown factor. He could turn violent."

"Gloria and I will both be careful," Marian promised him. "Presumably Vasquez won't be armed, but we'll proceed as if he were."

10

The restaurant was not a new one, but Marian had never been there before—had not, in fact, known of its existence. Called Avec Plaisir, it offered some of the same menu items as Le Cirque, arguably the best restaurant in New York. But unlike Le Cirque, Avec Plaisir did not place its tables so close together as to force shoulder-to-shoulder dining. The food was delicious, the service prompt and nonintrusive, the atmosphere one of quiet composure. Avec Plaisir was, from every point of view, a find. Leave it to Holland to have found it.

Something was bothering him. Broody and distracted, he barely spoke during the first half of the meal. Eventually Marian figured it out: he'd brought her there to apologize. Apologies did not come easily to Holland.

Finally he made a stab at it. "Saturday night . . . after the play. When you wanted to go to the Column Left. To go dancing."

"Yes?" It came out sounding more amused than encouraging.

"I, ah, I think I may have overreacted a trifle."

"Hm. When will you know for sure?"

"Oh, very well, I *did* overreact, and I'm sorry. There."

There. "What made you so angry?" Marian asked. "You'd think we'd asked you to help bomb IBM."

He leaned forward over his plate, as if to make sure she could hear him. "It was the music."

That didn't make much sense. "What music?"

"The music that's played at places like Column Left. I say 'music' because that's what other people call it, but it's not. It's uninventive noise, manufactured by the ungifted for the undiscriminating. It's music for people who don't understand music. Ear-shattering lullabies for the sleepwalking masses."

"Gawrsh," Marian said poker-faced. "I hadn't realized it was that iniquitous."

His eyes narrowed. "A joke to you, but a serious matter to me. Music like that is an insult. And I was outraged that you did not acknowledge it as such."

"Let's see if I understand you. You snubbed Kelly and walked out on me because you don't like the kind of music played at Column Left. Did I get that right?"

"Don't oversimplify."

"Have you ever been to Column Left?"

He made a dismissive gesture. "All those places play down to their listeners. It doesn't matter whether it's pop or rock or newage." Rhymed with "sewage." "It's such *bad* music. And when you go to places like Column Left, you simply encourage them, don't you see."

Marian made a noise of exasperation. "Holland, couldn't you have just said that? Couldn't you have said, 'I don't like that kind of music and I don't want to go'? We all understand English."

He spoke through clenched teeth. "That's what I'm apologizing for. The fact that I did *not* say that."

She kept a poker face. "Oh. Well, I'm glad we got that straightened out. But you don't fool me. I know what you're really after. You want to come to The Esophagus with me tonight."

He gave her a look of utter horror.

Marian laughed. "A joke. In fact, I want you to give me your word you will *not* come to The Esophagus tonight. I don't want to find you sitting in the next booth again, if The Esophagus has booths."

"Butt out?"

"Yep. Cops aren't supposed to take dates along on busts."

"Then you're going to wrap it up tonight?"

"Looks like it. It depends on whether Vasquez goes for some bait we're going to dangle in front of him. I think he'll bite."

"Then you'll be . . . finished."

With a shock Marian realized she'd not thought of that: if they found Ernie Nordstrom tonight, today was her last day of being a cop. She nodded dumbly.

"Excellent," said Holland. "Are you through eating? I have something I want to show you."

She finished her coffee and they left. Holland hailed a cab and gave an address on Lexington Avenue. After twelve minutes of Dodg'em, the taxi pulled up in front of a steel-and-glass tower.

"What's this?" Marian asked.

"Wait."

The lobby of the building had no furnishings to distract from the august starkness of the marble walls and floors. In the otherwise unoccupied elevator, Holland pressed the button for the eighteenth floor.

"*What?*"

"Wait."

The eighteenth floor had the same marble walls, but the floor was covered with deep charcoal-gray carpeting. Holland unlocked the door to Suite 1802 and gestured her inside. She stepped through and swallowed a gasp. The reception area alone was the size of her entire apartment. The place was new, modern, unspeakably expensive. The office suite was as yet unfurnished, so the place undoubtedly looked more spacious than it actually was; still . . .

Marian shot a sharp look at Holland. "I didn't know you had this kind of money."

He shrugged. "Look in here." He led her to a room in which the outer wall was glass. She could see the park, three blocks away. "This is your office," Holland said. "If you want it."

She was overwhelmed at the size of the gesture. But at the same time, she felt a flash of anger. "Holland—"

He held up a hand. "I'm not putting pressure on you. Of course there is no obligation on your part. None whatsoever. What I am trying to do, quite blatantly, is to tempt you. Is it working? You'd select your own furniture, set your own hours, turn down any case you didn't want—what else can I do to make this a dream job?" He paused. "I want you for my partner, Marian. Tell me what you want."

She couldn't think what to say. When the silence was beginning to grow uncomfortable, she surprised both of them by walking over to Holland and wrapping her arms around him. They stood there a long moment, holding on to each other, not speaking. Finally she said, "Wait until I have tonight out of the way. Then I'll be free to decide."

He didn't answer, but held on just a little tighter.

Marian was of the opinion that Gloria Sanchez's alternating of ethnic identities did not depend so much on the clothing she wore as on the way she wore them. Tuesday night Gloria had on a bright yellow tee with a safari jacket and jeans, plus enormous hoop earrings and lots of jangly bracelets. That morning's careful curls had been replaced by a hair style that could only be described as *wild*. Gloria had put on a lot of eye makeup; her nails were bright red and seemed to have grown an inch during the day. But most of all her walk was different, her hand gestures were different, the way she tilted her head while listening was different. She affected a Hispanic accent, but that didn't contribute to the overall picture so much as did the lilt in her voice when she spoke.

She's part chameleon, Marian thought, feeling very plain next to her colorful friend. They'd left the car in a delivery zone near Cooper Square and were making their way down Bowery; still a half hour before midnight, the street was crowded and noisy. A lot of the street people looked like college kids, acting cool. A lot of the others . . . didn't. Music seeped/poured/pounded out of half a dozen places; a loud-voiced argument raged nearby. The temporary team of Larch and Sanchez had decided to wait until Waltzing Brünnhilde's final set of the evening, so Vasquez would be free afterward.

"Here 'tis," said Gloria.

The management's sole attempt at exterior decoration was the hanging of a metal canopy on which the words "The Esophagus" had been painted. The frontage was quite narrow. "Must be a basement club," Marian said.

Sure enough, the door opened to reveal a landing from which a staircase descended. A man dressed very much like Gloria collected a fee from them, and they made their way down into what at first appeared to be almost total darkness. When Marian's eyes had adjusted, she was not pleased at what she saw. The low lights couldn't hide all the peeling paint, the grease on the walls several layers thick, the dirt and the litter. "It's a rathole," she muttered.

"Yeah," Gloria agreed. "An' a busy rathole, too." All the tables were taken; they made their way to the bar where one stool stood empty; Marian told Gloria to take it and squeezed in between her and a skinny young fellow who had his back turned.

Waiting for the next set, the crowd was good-naturedly boisterous and noisy. Marian checked her watch. "Still a few more minutes."

Gloria was reading the signs behind the bar. "I don' beliv it—yuppie beer for seventy-fi' cents? Hey, mon, bring me a Rollin' Rock!"

"Make it two," Marian said.

Now that her eyes had adjusted fully, Marian could see the room they were in was a large one, extending back perhaps even farther than the original depth of the building. The stage was opposite the bar at the far end; it was shallow and undecorated but surrounded by a small fortune in lighting equipment, none of it in use at the moment. The brightest thing in the room was a glowing red Exit sign on the left.

"Roberts was out sick today," Gloria said unexpectedly. "So guess who I got partnered with."

"Not Foley?"

Gloria made a face and nodded. "We went to check out a drive-by shootin'—nobuddy injured, jus' a lot of broken glass and damage. Your former partner gets it into his so-called mind that a new gang war's about to bust out. So he wan's to start roustin' all the gang members he knows, stir 'em up a little, you know? I kep' tellin' him he'd *start* a war, but he wouldn' listen. I had to go to Captain DiFalco to stop 'im."

"The man's a menace." Marian was quiet a moment, thinking of a time Foley's undependability had put her in danger. "Is DiFalco going to do anything about him?"

"Naw. We got a manpower shortage, remember?" Gloria grinned. "We don' even have a sergeant now."

"Hm."

Suddenly the stage lights blazed on, the stage erupted in a cacophony of electronic sound, and the audience started cheering and shouting. Waltzing Brünnhilde had arrived.

Marian looked, blinked, looked again. The four men on the stage were attired—if that was the word—in Jockey shorts.

"Why, those boys don' have no pants on!" Gloria yelled delightedly.

The band ripped into a number that drowned out every other sound in the place. The lead singer was wearing Beetle Bailey boots and a black shirt that had only the bottom button fastened. He swung his head and his long black hair swept over the dead white skin of his exposed chest. That plus garish make-up gave him a vampirish look, a look that the bare white legs somehow enhanced. Two of the other band members were wearing sneakers and the fourth had on sandals; all three wore plain shirts that didn't distract from the main man's Dracula persona. Two of the band had ponytails . . . but one of them was blond. Marian looked over the heads of the audience at the other one, the man they'd come to find. Vasquez was every bit as hunkish as Kevin Kirby but without the other man's attractive facial features and personable manner. Vasquez was big, heavily muscled, unsmiling. He held his guitar like a weapon, and he looked dangerous.

Waltzing Brünnhilde segued into a second song; it was aggressive, challenging—what had Kevin Kirby said? A *more pissed-off sound than even speed metal.* One or more members of the group frequently emphasized the fuck-you attitude of the music by giving the audience the finger. The audience loved it.

A brief pause followed the second song while the lead singer and the audience exchanged a few insults. Gloria said into Marian's ear, "Do you know who that is? That's Rex Regent. He useta be with the Sumo Surfers. What's he doin' in a dump like this?"

"I really don't know," Marian replied soberly.

The music started again. A strobe light was playing over the audience, while the stage went through a constantly changing play of colored light. Gloria gave Marian her bar stool as she herself started gyrating to the evening's rhythms. As Waltzing Brünnhilde moved from song to song to give-and-take with the audience, Marian began to think it was never going to end. At one point Rex Regent mooned the audience. A few members of the audience returned the compliment.

The act came to a premature close when five members of the audience, three women and two men, clambered up on the stage and jumped Waltzing Brünnhilde's lead singer. They tore his Jockey shorts off him and then fought among themselves for possession. Laughing, Rex Regent got to his feet and stood there a moment, making sure everyone got a good look, before turning and clomping off the stage, his army boots making hollow sounds in the wooden floor. The stage lights dimmed; the show was over.

Gloria looked at Marian in mock sorrow and said, "And you're goin' to resign a job that pays you to watch a dude get his underwear ripped off."

Marian had to laugh. "True, there aren't many jobs like that. But we've got a problem. How do you get through *that*?" *That* was about half the audience climbing up on the stage and pushing its way toward the backstage area. "You'll never get to Vasquez through that mob."

"They're after Rex Regent." Gloria leaned over the bar and gestured to the bartender. "Is there another way to the dressin' rooms?"

"See the Exit sign?" He pointed. "Don't go up the stairs. Go down the hall, straight back."

"Thanks, mon." She and Marian exchanged a silent

thumbs-up and Gloria headed for the Exit sign. Marian waited a few minutes and followed, but took the stairs up to the street instead of going backstage. She waited there, where they'd be coming out.

Once she was approached by a trio of young men looking for a lone woman to hassle, once by a man dressed as a clown who wanted to know how much she charged, and once by a uniformed officer who told her to move along. She got rid of all of them by flashing her badge.

It was nearly half an hour before Gloria and Vasquez appeared. Marian breathed a sigh of relief; the first hurdle was over. Keeping other people between them, she followed for about a block and a half, to a pizzeria; Vasquez was hungry after his gig. She peeked through the glass and saw Gloria doing the ordering for both of them. Marian checked the time: eleven minutes to two.

Gloria had twenty-four thousand dollars in her bag, twenty-four to avoid a too-pat round number. She was to tell Vasquez she could get her hands on three, maybe four more thousand. It was a nice piece of change for someone who played for scale in a rathole like The Esophagus and rented out his muscles to Ernie Nordstrom between gigs. Captain Murtaugh had had trouble getting the cash; the crime they were investigating was just too minor to risk that kind of money. But he had prevailed, somehow, and right now Gloria was doing her desperate-woman act, over pepperoni and anchovies. Thank god Xandria Priest had kept a diary.

Marian was stamping her feet to warm them when Vasquez finally came out—alone. He turned onto Bleecker Street; she fell in behind him and took a walkie-talkie out of her bag.

Before long it crackled. "Marian?"

"We're heading west on Bleecker." Just then two black

teenagers saw her coming and separated just enough to block her way. "Don't even *think* about it," she snarled and plowed through. They let her go, contenting themselves with yelling a few obscenities after her. "Gloria? He's going into the subway. IRT uptown."

"Shit." The radios would be useless. "I'll get the car and stay on Third Avenue until I hear from you."

"Right."

It was what they'd planned, in case Vasquez took a subway or bus; but Marian had been hoping he'd feel flush enough to stop a cab. She followed him down into the subway. Past the turnstile, Vasquez looked around with studied casualness, his gaze passing over Marian to linger on a nondescript man reading a newspaper. Marian edged behind a vending machine.

The train roared into the station. She got into the car next to the one Vasquez took and stood at the rear, where she could keep an eye on him through the double windows. The man with the newspaper had boarded the same car as Vasquez.

They rode only three stops. Marian stepped behind a pillar as Vasquez waited to make sure the newspaper man was not getting off. Only when the train doors slid shut did he turn toward the exit stairs.

Up on the street, Marian pulled out the walkie-talkie. "Gloria? We're heading east on Twenty-third, south side of the street."

"Gotcha."

Vasquez was turning right onto Second Avenue just as Gloria pulled up to the curb. Quickly she and Marian changed places, Gloria now following on foot. But Vasquez went only half a block farther, crossing the street to a white-stone apartment building. A doorman let him in.

So he's known there, Marian thought, pulling up by a fire

hydrant. She locked the car and met Gloria in the middle of the street, her heart beginning to pound as they got closer to their target. They ran up to the glass door of the building and banged on it with their fists, holding up their badges when the elderly doorman came to see what they wanted. He let them in.

"The man who just came in here," Marian said. "You know him?"

The doorman nodded. "Mr. Norris's nephew. He comes here a lot."

So he wasn't "Ernie Nordstrom" at home. "Which apartment?"

"Seven-oh-four. What's going on?"

Neither Marian nor Gloria answered as they hurried to the one elevator and hit the button. The elevator was already on its way down, so they didn't have long to wait. The doors opened . . . and Vasquez erupted from the elevator car like a sprinter training for the Olympics. "Stop!" Marian yelled.

He didn't stop. Gloria was hard on his heels, though, and brought him down with a flying tackle just as he reached the door. Then Marian was on top of both of them, struggling to get a pair of cuffs on Vasquez. When she'd finally succeeded, all three of them sat panting on the floor. The elderly doorman shuffled as close as he dared. "*What's* going on?" he complained.

Gloria pulled out her badge and held it in front of Vasquez's face. He sighed in resignation . . . and then did a double take as he recognized Gloria. "Yeah, it's me," she said. "Come on—get up."

"What were you running from?" Marian asked him.

"He can't understand you." Gloria repeated the question in Spanish, to be answered by a stream of words that seemed to involve a great deal of repetition. "He keeps saying he didn't do it." She and Marian exchanged a look of apprehension. "Oh-oh."

They got Vasquez to his feet and steered him toward the elevator. He hung back, until both women spoke to him in their tough-cop voices. He kept repeating that he didn't do it.

"I wish someone would tell me what's going on," the doorman said waspishly as the elevator doors closed.

All the way up, Vasquez kept up a steady stream of protest until Gloria finally told him to shut up. The seventh floor consisted of one narrow hallway with apartments opening off both sides. The door to 704 was standing ajar.

The apartment was cold. Although she already had a good idea of what to expect, Marian felt her heart sink when they walked in and found the dead man on the floor. He'd been strangled with a fancy tasseled pull rope, the kind that was used to summon servants in Victorian homes. His tongue protruded from one side of his mouth and both eyes were open. The dead man was short, stocky, and middle-aged, and he was surrounded by movie and theater memorabilia. Ernie Nordstrom.

An agitated Vasquez was still protesting his innocence. Marian bent over and laid her palm alongside the dead man's neck. "Rigor's started," she said. "Tell him we know he didn't do it. Nordstrom's been dead at least an hour, probably longer, since the room's so chilly. And we know where Vasquez has been the past . . . "—she looked at her watch—"three hours and seven minutes. Tell him we're his alibi."

Gloria spoke to Vasquez at some length, and gradually he began to calm down. Marian motioned them out into the hallway and used a handkerchief to pull the door to after her. "I'll go look for a phone and call it in," she said. "Will you be all right here with him?"

"Oh sure," Gloria said. "This boy ain't goin' nowhere."

Marian nodded and stepped back into the elevator. As the doors closed, she leaned tiredly against the side of the car. Whoever would have thought that her nice, easy, *friendly* little case was going to turn into a full-fledged homicide.

11

Captain Murtaugh looked as tired as Marian felt. Two uniformed officers had taken Vasquez in to be held for questioning, and the men from the Medical Examiner's office had removed the body. But the Crime Scene Unit was taking longer than usual to finish up; all the *stuff* Ernie Nordstrom had accumulated made their job difficult. Gloria Sanchez was standing straight up with her eyes closed; Marian was convinced she was sound asleep. None of them could sit down, because there was no place *to* sit.

Ernie Nordstrom had lived in a one-bedroom apartment, if living was what it was. The bedroom held a narrow cot and a chest of drawers; in the living room was a desk and a chair; on the desk was a six-inch TV of the brand taken from the Broadhurst. And except for a narrow pathway, every other inch of floor space was taken up with memorabilia. Clothes racks holding costumes, cardboard cartons marked with some cryptic code the dead man had devised, stacks of paper items, props, personal articles—Nordstrom had covered the spectrum of show biz collectibles. The kitchen cabinets were full of memorabilia, more costumes hung from the shower curtain rod and were draped across the foot of the cot, and the chair by the desk was stacked high with lobby cards. What little wall space there was, was filled with framed theater posters and photographs of actors and entertainers. Dealing was Ernie Nordstrom's entire life.

"Cold in here," Captain Murtaugh said. "Sanchez?" Gloria opened one eye. "The doorman claims Vasquez was Ernie Nordstrom's nephew. Anything to that?"

"Nope, that was just Nordstrom's cover story," she said in accent-free English, "to explain Vasquez's appearances here at all hours of the night." She managed to get the other eye open. "Vasquez told me about it while we were waiting for the CSU to get here. The two didn't look anything alike—it was a dumb cover. But Marian was right about Vasquez. He was just hired muscle. I don't think he even knew what was going down half the time. He just lifted and carried whatever he was told."

"Then Nordstrom must have spoken Spanish," Murtaugh pointed out.

"Must have."

Marian studied Gloria closely. Gone were the big earrings, the jangly bracelets, the bright yellow tee of earlier in the evening. The wild hairdo had been tucked under a black cap, and the safari jacket had been reversed to show a dark green corduroy—which she now wore over a black sweater. No wonder Vasquez hadn't recognized her at first; she was a different woman. She was neither Whoopi Goldberg nor Chita Rivera.

"Gloria," Marian said, bemused, "you look like . . . yourself."

"Yeah. I figured nobody'd know me this way."

Gloria and Vasquez had hit it off right from the start, backstage at The Esophagus. Everyone else was crowding around Rex Regent; so when Gloria made a beeline for Vasquez, he'd felt puffed up and receptive. He told her she looked like Elizabeth Peña; she told him he had better pecs than Ahnold. Matters were progressing nicely until the subject of the diary came up. It had taken Gloria a long time to get Vasquez to overcome his initial suspicion; but when they were in the pizza parlor, she'd shown him the cash she was carrying and promised to get more. That had started the wheels turning in Vasquez's head. If that diary was worth twenty-four-thousand-plus to this woman who'd appeared out of nowhere, might it not be worth even more to somebody else? In fact, couldn't there be dozens of people whose dirty secrets were recorded in the diary? The trouble was, Vasquez couldn't read much English.

Gloria had hit upon the strategy of saying all she wanted from the diary was one page or possibly two. She'd pay him all the money if he'd just let her destroy a couple of pages; then he could do whatever he damn well pleased with the rest of the diary. She even offered to translate for him. That appealed to him; he liked the idea of being on to something that even Ernie Nordstrom didn't know about. So he'd gone for the deal. He'd told Gloria to order another pizza and wait until he got back. But finding Nordstrom dead had scared him so much he'd not even stopped to look for the diary.

"Okay, Captain, we're finished." The three men and one woman from the Crime Scene Unit packed up their gear and left.

"Quick sweep," Captain Murtaugh said to Marian and Gloria. "Just get an idea of what we've got here. Leave a detailed examination until after we've had some sleep. I'll take the desk."

Gloria went into the bedroom to look through Ernie Nordstrom's chest of drawers, and Marian started a quick sort through the stacks of papers everywhere. After a while she found what she was looking for. "Captain. The *Apostrophe Thief* scripts."

Murtaugh looked up from the desk. "That nails it, then. Nordstrom's our Broadhurst thief, assisted by Vasquez and . . . ?"

"Kevin Kirby," Marian supplied, "neither of whom killed him."

"You're sure of that?"

"The man from the ME's office estimated he'd been dead about two hours, so that rules out Vasquez. And I don't think Kirby even knew where Nordstrom lived."

"Pick him up tomorrow for questioning. You have his address?"

"Yes."

Gloria came back from the bedroom. "Nothing in the bureau except clothes and personal items. He used only half the closet for clothes—the rest is stacked up with *Playbills*. He even has *Playbills* under the cot. What's in the boxes?"

"Haven't looked yet," Marian said. "Captain, did you find any kind of inventory list or such? All those cartons have some sort of code number marked on them."

He handed her a small loose-leaf notebook. "Take a quick look for any other Broadhurst items."

"Well, that television on the desk may be one of them. Let's see, here." She flipped through the pages until she spotted something familiar. "Ah . . . 'framed, autographed picture of Geraldine Page'—yes, that's from the Broadhurst. Code PFA.BT94."

Gloria helped her locate the right carton. When they opened it, they found it filled with signed photographs in frames, each one carefully wrapped in a foam rubber sheet. The Geraldine Page photo was on top.

"My god, will you look at this?" Gloria said, unwrapping some of the others. "Ethel Waters. That goes back a ways."

"Mikhail Baryshnikov," Marian murmured. "And Clifford Odets."

"Who?"

"Playwright," Captain Murtaugh interposed. "All right, I've seen enough for now. Let's get out of here before we all freeze. Sergeant, I'll want you to come back tomorrow and check exactly how much of the Broadhurst loot is here. You can finish going through the desk as well." He turned to Gloria. "Detective Sanchez, you did good work tonight, and I'll make sure Captain DiFalco knows it. You helped us out when we needed you, and we—"

"I know," Gloria interrupted with a yawn. "You couldn't have done it without me. Thank you, Captain. You tell that to DiFalco *on paper* instead of over the phone and we'll call it even."

He gave her a tired smile. "Consider it done."

After five hours' shut-eye, Marian drove to Hastings Street and rousted Kevin Kirby out of a deep sleep. He was a slow waker, and was dressed and handcuffed before he started to get worried. At Midtown South, Marian and Murtaugh had a go at both Kirby and Vasquez; a detective named Sergeant Campos, just back from picking up a prisoner in Miami, acted as interpreter for the latter. The story they told was the same.

Ernie Nordstrom had recruited them for what he claimed was an inside job. He knew what time the cleaning crew showed up in the morning and how long they'd have to go through the dressing rooms before the stage doorkeeper was due to arrive—the information provided by Nordstrom's contact inside the Broadhurst. That was all Kevin Kirby knew, except that he'd tucked away Kelly Ingram's hairbrush as a souvenir. Vasquez added that the contact's cut was to be one specific item Ernie was to take. What item? Vasquez didn't know. Who was the contact? Ernie never said.

Kirby had been scared witless when he learned Nordstrom had been murdered. Marian believed his reaction; she didn't think he was that good an actor. But he had an alibi for the night before, he said; he'd been rehearsing a part in a new Off-Off-Off-Broadway play—well, New Jersey, actually. But they'd been doing an early run-through in the writer-director's apartment in Chelsea and didn't stop until nearly two in the morning; then four of them had gone out for something to eat. Murtaugh gave Perlmutter the job of checking out the alibi.

"So have we got a motive?" Murtaugh asked Marian later in his office. "An insider at the Broadhurst wants something that's kept backstage. He wants it so badly that he lines up Ernie Nordstrom to do a sweep of theater 'collectibles'—a variety of thefts to hide one particular one. Then say Nordstrom holds out on him. The contact tries to get whatever it is away from Nordstrom and ends up killing him. Is that how you read it?"

"Just about," Marian agreed.

"Is 'Nordstrom' his real name? See if you can find out. The doorman knew him as Mr. Norris. When are you going back to his apartment?"

"Right now. And the first thing I'm going to look for is Xandria Priest's diary."

Murtaugh pressed his lips together, eyeing Marian carefully. "Larch, you're not going to quit on me in mid-investigation, are you?"

Her eyebrows went up. "I wouldn't dream of it."

"You've given up the idea of resigning, then?"

"No, but not until this case is wrapped up. I told you that yesterday, Captain. True, it's turned out to be a bit more than I bargained for, but it's *my* case . . . it is my case, isn't it? You're not giving it to someone else?"

He smiled. "I wouldn't dream of it," he said, echoing her. "No, your assurance that you're going to stick is enough for me."

"Well, you've got that," Marian said emphatically. "Now, I'd better be moving."

He waved her out.

Marian left the car and walked down to Thirty-fourth to

catch a crosstown bus. At Second Avenue she transferred to a downtown bus for the short ride to the block where Ernie Nordstrom's building was located. A different doorman was on duty; he too referred to the dead man as Mr. Norris when she asked. Upstairs, a uniformed officer stood by Nordstrom's door; crime scenes were guarded for twenty-four hours. Marian identified herself and was let into the apartment.

She looked through Nordstrom's inventory book and located the code number for Xandria Priest's diary, praying the dead man hadn't already disposed of it. She found it in a box containing letters and postcards written by celebrities; there was even a bank card with Greta Garbo's signature on it. Marian opened the diary and began to read.

After the first three or four pages, she started skimming. Compliments! Page after page of compliments! Xandria's "diary" was nothing but a record of the day-by-day compliments that had been paid to her. Occasionally there'd be the plaintive entry, "Nobody said anything nice today." But there was some sort of entry for every day of the year. It took a certain amount of discipline to keep a diary at all, but *this*. . . ! It was as if the compliments would evaporate unless they were written down quickly. Young Xandria needed a *lot* of reinforcement.

Marian cleared a place on the top of Ernie Nordstrom's desk and put the diary there. Then she began a systematic check of her list of items stolen from the Broadhurst. It took a long time; she worked right through lunch, ignoring her growling stomach as she opened boxes and rummaged through them. Nordstrom's inventory record had lines drawn through two entries, those for a vase and for Kelly Ingram's sneakers; Marian assumed that meant the items had been sold. Kelly would be amused to learn her old sneakers had some value after all. Or maybe not; it depended on how funny Kelly thought foot fetishism was.

Aside from those two items Nordstrom had disposed of, Marian found six others missing. Three costumes: the much-missed Sarah Bernhardt jacket, a gown worn by Xandria Priest, and an imitation fur coat worn by a woman named Frieda Armstrong, who played Kelly's and Xandria's mother in *The Apostrophe Thief*. Also: Kelly's hairbrush, Ian Cavanaugh's shaving mug, and the notebook computer belonging to Mitchell Tobin.

Tobin—he was the one who'd had all the electronic gadgets in his dressing room. Kevin Kirby had pinched Kelly's hairbrush, so that brought the list of missing items down to five. Marian was sorry Cavanaugh's shaving mug was gone; he wanted it back so very much. But everything else was there: all the scripts, the rest of the costumes, the few props that had been taken, the two paintings, the personal items—even Kelly's hand lotion was there.

Three costumes. A shaving mug. A notebook computer. Ernie Nordstrom had been killed for one of them.

That part of her job finished, Marian sat down at the desk to see what she could learn about the murdered man. No personal letters, no checkbooks, no income tax papers. She found an assortment of money order stubs, bundled together with rubber bands. Nordstrom had paid his rent and utility bills that way—the unavoidable bills. But you didn't need to give a social security number when buying money orders, the way you did when opening a bank account. No telephone bills, because there was no telephone.

Marian found a lease made out to Eddie Norris. So was that his real name? "Eddie Norris" sounded more like a made-up name than "Ernie Nordstrom" did, though; "Norris" was probably for the purpose of renting the apartment. That way he could use his own name for all his dealing without worrying someone would track him down. And Nordstrom had had an elaborate burglar alarm system installed in the apartment. Perhaps all dealers did, just being *precautious*, as Luke Zingone would say.

But the alarm had been off and the door open last night. Vasquez swore that was the way he'd found them. So Nordstrom had let the killer in, not suspecting anything.

The bottom drawer of the desk turned out to be a built-in safe; Marian made a note to request a police locksmith. There hadn't been much loose cash in the apartment, a couple of hundred dollars. And Nordstrom didn't seem to care for banks much. It could be his whole stash was right there in the desk safe.

The only other thing Marian found of interest was a small book of addresses and phone numbers. All dealers and collectors, most likely; the Zingones were listed there. There was no "Norris" or "Nordstrom" listing—did that mean he had no family? Since the dead man was so wary about putting his name on legal documents, he probably hadn't made a will. But if Nordstrom or Norris had died intestate and indeed had no living relatives, then the City of New York had just become the legal owner of an impressive collection of show biz memorabilia.

With a sigh Marian dropped the address book in her handbag; everyone listed there would have to be contacted. She might as well go back to Midtown South and get started.

At the end of the day Marian went home no closer to an answer than she'd been before she began her marathon telephoning session. Every number in Ernie Nordstrom's book was that of a dealer or collector, everyone with whom he did business or with whom he might do business in the future. No friends. No relatives. No number for the Broadhurst Theatre or for any of the cast or crew of *The Apostrophe Thief*. Whoever had set up the backstage burglary, he was as faceless as ever.

Marian had called Kelly after her Wednesday matinee to let her know what had happened. When she finally got her friend calmed down enough to listen, she asked her to break the news to Ian Cavanaugh that his shaving mug was not part of the recovered loot. Marian said she'd probably be coming in to the theater tomorrow or the next day.

Perlmutter had reported that Kevin Kirby's alibi checked out. And the police locksmith had gotten Nordstrom's safe open, to find it filled with cash. Ninety-one thousand dollars, squirreled away by a man who lived in a cramped, claustrophobic apartment that was little more than a high-rise warehouse. Nothing else was in the safe.

Ernie Nordstrom had been a man with an obsession, an obsession so great it had blotted out everything else from his life. Nothing at all mattered to him except Elizabeth Taylor's eyeliner, or Katherine Cornell's monogrammed handkerchief, or a restaurant menu Anthony Hopkins had autographed. Nordstrom didn't mind breaking the law if it netted him a few more treasures to trade/sell/keep. Someone with *The Apostrophe Thief* had known of that obsession and used it to get what he wanted. And he'd paid Nordstrom off by killing him.

It was dark by the time Marian got home. She parked in her usual place, a delivery zone belonging to a printing company that closed promptly at 5:00, and walked toward her building. Parked directly in front of the entrance was a black Jaguar; the door opened and Holland got out.

"You worked today," he said flatly. "That means you didn't find your man last night."

"I found him," she answered in an equally flat tone. "I found him dead. He'd been strangled."

There was a pause, and then he came up to her, his eyes like ice. "Why didn't you call me?"

"What?"

"You walk in on a murder and you don't bother to tell me about it? You should have called me."

"Why? I didn't get home until after four, and there wasn't anything you—"

"*You should have called me.*"

Marian was puzzled; it wasn't like Holland to play the protective male, and she didn't think that was what he was doing now. "Explain it to me," she said quietly.

"I would have hoped," he said stiffly, "that you'd want me to know when something significant happened in your life. Yesterday you were an inch away from resigning. Today you're out looking for a murderer, still carrying that badge and doing your usual job. That's a big turnaround, isn't it?"

"Holland—"

"Not that I expect us to *report in* to each other," he went on coldly, "but I had presumed a connection existed between us. I was wrong, I now see. If you wish to exclude me from your life, I would appreciate your telling me so right now."

Oh lord, he was feeling she'd turned her back on him. And she *had* remembered to call Kelly. "I would have told you in time," she said. "I just hadn't gotten to it yet. Look, can we go get something to eat? I missed lunch and if I don't get something in my stomach soon I'm going to keel over. I'll tell you all about it over dinner."

"Why, *thank you*," he said sardonically.

Marian punched his shoulder. "And don't you get sarcastic with me! Dammit, I'm *trying* to make it right."

He sighed, the anger beginning to drain out of him. "I know. It's just that when I didn't hear from you all day . . . well." He cleared his throat. "Dinner, you say. Sonderman's all right? I'll drive."

She eyed the car. "Where'd you get the Jag?"

"I stole it."

"Holland, I never know when you're joking!"

"I'm joking. It's leased. Get in."

Marian got in, thinking that *just once* she'd like to share a meal with him without some misunderstanding that had to be patched up.

12

This time when she woke up the next morning, he was not gone. He was awake, though, and watching her. Marian stretched luxuriously and smiled, not wanting to think about getting up just yet.

Holland touched her cheek. "All right?"

"Never better. I'd like to stay here all day."

"Can you? I wouldn't mind that myself."

She struggled to a sitting position. "You know I can't."

He put his head down on her thigh. "Ah, but an occasional day of lolling about replenishes the soul, not to mention what it does for the body. If we get bored, I'm sure we can think of something to do."

"I'm thinking of it already," Marian said with a laugh, "but it's going to have to wait." She eased her leg out from under his head and got up. "A skillion things to take care of today."

Holland sighed dramatically. "I'll bet you never called in with blue flu in your life."

"Once I did. One of those horrible days when nothing goes right—I burnt myself, I didn't have a clean shirt, my hair looked awful, I was late, and a pipe sprang a leak under the kitchen sink. So I called in sick."

He got out of bed. "How did things go the next day?"

"Like clockwork."

When they'd showered and dressed and were rummaging in the kitchen for something to eat, Holland said, "You don't have a CD player, do you?"

"Nope."

"Nor a tape deck or stereo? What do you do for music?"

"There's the radio." In truth, Marian didn't listen to music often.

"Pity. There's a new recording of *Don Giovanni* I'd like you to hear."

Don Giovanni! "Er, uh . . . why?"

"Why? For one thing, to provide you with a proper antidote to that travesty that assaulted your ears on Tuesday night."

"Waltzing Brünnhilde? Gloria liked them."

"Gloria has odd tastes at the best of times. What about you? Did you like it?"

Marian shrugged. "It was okay. Kind of hostile."

"Well, Mozart isn't. Listener-friendly, in fact. I'll see what I can do about it."

The coffee smelled done; Marian poured them each a cup. "What are you going to do today?"

"Buy computers for the office. Interview three operatives I'm thinking of hiring. Meet with the telephone people who are installing my lines. Look at office furniture. Go to the printer's. Set up an account with an office supply house."

"Uh-huh. But what are you doing *after* lunch?"

"Making a dinner reservation for tonight."

Marian shook her head. "I want to go to the Broadhurst tonight—I'll just grab a bite on the run. Why don't you meet me there, after the play? If you've got any strength left, after all the buying and meeting and interviewing."

"I'll draw upon my hidden reserves. We'll go for a late supper. Ten, ten-thirty?"

"Thereabouts."

It was after they'd gone their separate ways when it occurred to Marian that that was about the most *un*romantic morning-after imaginable. No declarations of undying love, no long lingering soulful looks, no was-it-good-for-you. She laughed aloud; the idea of Holland playing that game was hilarious. And she was grateful. If they could just keep it *comfortable*, with no role-playing or scene-acting . . . well, they just might end up not hating each other.

As hard as it was, she put Holland out of her mind and concentrated on the day's schedule. Today she was going to try to find out why one of the five articles missing from Ernie Nordstrom's Broadhurst cache was so special that it was worth killing for. She stopped by Midtown South long enough to report in to Captain Murtaugh and to collect some addresses.

Xandria Priest first.

Xandria-Holier-Than-Thou-Female-Priest, as Kelly called her, was still asleep when Marian got to her apartment. With difficulty she persuaded the young woman who'd answered the door to go wake her up. The young woman did, and then rushed off, muttering something about a cattle call. Another young woman wandered out of the kitchen holding a cup of coffee, smiled vaguely at Marian, and disappeared.

Finally the young woman she'd come to see wandered in—sleepy-eyed, tousle-haired, and wearing a robe; she still looked fresh-faced and pretty, in the way only the young can. She ducked her head and peered at Marian through long eyelashes. "You're Kelly's police friend."

"Sergeant Larch, NYPD," Marian said crisply. "I'd like to ask you a few questions, Ms Priest."

"Xan. Call me Xan."

"Er, Xan. You're aware that the man who burglarized the Broadhurst has been murdered, aren't you?"

"Yes, I *know*," she said, now wide-eyed. "I've never had anything to do with a *murder* before!"

Funny way of putting it. "Did you ever meet Ernie Nordstrom? He was also known as Eddie Norris."

"I never even *heard* of him. Did you get my diary back?"

"Yes, it was recovered. But a gown you wear—"

"Oh, I'm so *relieved!*" She smiled prettily. "I would just *hate* it if anyone read my diary. There are things in there, you know, about other people? I don't want to *embarrass* anyone."

Marian remembered the innocuous nature of the diary with its compulsive listing of compliments and said, "I'm sure you don't. But it's one of your costumes I want to ask you about. A white gown—you wear it toward the end of the first act."

"You've seen the play? What do you think?"

"I think it's terrific. The performances are terrific. Everything's great. Now, about this gown—"

"Yes, but . . . " Xandria Priest moistened her lips, leaned forward provocatively, and said breathily, "What did you think of *my* performance?"

Kelly had said Xandria didn't know how to communicate without flirting; Marian was beginning to see what she meant. "I think your performance was outstanding," she said gently to the younger woman, "and you have a wonderful and exciting future ahead of you."

That was what Xandria wanted to hear; she beamed at Marian and said, "Thank you. How kind of you to say so."

Marian wondered if she'd bought a new diary to replace the stolen one; if she had, what Marian had just said was sure to be recorded for posterity. "Tell me about the white gown. Was there anything special about it?"

"Special? Well, it didn't drape exactly right in the back— "

"No, I mean was there anything that made it, well, valuable? More valuable than the other costumes, say?"

She looked puzzled. "It was just a dress."

"Did anyone ever offer to buy it from you?"

"No, why should they?"

It was clear Xandria Priest knew nothing, but Marian made one more stab at it. "Do you collect theater memorabilia? Play programs, autographs, like that?"

Xandria's pretty mouth turned down. "That's for *fans*. I'm a *professional*."

That says it all, Marian thought. "Well, I guess that's it. Sorry I had to wake you up."

"Um, how did you and Kelly meet?"

"During an investigation I was conducting."

"A *murder* investigation?"

Oh, dear. "Yes, someone she knew had been killed."

Big eyes again. "Then this is the *second* murder Kelly's been involved in?"

"She's about as 'involved' as you are. Now I must be going. Thanks for your time."

"I'd just *love* to hear about that other murder. Maybe we could get together sometime and talk?" She actually batted her eyelashes.

"Why don't you ask Kelly if you want to know?" Marian smiled to take any sting out of the words. She thanked her again and left.

Gene Ramsay next.

Ramsay's office on West Forty-fourth, not far from the Broadhurst, was laid out like a little kingdom. Marian had to make her way through a sort of petitioners' receiving room, where agents and actors and writers and directors were growing cobwebs waiting to be admitted to The Presence. A harried receptionist checked with her boss when she saw Marian's badge and then motioned her on through. Next came a series of cubicles, each occupied by a man or woman talking on the phone while trying to read playscripts or portfolios or the latest issue of *Variety*. The last barrier was Ramsay's secretary, a woman who looked as if she'd seen everything. She ordered Marian to go in.

The private office that Marian entered had been designed with naked intimidation in mind. Chairs and low tables had been arranged in a way that forced the visitor to travel a long aisle that ended at Ramsay's enormous desk; it was like approaching a throne. The producer sat with his back to the window, watching Marian without speaking, giving her the full treatment. When she managed to make the journey without collapsing from fear, he turned friendly. "Hello, Marian," he said, coming from behind his desk to greet her. "Or perhaps I should go back to 'Sergeant'? I'm sure this isn't a social call."

"'Marian' is fine." She took the chair he offered as he sat in another opposite her. "You know why I'm here, I'm sure. Did you know Ernie Nordstrom?"

He shook his head. "That's the burglar who was murdered? No, I didn't know him. In fact, I don't think I ever heard the name before."

"What about Eddie Norris?"

"No. Who's he?"

"Same guy. You told me—"

"When do we get the costumes back?" he interrupted. "And the other things that were taken?"

"I'm sorry, I don't know. Some of the items will be needed as evidence for the prosecution of Nordstrom's accomplices." She took a deep breath. "And I'm even sorrier to tell you that some of items have not been recovered. The Sarah Bernhardt jacket is one of them."

"It's gone?"

"I'm afraid so."

"God *damn* it!" His face darkened, and he worked his jaw back and forth for a moment. "The *one* thing I wanted back . . . they could keep everything else as far as I was concerned. We were insured, and everything's been replaced anyway. But that jacket was one of a kind. *Damn* it!"

"Maybe we can get a line on it later, if whoever has it tries to make a sale." Neither one of them believed that. "You told me you were on the board of directors of a costume museum?"

"The New York Museum of Theatrical Costuming, yes."

"Did that ever bring you into contact with memorabilia dealers, people like Nordstrom who bought and sold costumes and other things?"

"No, I left all that to the museum's director. He's responsible for purchasing." Ramsay looked at his watch.

"And yet you bought the Bernhardt jacket."

He smiled. "That was a fluke. I was in Paris on other business when I learned of the auction. My intention was to donate the jacket to the museum and claim a tax deduction rather than draw on the museum's limited funds. But before that, I wanted to take advantage of its publicity value by having Kelly wear the jacket for a while in *The Apostrophe Thief*. I would have replaced it in another few days. The jacket was in good condition, but it *was* old."

And Kelly thought his letting her wear it had been a vote of confidence. Marian thought back: the list of stolen costumes the wardrobe mistress had provided designated the value of the jacket as unknown. "Gene, how much did you pay for it?"

"In American currency, a little over twenty-two thousand dollars."

Marian was impressed. "For one jacket?"

Gene laughed shortly. "For *Bernhardt's* jacket. It was a steal."

"Was it insured?"

"Of course." He looked at his watch again.

"I'd like to see the receipt," Marian said, "from the Paris auction house. Better still, I'd like a photocopy to take with me."

"You got it." He stood up and went to the phone on his desk. When he'd finished telling his secretary what he wanted, he said to Marian, "Edie's making you a copy. Now, if there's nothing else, I have a full schedule this morning."

"That's all for now," Marian said, getting up. "Thanks for your time."

By the time she reached the door, he was already on the phone, chewing out someone named Manny. In the outer office, Edie the Efficient had the photocopy ready and was putting it into an envelope, which she handed to Marian with a look of wordless reproach—for taking up Gene Ramsay's precious time over foolish things like receipts, Marian supposed.

Two down. Mitchell Tobin next.

"I just used it for correspondence," Tobin was saying with irritation. "The only program I put on the disk was a word processor." He was feeling his thirty-two years this morning, but his baby-faced good looks were still enough to permit him to pass for the college student he played in *The Apostrophe Thief*. He'd just gotten up when Marian arrived at his apartment and he was still grouchy.

"Mr. Tobin, how long had you had the notebook computer?" Marian asked.

"That was just it—it was brand new! I hadn't had it even a week!"

"Then that's probably why it's gone. A virtually new computer . . . that would be easy to dispose of. What about the printer? You didn't report one stolen."

"I used my old printer. The one I keep here."

"Ah. Is there a chance something was on the notebook disk that was important to someone?"

"What? I told you, I just used the thing for correspondence."

A young woman whose face Marian was sure she'd seen on magazine covers drifted in from the back of the apartment, smiled mechanically at no one in particular, picked up a purse from a table, and drifted back out again. Tobin ignored her.

With an effort, Marian did the same. Back to business: "Did you back up the disk, or make hard copies to file?"

"No, no, it's all gone." Tobin took a long swallow of coffee, trying to work himself out of his cantankerous mood. "I'm sorry, Sergeant, there just wasn't anything there of value to anyone other than me."

"Tell me what kind of correspondence."

"Letters to my agent and money manager, mostly. One letter to my mother. And I answered a few fan letters."

"That's it?"

"That's it."

"The letters to your agent and your money manager—what were they about?"

Tobin stood up and stretched, then walked over to look at himself in a wall mirror . . . of which there were three in the room, Marian noticed. "My agent's trying to get me TV guest roles that can be shot in four days," he said, "so I won't have to miss the Wednesday matinee. I sent him two or three letters about shows I did and did not want to appear in. If I told him over the phone, he'd just forget."

"And your money manager?"

"Two letters—I remember now, I wrote him two letters. They were both just cover letters, accompanying some receipts."

Nothing there, evidently. Not expecting anything, Marian asked, "Did you know Ernie Nordstrom?"

Tobin turned away from his mirror and frowned. "You know, I may have met him once. I don't believe I ever heard his last name, but I'm sure the first name was Ernie."

"What did he look like?"

"Short and stout. He had a respiratory problem, as I recall."

"That sounds like Nordstrom," Marian said. "When did you meet him?"

"Oh, eight or nine years ago. I was still struggling and taking any job I could get. At the time I was understudying two roles in *Lockhart's Lie*, and this Ernie offered me a hundred dollars to get him a bullwhip that was used in the play. I needed money, but not so badly that I'd stoop to stealing stage props for some leech I didn't even know. So I told him to get lost. But about a week later the whip did disappear, so he got to somebody."

He told the story so guilelessly that Marian believed him, not forgetting the man was an actor; but if Tobin had himself taken the whip, he'd have denied knowing Nordstrom. "Did you ever see him again after that?"

"Never did." Tobin sat back down, crossing his legs with a studied elegance. "In fact, I didn't even think of him when our stuff was taken from the Broadhurst. It was only when I read the name 'Ernie Nordstrom' in the paper that I began wondering if it was the same man. By the way, when do I get the rest of my things back?"

Marian explained that that was up to the DA's office and took out a card. She scribbled the number for Midtown South on it and handed it to Tobin. "If you remember anything else on your computer disk, please call me. It doesn't matter what it is."

He shrugged but took the card. "Why was this Ernie killed, Sergeant? Does it have anything to do with our play?"

"I'm afraid it does, Mr. Tobin. You'll be seeing me again."

"Good god, am I a suspect?"

"Everybody's a suspect, and nobody is." Her rote answer. "No, I meant I'd be at the Broadhurst tonight, that's all."

He didn't look especially reassured. But he said, "Have you seen the play?"

"Twice."

"Ah. What did you think?"

Marian's earlier experience with Xandria Priest warned her he wasn't the least bit interested in her opinion of the *play*. So she gave him the praise he craved and left him in a much better frame of mind than she'd found him. He saw her to the door, checking his profile in one of the mirrors as he did.

Good timing; her stomach was beginning to make noises.

Marian was in the mood for something green and crunchy, so she stopped at a small eatery that had a fairly decent salad bar. As she chewed on a cucumber slice, she took out her notebook and flipped through the pages. The fact that Mitchell Tobin had once met Ernie Nordstrom didn't mean much, she felt. Considering the line of work Nordstrom had been in, it was not unreasonable that he'd once crossed paths with someone from the *Apostrophe Thief* bunch. And unless Tobin was lying, there was nothing on his computer disk that anyone wanted.

Xandria Priest's costume was just that, a costume; nothing special about it. But the Bernhardt jacket—that had turned out to be more valuable than she'd realized. People killed for a lot less than $22,000. Marian still had to see Frieda Armstrong about her missing fake fur coat; and she supposed she ought to check with Ian Cavanaugh about that shaving mug he'd made such a fuss over. But at this point it looked as if four of the missing items had been taken only to confuse the issue, to prevent the police's attention from being focused on the fifth.

That's the way the original burglary at the Broadhurst had been set up, a lot of thefts to obscure one particular one.

Marian finished her salad and idly pushed a black olive around her plate. Captain Murtaugh was sending out a list and description of the five missing items to all the precinct houses, but the chances of anything coming of that were slight. Maybe she'd been too quick to dismiss Mitchell Tobin's brief contact with Ernie Nordstrom, because maybe it wasn't that brief. Perhaps Tobin was protecting himself by admitting he'd known the dead man, in case someone saw him recently with Nordstrom. But if that were so, he wouldn't have claimed his one and only meeting with the dead man had taken place eight or nine years earlier. Marian sighed; no point in trying to figure it out until after she'd spoken to Armstrong and Cavanaugh. She popped the olive into her mouth and left.

Marian was looking forward to her next interview. Frieda Armstrong was something of an institution; she'd been acting longer than Marian had been alive, on the stage and in the movies and on television. Not everyone knew her name, but few people in the country would fail to recognize her face. Armstrong had never been a leading lady; she'd made a career out of playing mothers, or at least motherly women. Her very first role, at age eighteen, had been a thirtyish mother, and she'd been playing mothers or mother-types ever since. Sometimes she was a loving aunt, or a best friend, or a helpful next-door neighbor; Marian remembered one movie set during the Depression in which she'd founded an orphanage. Her role in *The Apostrophe Thief* was a slight departure; still a mother (Kelly and Xandria's), nevertheless she somehow wasn't quite *nice*. A mother that made the audience just a trifle uncomfortable—by design. It was a smart touch, thanks to Abigail James; and smart casting . . . thanks to John Reddick?

Frieda Armstrong lived in an older apartment building on

the West Side that looked like an Art Deco set for a Marx Brothers movie. The door to her apartment was opened by a maid or housekeeper, who made Marian wait in the hallway while she took Marian's card in to her employer. But she returned quickly, and Marian was ushered into a formal sitting room.

The woman she'd come to see was sitting at a writing table by a window, the afternoon sun throwing her partially into silhouette and creating an attractive picture suitable for framing. Armstrong finished what she was writing and then looked up. "Well?" she said sharply. "Have you come to tell me my fur coat has been found? My very *expensive* fur coat." There was no mistaking the sarcasm in her voice.

"Just the opposite, I'm afraid," Marian said. "I came to tell you it has *not* been found."

The other woman made a noise of exasperation. "I don't know why I'm surprised. Or even why I care. It was a cheap coat . . . still, it was better than the one they replaced it with. Oh, do sit down—don't *hover* over me like that! I suppose now you want to ask me questions."

Marian sat down, amused. She knew better than to confuse actors with the roles they played, but evidently all those years of kindhearted motherness had begun to wear on Frieda Armstrong. "Ms Armstrong, was there anything special about that coat, anything that might make it valuable to someone else?"

A look of such scorn appeared on her face that Marian had to fight down an urge to apologize. "*That* coat?" the matronly actor exclaimed in ringing tones. "Surely you are jesting . . . "—she glanced at the card Marian had sent in—"Sergeant Larch. *That* coat belongs in a Goodwill Industries used-clothing store! I wouldn't be surprised if that's where it came from. I've never known Gene Ramsay to squeeze a dollar the way he's done with this play. For something as pivotal to the plot as the fur coat is—but then, I don't suppose you've bothered to see the play."

"I was there opening night," Marian said, trying to sound humble.

"Were you indeed? Well, then, you know how important it is that I wear a good fur coat. The whole plot turns on it!"

Well, not the whole plot, Marian thought. In one scene young Xandria got on her mother's case about wearing fur; Kelly eventually backed her sister, although suspicious of Xandria's sudden interest in animal rights. The mother seemed willing to alienate both her daughters rather than give up her fur coat; it was one of several minor issues deliberately left unresolved in the play, to show the family looking for things to squabble about rather than grapple with the big problems that faced them. "Yes, I can see why real fur would be better," Marian said diplomatically.

"But Gene Ramsay absolutely refuses to get me real fur," Frieda Armstrong went on, "because, he says, from the stage the fakes *look* real." She sniffed. "As if anyone who's ever worn fur would be fooled by those conspicuous imitations!" She put her fingertips to her throat and posed for a moment, and then said, "I see *The Apostrophe Thief* as a female *King Lear.* 'How sharper than a serpent's tooth it is to have a thankless child!' Here's this woman who's given her entire life to two selfish daughters, who turn on her when she finally has a bit of luxury to indulge herself in! However, I can't say I care much for the ending of Abby's play . . . it's a bit equivocal, don't you think?"

Marian made a noncommittal sound; the play's ending had seemed quite *un*equivocal to her. The mother played only a small role in that ending, though—that's what grated on Frieda Armstrong. "Did anyone try to steal the fake fur earlier? Or buy it from you?"

A scornful laugh. "Most burglars wouldn't take the trouble. As to buying it—no, of course not. Who would want it? Other than that contemptible little man who robbed us and then got himself murdered."

Uh-huh. "How did you know he was little?"

"He was a thief, wasn't he? He was little."

"Did you ever meet Ernie Nordstrom?"

"Certainly not!"

"Perhaps you knew him as Eddie Norris."

"Sergeant, I didn't know him as *anything*! There are hundreds just like that man, swarming around every play, looking for things they can pick up to keep for themselves or to sell. And in cinema and television, they number in the thousands! These people are leeches—faceless, nameless leeches. They get their identities from us. They're not true fans, you know. True fans show respect. But these *collectors* respect nothing except their own collections. Take their collections away from them and they'd wither up and blow away, I'm sure of it."

Marian was thinking Holland would probably agree with her. But that was the second time that day Marian had heard Ernie Nordstrom called a leech, and she wondered what had prompted Frieda Armstrong's tirade. "You've been ripped off before, haven't you?" she ventured.

Instantly a change came over the woman; gone was the imperious denouncer of collectors, and in her place emerged a sweet, long-suffering woman of sturdy backbone and cheerful demeanor. Mom had arrived. "All my life," she said in a gentle voice. "As far back as I can remember, people have been taking from me. But I try not to let it dishearten me. I don't let myself feel like a victim. That's all one can do, isn't it? Keep on keeping on? It's a burden one simply must bear."

The scene would have benefited from music swelling in the

background, but it still played pretty well the way it was. "You're very brave," Marian said solemnly.

"I try to be. To set an example for the younger ones in the cast, you know. They don't yet understand it's better to be stolen from than to have to steal."

Marian felt sure that was a line from a movie. On the whole, she'd been enjoying Frieda Armstrong's performance, but she wasn't getting any answers here; reluctantly Marian got up to go. "Thank you for your time, Ms Armstrong—"

"Oh, you aren't leaving, are you, dear?" Mom said. "Wouldn't you like a nice cup of tea before you go? Or are you a coffee drinker? Perhaps cocoa is more to your taste."

"Nothing, thank you," Marian said with difficulty. "I just finished lunch."

"Well, then, some other time."

"That would be nice. Goodbye."

Marian tried to hold in her laugh until she got down to the street; but in the elevator it exploded from her in a rush, frightening an elderly man cradling a small dog close to his chest. "Sorry," she apologized, "but a visit to my mother always affects me like that."

13

Ian Cavanaugh lived with Abigail James in a brownstone on West Thirty-fifth, right down the street from Midtown South. Marian climbed the stoop and rang the bell, positioning herself in front of the eye hole set into the steel door.

The sound of a chain being removed reached her ears and Ian Cavanaugh opened the door. "Sergeant Larch—come in, come in!" He stood back to allow her to enter. "You'll have to excuse me for a moment . . . I'm in the middle of a fight with Abby. Make yourself comfortable." He waved a hand vaguely and headed toward a staircase that looked newer than the rest of the house. "I *told* you to wait until I could help!" he called up. "Now the neighbors have complained about all the racket you've been making and called the police! Sergeant Larch is here."

Abigail James's muffled voice floated down from upstairs, the words indistinct.

Cavanaugh was at the top of the stairs; he took a left turn and disappeared from view. "What's that? Speak up!"

This time the playwright's voice came loud and clear. "I'm *stuck*."

"Stuck?" Cavanaugh's voice was growing fainter. "How can you be stuck?"

Curious, Marian walked to the foot of the stairs and looked

up; she could see nothing, but she could hear a thumping noise and an occasional swear word. Then: silence.

"Can you use some help?" she called up.

"Yes!" two voices floated down.

She ran up the stairs and paused, looking for them. "Where are you?"

"Here!"

"On the staircase!"

Marian walked back to where the next staircase began, and found them: they were both stuck. Abigail James had been trying to move a cardboard carton large enough to hold a four-drawer file cabinet; in fact, the markings on the box indicated that's what it was meant to contain. But halfway between the third and second floors, the box had slipped sideways just enough to wedge both its handlers firmly in place. Ian Cavanaugh was pinned against the wall with one leg stretched out, his foot braced against the banister. Abigail James had somehow got herself *under* the carton; one of her legs was hooked over Cavanaugh's waist.

"Don't just stand there laughing!" the actor snapped at Marian. "Get us out of this!"

"Sorry. But you do look funny."

"*Delighted* to provide you with a moment's amusement. Now will you *do* something?"

"Watch your foot, Ian," the playwright said. "You don't want to break the banister."

"Never you mind my foot. If you'd *waited* the way I asked—"

"I know, I know."

Marian climbed up to them; if she could somehow get *him* loose, then they could just slide the box off *her*. She reached over Cavanaugh's outstretched leg and worked her hands under the carton; it wouldn't budge. "What have you got in this thing—bricks?"

Cavanaugh sighed. "Next thing to it. Books."

"Bend over."

He did; Marian leaned over his back and managed to rock the carton upward a little. "Can you get out?"

"Not yet."

She pushed a little harder. Abigail James groaned and said, "You do realize you're flattening me, don't you? I just want to make sure you realize that."

"Just a smidge more."

Finally Cavanaugh was able to slip out; but once his body was no longer wedging the carton in place, it began to descend the stairs under its own volition. He and Marian desperately tried to stop its advance . . . but to no avail. The box hit the newel post and split open, showering them with books. Marian yelled; the books *hurt*. She lost her balance and fell. After a moment she sat up, covered with books. Ian Cavanaugh lay on the floor next to her, a *What-happened?* look on his face.

Abigail James was sitting primly on one of the steps, elbows on her knees and chin resting in her hands. "Now, *that's* funny," she said.

With a lot of groaning and complaining, they got the books stacked up in fairly neat piles. They disposed of the now-useless carton; and by the time they ended up downstairs in the kitchen, Marian was on a first-name basis with the other two.

"I like these big old kitchens," she said, sitting across the table from Abby. "You don't see them much anymore."

The playwright smiled. "There's another one two floors up."

"Abby's kitchen is even bigger than this one," Ian said, as he made the coffee.

"*Abby's* kitchen?"

They explained that the brownstone was divided into two two-story apartments. Abby had been living in the top apartment for eons when Ian bought the downstairs apartment from the couple living there. Then they put in a new interior staircase; Abby had been using an outside entrance before. But other than that, they'd left the two apartments pretty much the way they were. Upstairs was her stuff, downstairs was his.

"Except that her stuff has a way of creeping down to encroach on my stuff," Ian said, pouring them coffee. "She'll say, 'You're not using this wall space here, are you?' And the next thing I know, a new bookcase has gone up."

Marian asked, "What were you doing with all those books you were trying to get down the stairs?"

"Giving them to Goodwill," Abby said. "There's just never enough shelf space."

Ian brought a plate of cookies and sat down at the end of the table. "Have a cookie."

Abby sighed. "You're a better hostess than I am. Where'd these come from?"

He smiled a stage smile. "Xandria made them. With her own lily-white hands."

"I'll bet." The two women each took a cookie. "Not bad," Abby said. "Did she bring cookies for everyone, or just for you?"

"Just for the men." Ian laughed. "You should have seen Leo Gunn's face."

Marian finished her cookie and reached for another. "I think I'm supposed to be here on police business. Just thought I'd mention it."

"And now that you've mentioned it," Abby said, "we can forget about it?"

"'Fraid not. This will take all of thirty seconds, so brace yourselves." Marian pointed a finger at Ian. "Honest-to-god truth, now—how much was that shaving mug worth?"

He took a swallow of coffee and said, "Honest-to-god truth, I haven't the foggiest. I put a five-thousand-dollar price tag on it the night it was stolen because I was furious at being robbed—but my grandfather could have gotten it at Woolworth's for all I know. Kelly told me it was missing from the things you recovered, is that right?"

"Unfortunately. I'm sorry, but I doubt if you'll ever get it back now. Did anyone ever offer to buy the mug from you?"

"Good heavens, no. Although come to think of it, Abby did try to throw it away a couple of times."

"I did not. I simply bought you a new one last Christmas, that's all."

"Which I now use dutifully every day, thank you very much."

"So the missing mug would have no value for anyone else?" Marian persisted.

They both sobered at her tone. Ian said, "No, it has no intrinsic value. It's just an old shaving mug."

Marian nodded. "Okay, that's my thirty seconds' worth. That's all I wanted to know."

The other two exchanged a look. Abby said, "Marian, who was this Ernie Nordstrom? Was his burglarizing the Broadhurst what got him killed? What's the connection?"

Marian gave them the *Reader's Digest* version. "Ernie Nordstrom was a man whose whole life consisted of dealing show business collectibles. He was killed by someone who set up the Broadhurst burglary for him. The killer's cut was to be one specific item that was kept backstage—we don't know what. But it looks as if Nordstrom welshed on the deal and was killed for it, and then the killer simply took the item he wanted. But before he left Nordstrom's apartment, he grabbed up as much other stuff as he could carry—to muddy the waters a little."

"And my shaving mug was one of the things he grabbed," Ian said.

"That's right. The mug's most likely been broken and the pieces scattered by now."

"Damn. Is the killer connected with *The Apostrophe Thief*?"

"He has to be," Abby interposed, "if he was able to set up the burglary. What else was taken besides the shaving mug?"

"Three costumes and a notebook computer," Marian said. "Everything else is accounted for."

"Mitchell Tobin's the only one who had a notebook," Ian remarked. "One of the costumes must have been the Bernhardt jacket, right? What were the other two?"

"A dress worn by Xandria Priest and Frieda Armstrong's fake fur."

Abby and Ian looked at each other and shrugged. "The Bernhardt jacket," Abby said.

Ian concurred. "It's the most valuable thing there."

Marian was inclined to agree. "I'm trying to rule the items out, one by one. So far, I'm about as certain as I can be that it wasn't the shaving mug or the other two costumes. That computer is still a question mark, though."

"Tobin hadn't had it long," Ian said. "I remember how excited he was with his new toy."

"Have you asked Xandria and Frieda about their costumes yet?" Abby asked. When Marian said yes, the playwright smiled. "Did Frieda give you her *King Lear* interpretation? About how *The Apostrophe Thief* concerns a mother with two ungrateful daughters?"

Marian laughed softly. "She certainly did. She really thinks your play is about her character, doesn't she?"

"That's why she was cast," Abby explained. "Frieda Armstrong has spent her life playing warm, nurturing, concerned women—but she's one of the most self-absorbed actors in theater . . . and that's saying something. John Reddick has done a marvelous job of getting her to let that aspect of her personality show through. The reviewers all mentioned the 'new subtlety' in her performance or some such flapdoodle. One of them even praised her courage in revealing the dark side of a stereotype she's played so successfully in the past."

"Frieda's going to win a Tony for this role," Ian proclaimed wryly. "You wait."

"She said something to me that I'm sure is a line from a movie," Marian remarked. "What's this from? 'It's better to be stolen from than to have to steal.'"

The other two frowned in concentration. "British," Ian said at last.

"And it's a man who says the line," Abby added.

But neither of them could remember which movie. Marian looked at her watch and stood up. "Thanks for the coffee . . . and the cookies."

Abby looked surprised. "You're leaving?"

"I have to report to my captain. And I want to get away in time to come to the theater tonight."

"Can't stay away, hm?" Ian asked smugly.

"Positively can't," Marian answered with a smile. "See you later."

When she'd left, she thought it just as well she hadn't told them that one of the reasons she was going to the theater was to talk to the wardrobe mistress, not to see the play. The woman lived on Long Island, and Marian simply didn't want to make the drive. But while she was at the Broadhurst, it might not hurt to have a word with Leo Gunn as well. Who was in a better position to know cleaning-crew and doorkeeper schedules than the stage manager?

She got back to Midtown South to find storm clouds brewing. Captain Murtaugh was talking heatedly on the phone; he made an angry arm gesture for her to come into his office. She closed the door behind her.

"Out of the question," Murtaugh snapped. "It's our jurisdiction." He listened a moment. "That doesn't make any difference. She's on loan to us, she called in the murder, it's her case."

Marian sank down on a chair; *she* was the "she" he was talking about.

"Yes, I know—we've all got a manpower problem. But the investigation stays at Midtown South, whether you pull her back or not," Murtaugh was saying. "If she goes back to the Ninth, I'll put a gag order on her. The Nordstrom case stays *here*. It's still a jurisdictional matter." He listened some more. "You do that." He slammed down the receiver.

"DiFalco?" Marian asked.

Murtaugh was fuming. "He wants me to transfer the Nordstrom case to the Ninth Precinct and you along with it. He's threatening to go over my head."

"Can he do that?"

"I don't know—what kind of connections does he have?"

Marian thought back. "I know he has a pipeline to the Chief of Patrol's Office. Maybe to the Chief of Detectives as well."

"Hell!" Murtaugh brooded a moment. "He might be able to pull it off, but it'll take him a while. Can you wrap it up in forty-eight hours?"

"I don't see how. I don't have a suspect."

Murtaugh swore. "DiFalco seemed sure you'd nail the killer . . . what's it to him? Credit for the bust?"

"Exactly. It's a glamour case—Broadway stars and like that. The way he thinks, he probably feels he has a right to the case, what with Gloria Sanchez in on it as well as me."

The captain looked at her oddly. "Those are precisely the words he used—'I have a right to the Nordstrom case,' he said. 'My detectives, my case.' He doesn't really *believe* that, does he?"

Wordlessly, Marian nodded her head.

Murtaugh sat down at his desk. "I'm beginning to see why you don't want to go back to the Ninth. I don't know how big a stink DiFalco can raise, but we can't cross that bridge 'til we come to it. So, fill me in. What have you got?"

"It looks as if it's the Bernhardt jacket," she said. She pulled out the photocopy of the receipt Gene Ramsay had given her. "Could we fax this to the French Sûreté, get them to check its authenticity? Gene Ramsay paid twenty-two thou for the jacket."

"That much?" Murtaugh took the receipt. "Nothing else valued that high, right?"

Marian summarized what she'd learned and ended by asking if she could borrow Perlmutter the next day. "I need somebody to show photos of everyone connected with *The Apostrophe Thief* to the doormen at Nordstrom's building, especially the one who was on duty Tuesday night."

"I'll put him on it tomorrow. What else?"

"Mitchell Tobin's the only one to admit to knowing Nordstrom, but he says it was only one encounter eight or nine years ago."

"Did you believe him?"

"Yes, I believed him, about Nordstrom. I'm more concerned about that missing computer of his . . . a loose end there's no way to tie up. I'm going to talk to the wardrobe mistress and the stage manager tonight, see if they can tell me anything."

"What about your connection, uh, Augie? Have you checked with him?"

"He doesn't know anything, Captain. I think I'd have better luck with the Zingones."

"Zingones—ah, the biblical brothers and . . . Janet, is it?

But they're *dealers*. You don't think the killer'd be stupid enough to peddle the things he took from Nordstrom's apartment, do you?"

Marian slumped in her chair. "No, I don't. But I'm running out of leads, and I am in a position to put a little pressure on the Zingones. Receiving stolen goods. If any of the Nordstrom stuff *is* moved, the Zingones would know about it."

"All right, but it sounds like a long shot." He paused. "Change of subject. Lieutenant Overbrook's coming back next week."

"Ah! That's good. Full time?"

"Not at first. We'll see how it goes. But you know he'll be here only a matter of weeks before he retires." He looked her straight in the eye. "And you did take the Lieutenants Exam."

Marian's stomach knotted. "Captain, I—"

"I checked the eligibility list. You're right at the top."

"I was right at the top last time, too," she muttered.

Murtaugh raised an eyebrow. "So now you're sulking because you were passed over?" He sounded amused. "Oh, of course—that's never happened to anyone else. But it isn't *all* DiFalco, then."

"I never said it was," Marian answered, a little too defensively.

"Under the circumstances, I imagine you're right to resign," Murtaugh went on blandly. "Obviously you'll be satisfied with nothing less than perfection in a job, and I rather doubt you'll find that in police work."

"Damn it, Captain, don't patronize me! It took me a long time to reach the point of deciding to quit, and . . . and . . . "

"And now that you've made up your mind, you don't want to have to *un*make it? Reconsideration is a sign of weakness?" He dropped his needling tone and said earnestly, "You've been going after Ernie Nordstrom's killer like a *cop*, not like some deadbeat just counting the minutes until she's out of here. You're a *cop*, Larch. You'd be miserable doing anything else." He paused. "Just thought I'd mention it."

Marian threw up her arms. "Just thought you'd *mention* it?"

He laughed. "Yes, well, let's put that on hold for now. I want to change directions on you again. I'm going to drop by the Broadhurst myself tonight. Will you be there before or after the performance?"

"Both. I like the play. Are you going to tell them one of them is a murderer?"

"Certainly. They have a right to know, if they haven't already figured it out. And something helpful might come out of it. I'll wait until they finish their performance and then make an announcement."

"Alibis?"

"Right after the announcement. I know you could handle it alone, Sergeant, but I haven't met any of those people and I want to get a feel for the place." Murtaugh shifted his weight. "If you don't have anything else, go home. It's going to be a long night."

"Right," said Marian, and got out as fast as she could. She stopped at a deli for take-out; she'd have time to shower and change and still get to the theater well before curtain time. But even while wavering between artichokes and linguine salad, she couldn't get Murtaugh out of her head. The way he'd dangled the lieutenancy in front of her—*making* her think about it! Murtaugh didn't decide who got promotions, but his recommendation would carry a lot of weight with Personnel. And what about the man himself? Marian didn't know another captain in the entire NYPD who'd want a woman as his lieutenant.

I can't think about this now.

At home, the message light on her answering machine was blinking. It was Gloria Sanchez: *Call me immediately.*

Marian tapped out her home number. "Gloria? What's up?"

The other woman took a deep breath. "Are you ready for this? Foley's been suspended. Pending an investigation."

Marian gasped. Her old partner, the worst cop she'd ever known. She'd pleaded with Captain DiFalco to take Foley off the streets, and now . . . "What'd he do?"

"Oh, he fucked up regally. A gorilla named Jimmy Ybarra was beating on his family so bad that one of the kids called the police. Foley was told to investigate, but he didn't even bother going to the home. He just got Ybarra on the phone and asked if he was abusing his family. The guy said he wasn't, natch— and Foley wrote in his report that he'd found no evidence of domestic violence."

Marian could see what was coming. "Who?"

"The wife. She's in the hospital now with a broken back. She may die."

Marian closed her eyes and gritted her teeth. A *broken back. May die.* That woman should have been safe if Foley had done his job. "And DiFalco had to wait until something like this happened before he'd suspend him."

"That's not all," Gloria said. "With Foley on suspension and you cozying up with Captain Murtaugh, DiFalco's short two detectives. Marian, he's going to pull you back."

"I know—he's already made his first move. But it's not me he wants, it's the Nordstrom murder. Since you and I both worked on it, he's claiming it for his own."

"But that's stupid! It's not a Ninth Precinct case."

"That's what Murtaugh is saying. But DiFalco's threatening to go over his head."

"Oh shit. How hard will Murtaugh fight to keep it?"

Marian thought a moment. "Hard, I think. He doesn't like being strong-armed."

"So, what are you going to do?"

Marian was silent for a long while, and then said, "Gloria, I haven't the faintest idea."

14

Leo Gunn was using his mechanical hand to flip through the pages of his newly marked script. When he looked up and saw Marian, he sighed. "I was wondering how long it'd take you to get around to me."

Knowing a gift when she saw one, Marian simply said, "You want to save me some time and tell me straight out?"

"There's not all that much to tell," he said. "I barely knew him. I never did business with him, if business was what it was. I didn't even know where he lived."

"Few people did. Where'd you meet him?"

"In a bar—on West Forty-seventh, I think. My roommate introduced him. He thought he was an antiques dealer." Gunn smiled sourly. "I kind of felt sorry for the guy."

"Why's that?"

Gunn made a *huhn* sound. "Because he was fifty years old and still starstruck. He sat there at the bar wheezing away, telling us he had this star's dressing gown and that star's make-up kit. He was like a kid, bragging about his treasures."

"What did he want from you?"

"Can't you guess? He wanted an 'arrangement'—I'd steal stuff from the shows I was working, he'd sell it and split the profits." The stage manager closed his script. "When I told Ernie I'd been in this business too long to start going in for petty theft now, his face just crumbled. I thought he was going to cry. Excuse me a minute."

He broke off to tell one of the stage electricians to check a spotlight he thought was slipping its brace. When he came back, Marian asked, "When did all this happen, Mr. Gunn?"

"Oh, three, four years ago. I was working a fake Shakespearean musical called *Alarums and Excursions* that was loaded with glitzy props and special stage effects. Ernie was just itching to get his hands on the stuff."

"Did you tell anybody you'd been approached?"

"Yeah, I warned the director and the producer. The show didn't run long, and the props were all sold off quickly or destroyed. I don't know if Ernie ever got anything or not."

"Did you ever see Nordstrom after that time in the bar?"

"Oh sure. Every time I'd open a new show, there'd be Ernie, asking if I'd changed my mind."

"When was the last time you saw him?"

"Months ago. Before rehearsals for *The Apostrophe Thief* even started." The stage manager rubbed his chin. "That's right, he didn't come around this time. I hadn't thought of that."

"Didn't you suspect him after the burglary?"

"He's about the last one I would suspect." Gunn paused, gathering his thoughts. "Sergeant, I don't quite know how to explain it, but Ernie Nordstrom was a *mild* man. Don't get me wrong—there was a generous helping of sleaze in his nature. But he wasn't aggressive and fearless in his pursuit of collectibles. He dearly loved every piece of memorabilia that passed through his hands, and he honestly didn't see anything wrong in working a shady deal now and then if it brought him some new trophy. The collection was everything . . . all else was secondary."

"Yet he did manage a rather aggressive burglary," Marian pointed out.

"Yes, that's just it! That whole thing is so *un*typical. Mounting a full-scale assault on a theater? Why, he must have been scared to death! That just wasn't Ernie's style. You know what I think? I think somebody else was behind it. Ernie would never have thought it up on his own. That's what I think."

"And I think you're right. Any idea who it might be?"

Gunn wouldn't venture a guess. "But whoever he is, he took advantage of Ernie's obsession to get him to do his dirty work. And then he killed him." He shook his head. "Ernie wasn't dangerous. He was just doing the best he could. He didn't deserve to die like that."

Marian was silent; those were the first kind words she'd heard spoken about Ernie Nordstrom, and they were spoken by a man who hadn't even liked him much. She reached into her bag and pulled out a list of the missing items. "Tell me what's the most valuable thing there."

He read the list. "Sarah Bernhardt's jacket, I'd say."

"And the next most valuable?"

"The computer. Neither of the other costumes would have cost as much as a notebook, and Ian's old shaving mug wasn't worth anything."

"Ernie Nordstrom was killed for one of the items on that list."

"No shit. One of these five? Well, it's got to be the jacket. I'd say you need to look for a collector or another dealer, Sergeant."

That was beginning to seem the only logical assumption. She thanked Leo Gunn and headed for the costume room; she still had forty-five minutes before the curtain.

Her interview took less than five. The wardrobe mistress was a plump, fortyish woman named Anne-Marie St. John, which she insisted was pronounced *Sinjun* even though her accent was as Bronx as Augie Silver's. She was using a blow-dryer to fluff up a fake fur coat.

"Is that Frieda Armstrong's new coat?" Marian asked.

"It is. It's identical to the first one, but Frieda keeps saying it's inferior. Bitch, bitch, bitch."

"About that first one. Could that by any chance have been a real fur?"

The woman laughed, raucously. "Are you kidding? The day Gene Ramsay shells out for real fur is the day I play Juliet opposite Kenneth Branagh. No, I bought that coat myself, and I handled it every night. It was as fake as they come. Here, look for yourself—this one's just like it."

Marian read the label, which conscientiously listed all the synthetics that went into creating "a fur experience"; it was fake, all right. "Okay, what about the white dress Xandria Priest wears? Anything special about that?"

"Whaddaya mean, special?"

"Was it especially valuable?"

"Naw. Four, five hundred dollars is all. I gave you a list of what everything cost, back on the night we were cleaned out."

"I know. I'm just trying to find out if there's any reason someone would want *that* coat or Xandria's dress especially. Would they have more value to a collector than, say, this dress?" She pointed to one at random hanging on a rack.

"Not that I can see," Anne-Marie St. John said. "'Course, with collectors you're never really sure what's going on. They're all crazy, you know."

Just then a young man stuck his head through the door. "Elsie, Xandria's got a ripped hem she wants you to fix."

"Be right there." The young man left and the wardrobe mistress shot an embarrassed look at Marian. "'Elsie' is just a pet name they have for me here."

"Oh." Marian followed her out and watched her head toward the dressing rooms. Once the other woman was out of sight, Marian stopped by the stage manager's desk. "What's Anne-Marie St. John's real name?"

Leo Gunn grinned. "Elsie Greenbaum."

What she'd thought. Marian's watch told her she still had a little time, so she crossed to the other side of the stage where the dressing rooms were. She knocked on Kelly's door and said, "It's me."

"Come in come in come in!"

Kelly was in costume and in the process of putting on her make-up. On her dressing table was half a glass of white wine. Kelly waved a hand toward an ice bucket and said, "Help yourself. John brought it."

Marian poured herself some wine and sat down. "What's this line from? 'It's better to be stolen from than to have to steal.'"

"*The Red Shoes*," Kelly said promptly. "The ballet director says it to the young composer, early in the film. Why?"

"Oh, Frieda Armstrong said that to me earlier today, and I thought it sounded like direct quotation." She took a sip from her glass. "This is good wine. John Reddick brought it? Is he here tonight?"

"He's around somewhere. Giving Xandria a good talking-to, I hope."

"You still having trouble with her?"

"*Bleaghh.* The best acting I do is in those scenes where I'm supposed to show how much I love my sister."

"Why don't you try upstaging *her*?"

"That's for amateurs." Kelly stopped what she was doing and turned to face her friend. "Are you just going to go on sitting there making chitchat? For crying out loud, Marian, tell me what's going on! Why was this Ernie Whatsisname killed? What's it got to do with us?"

Marian sighed. "My boss is going to make an announcement here later this evening. Ernie Nordstrom's killer is right here at the Broadhurst. He put Nordstrom up to the burglary—there was something among the loot that he wanted." She went on to explain about the five missing items, and how it looked as if the one the killer wanted was the Bernhardt jacket.

Kelly's eyes were big and round. "My jacket? A man was killed for my jacket?"

"Gene Ramsay paid twenty-two thousand for it. To a hard-core collector, it'd be a real prize. Kelly, who here collects theater memorabilia? Do you know?"

"Oh boy. Oh boy."

"Kelly . . . who?"

"Only one that I know of. Oh boy."

"Dammit, *who?*"

"John."

Whew. Marian thought about that a while. "Have you seen his collection?"

"Yes. He's given over a whole room in his apartment to his theater stuff. Marian, John's the only one I *know* about. There could be others."

"That's something I can check on." She finished her wine and stood up. "Don't say anything about this, Kel."

"I won't."

Just as Marian left Kelly's dressing room, she saw Mitchell Tobin coming out of his. "Mr. Tobin—a moment, please."

"Yes?" He waited for her to catch up with him.

"Have you ever seen John Reddick's theater collection?" she asked.

He looked surprised. "You don't suspect *John*, do you? But to answer your question, yes, he showed it to me once. Not much there, really—two or three items other collectors might want, but mostly it's play programs and scripts, other direc-tors' notes. Letters, a lighting plot or two. John's a director, and he's interested mostly in things to do with directing."

"Is anyone else here a collector?"

"Not that I know, and I'm not sure even John Reddick would qualify as a real collector. Leo Gunn keeps souvenirs from the plays he works—hell, we all do that, a little. But Leo usually manages to get the best stage props."

"You mean he just steals them?"

"Oh, I don't think so. I don't know what kind of arrange-ment he has."

The call of *Places, please* was sounding backstage, so she let Tobin go. Ian Cavanaugh was already on the stage, concentrat-ing; he looked right at Marian and didn't see her. Frieda Armstrong sailed up to join Mitchell Tobin; they were to enter together and stood silently until their cues. Marian looked across the stage and saw Kelly waiting on the other side.

John Reddick. Leo Gunn.

Finally it was time. The stage lights came up, the curtain opened, and the audience applauded the sight of Ian Cavanaugh standing there looking through an address book. That had impressed Marian the first time she'd seen it and it impressed her now, how the man could draw applause just by being there. After some stage business the actor had, Tobin and Armstrong made their entrance, and Marian listened as the now-familiar dialogue began to unfold.

She stood rooted to the spot until Kelly made her entrance; then she had to resist the urge to do a little dance at the way her friend marched out and took over the stage. Kelly and Ian were antagonists in the play; they squared off nicely in this first scene, and *The Apostrophe Thief* was off and running.

Marian felt a light touch on her arm; she turned to find the play's author standing next to her. Abby James crooked a finger at her and walked away; Marian followed.

When they were near the stage door, Abby said in a low voice, "Care to join me for a drink?"

"I'd love to," Marian whispered.

"Don't whisper. Whispers carry."

Marian nodded, and was surprised to see the other woman leaving through the stage door; she'd thought they'd be going to Ian Cavanaugh's dressing room or someplace like that. Outside, she said, "Don't you want to watch the play?"

Abby said no. "I agonize too much. When it's been running six weeks or so, then I can watch with a little objectivity." A thought occurred to her. "Oh—I'm sorry! *You* want to watch."

"I wouldn't get to see all of it anyway," Marian said, "so I might as well have a drink while I can. Where are we heading?"

Abby led her to a bar about half a block away that was virtually empty. "This place will be packed during intermission. Do you mind sitting at the bar? Hello, Fred." Fred took their orders and brought their drinks. "Ah, that helps," Abby said after her first swallow. "By the way, where's your friend who talks in blank verse?"

"Uh, Holland? He'll be along later. Blank verse? Really?" Then she realized. "Oh, dammit!"

"What's the matter?"

"We're supposed to go for a late supper—but I can't make it and I forgot to let him know."

"There's a pay phone on the wall."

"Wouldn't do any good. The only number I have for him is a voice service, and he won't be checking this late."

"Well, how far away does he live? You could grab a cab—"

Marian groaned. "I don't know where he lives!"

"Hm. You don't know his home phone, and you don't know

where he lives—just what do you know about the man?"

"Not a hell of a lot. He's a very secretive person. He's never mentioned his childhood, or anything earlier than the recent past that I already know about . . . how can he do that? How can anyone *never* mention what's happened to him?"

"I don't know. I couldn't. Ah, well—you're a detective, you like mysteries."

"I hate mysteries. What I like are *solutions*."

Abby laughed. "And you like Holland."

"Yes. Dammit."

"Well, you'll just have to wing it when he gets here. Why can't you keep the date?"

"Police business." Then, realizing how abrupt that sounded, Marian explained. "My boss is coming tonight, and he's going to inform everyone at the Broadhurst that Ernie Nordstrom's killer is one of them. Then he and I will take statements from everyone—we're looking for alibis."

"Oh, dear."

"Abby, you mind saving me a few minutes?" Marian pulled out her notebook. "What time did you leave the theater Tuesday night?"

"Tuesday . . . I didn't go in Tuesday night. Something I ate didn't agree with me, and I was afraid to get too far away from a bathroom. Ian came straight home after the performance."

"So you were both at home from about midnight on?"

"From before midnight, yes."

Marian thought a moment. "Abby, how well do you know Leo Gunn?"

"Very well, both professionally and personally. We go back a long way. Why?"

"The souvenirs he takes home from each show he works. How big a collection is it?"

Abby was shocked. "You can't suspect *Leo*! Leo Gunn is a decent man—he wouldn't stoop to theft, much less commit murder!"

"He knew Ernie Nordstrom. He's a collector."

"Of *souvenirs*, personal souvenirs! It's a perk he arranges with producers before he'll accept a job . . . he has the same deal with Gene Ramsay for *The Apostrophe Thief*. And what if he did know Ernie Nordstrom? A lot of people must have known him. Marian, take my word for it, you're on the wrong track there. Leo and Ian and I have been through a lot together, and I *know* Leo. He's not your killer."

Marian knew there was no point in arguing with that kind of conviction, so she said, "John Reddick's a collector, too, isn't he?"

Abby almost fell off her stool. When she'd composed herself, she said, "John's interested only in materials about directing. He keeps saying he's going to write a history of contemporary directing, postwar theater to the present. I don't know if he'll ever get around to it, but that's the only sort of thing he 'collects'—the Bernhardt jacket would be of no use to him."

"Yet he's given over an entire room of his apartment to this noncollection."

The playwright looked surprised. "How'd you know about that?"

"Then it's true?"

"Yes, but only because John's a bit of a procrastinator. If he'd ever sit down and sort through what he's got, he could get rid of a lot of the stuff. Marian . . . I know you can't just take my word for it, but John's no murderer, either. The thought of having to kill someone would drive him wild. He'd be more likely to run away and hide until the trouble blew over."

"All right, then, tell me who else is a collector."

"Why, I don't think anyone is. The kind of collecting you're talking about, that's a fannish sort of activity. I don't know of anyone with the play who goes in for that. If Ernie Nordstrom was indeed killed for the Bernhardt jacket, I'd say the killer was someone who needed cash, not necessarily a collector. Didn't you say Gene paid twenty thousand for the jacket?"

"Twenty-two." Leo Gunn had thought the killer must be a collector, but Abby's argument made sense. But the killer would have to have a buyer lined up, if all he wanted was money.

"Oh, there's John," Abby said. "Must be close to intermission."

John Reddick took the stool next to the playwright and started talking. "Who*ee*, are they 'on' tonight! You should have been there, Abby! Hello, Larch-Tree, why aren't you watching the play? Fred—scotch, please. You should have seen Ian, Abby. In the passport scene, he got so into it that he actually picked Kelly up and threw her against the sofa!"

"Oh, my god!" Abby said. "What did she do?"

"Bounced right back up, of course! For a minute there I thought they were going to start swinging!"

"Are they mad at each other?" Marian asked, puzzled.

John laughed. "Anything but, Larch-Tree! They came off the stage grinning like hyenas and congratulating each other. They'd pulled off a good one."

Abby said, "You were watching from backstage?"

"I started out front, but then I went back to see Leo—one of the spotlights looked crooked to me. God, Abby, I wish you could have seen it."

"Are you going to keep the sofa-bouncing bit?" she asked.

"I don't know. That kind of macho physical explosion isn't really in character, not that early in the play. But Ian did it so *gracefully*, it made a terrific bit of stage business. Theatrical as hell. I may tell him to keep it in, but only when the momentum is right. That way Kelly will never know what to expect. It'll keep her sharp."

By then the bar was crowded with playgoers trying to snatch a quick libation between acts. Fred kept shooting glances at Marian's empty glass, so she told Abby and John she'd see them back at the theater. She worked her way through the crowd, trying not to jar people holding drinks in their hands. Just as she was leaving she heard someone say, "And when he threw her against that sofa, I thought she was going to *kill* him!"

And Marian had missed it.

15

Captain James T. Murtaugh stood on the stage of
the Broadhurst Theatre, his back to the empty auditorium.
Facing him were the cast and crew of *The Apostrophe Thief*,
displaying varying degrees of irritation and/or curiosity. A uniformed officer stood by the stage door, his function being to
dissuade any member of the company from departing prema-
turely. A second uniformed officer was stationed in the lobby,
and a third was positioned behind Marian Larch at the side of
the stage. Marian looked around for Holland; no sign of him.

Captain Murtaugh introduced himself. "I'm sure you all
know by now," he said, "that the man who burglarized the theater was murdered Tuesday night. His name was Ernie
Nordstrom, alias Eddie Norris. We now feel certain he was
killed for the velvet jacket that once belonged to Sarah
Bernhardt."

If the captain expected a murmur to run through the
crowd, he was disappointed. Murtaugh went on, "Someone
with this play set up the burglary for the sole purpose of
obtaining that jacket for himself. We don't know if he planned
on killing Ernie Nordstrom all along or if it was just a case of
thieves falling out. We suspect the latter, because the killer
hurriedly grabbed up several other items to divert attention

from the *one* item he wanted, the jacket. If the murder had been planned in advance, the killer would have taken his time and picked out more valuable items—items that would have done a better job of confusing the issue."

"Wait a minute," John Reddick said. "You're accusing one of us? Of murder?"

"That's exactly what I'm doing. You are . . . ?"

"John Reddick. What makes you think someone in the company set up the burglary?"

"The fact that Nordstrom knew the layout here well enough to pull it off. That plus the admission of his two accomplices."

The director didn't have a comeback for that; he nodded and fell silent.

"What we want from you now," Murtaugh continued, "is a statement of where you went following Tuesday night's performance." The autopsy report had said that because of the low temperature of Nordstrom's apartment, he could have died as early as eleven-thirty. Between eleven-thirty and two was the crucial time—but there was no need to make that public just yet. "We'll ask you two or three other questions as well. Sergeant?"

Marian walked out on the stage. "This shouldn't take long. If you know anything at all about Ernie Nordstrom or the Bernhardt jacket, now's the time to tell us. Please come forward when Officer Dowd calls your name."

The uniformed officer had the stage doorkeeper's list of everyone in the company. Leo Gunn had set up two small tables with chairs on both sides for Marian and the captain to use. Officer Dowd called out two names, and the questioning began.

In addition to inquiring about alibis, Marian and Murtaugh also asked each interviewee if he or she knew of anyone in the company who collected theater memorabilia, rather than use the more direct *Are you a collector?* Additionally, they were all asked about Nordstrom/Norris and given a phone number to call if anything occurred to them later.

Marian's prediction turned out to be right; it didn't take long. Most of the company alibied one another. The rest gave names of people they'd been with and where they'd gone after the final curtain. Evidently no one in theater just went home to bed after the night's work was done. Only Mitchell Tobin and Leo Gunn admitted to having known Ernie Nordstrom, and no new collectors emerged from the crowd. To Marian's mind, the whole thing was a waste of time; but procedure demanded it be done.

She looked for Holland again and was wondering whether to get mad at being stood up when Murtaugh announced everyone could go. He came over to Marian's table. "I got nothing. What about you?"

"Same here. Alibis all around, nobody knows anything about the jacket. There's one person who wasn't here—Gene Ramsay, the producer. I'll check with him tomorrow."

"Why would Ramsay steal his own property?" Murtaugh mused. "He hadn't donated it to the museum yet, had he?"

"Not yet. But I'll get his alibi just the same. When you said everyone could go, did you mean me too?"

"You and me both. I think I'll just take a look at the layout of the dressing rooms before I leave. See you tomorrow, Sergeant."

As soon as he'd left, Marian heard, "Psst! Hey! Marian!"

She turned to see Kelly gesturing to her from the wings. "Psst, hey, Marian?" she repeated wonderingly.

"Are you off duty now?" Kelly asked in a stage whisper.

"Yes. Why are you whispering?"

"Oh, well, that's all right, then," Kelly said in her natural voice. "Your date's here. Come on."

"Holland's here?" He was, standing behind a tormentor, talking to Abby James. "Has he been here all this time?"

"He has," Abby said.

"And a very *long* time it has been indeed," Holland said archly.

"I'm sorry, I should have let you know. I goofed."

"He wouldn't let us tell you he was here," Kelly said. "Not until you were finished."

Abby smiled. "Preferring to suffer nobly, unseen and unheard."

"So long as suffering finds its just reward," Holland announced, "in ample gustatory compensation."

"There," said Abby. "That's blank verse."

"You mean you're hungry," Marian said.

"I mean I'm hungry."

"So am I," said Kelly. "But I wouldn't dream of intruding." She batted her eyelashes in mock coyness.

Marian laughed. "Not much you wouldn't. Come along, then. What about you, Abby?"

"Thought you'd never ask. Do you mind, Holland?"

"Do I mind escorting *three* ladies to supper?" He raised an eyebrow. "And run the danger of being the envy of New York? I'll risk it."

"Good. I'll go get Ian."

Holland stage-sighed. "If you must."

Kelly went with Abby, to pick up her purse and coat. Marian turned to Holland. "I'm sorry you had to wait. Captain Murtaugh sprang this question-and-answer session on me late in the day, and I just didn't think to call you."

"It doesn't matter. How is Murtaugh to work for?"

"So far, just fine."

"Not another DiFalco?"

"No, thank goodness! Murtaugh was doubling for his lieutenant tonight—Lieutenant Overbrook's recovering from a coronary."

"Then I imagine he'll be retiring soon."

How quick he was! "Yes."

He was quiet a moment. "You want his job." Not a question.

Marian took a deep breath. "That's what I'm trying to decide, Holland."

"I see."

An uncomfortable silence growing between them, they moved automatically toward the stage door. Captain Murtaugh returned from his inspection of the dressing rooms and said, "Security isn't the greatest here, is it?" Then he spotted Holland. "Hello. Who are you?"

Marian introduced the two men, neither of whom offered to shake hands.

"Are you with the play?" Murtaugh asked. "Your name isn't on the doorkeeper's list."

"No. I'm not with the play." No further explanation.

Murtaugh's eyes narrowed at Holland's curtness. "Then may I ask what you're doing here?"

"Yes. You may ask."

The captain was aware that Holland was giving him the once-over, and he didn't like it. Murtaugh was the taller of the two, towering over Holland by nearly a full head, but they still managed to lock eyes. Marian waited, but neither man seemed inclined to speak. "He stopped by to pick me up," she said tiredly.

"Ah. Well, I'm sorry to have kept you so late, Sergeant. A policeman's lot and all that. Good night." He nodded to Holland and went on out.

Holland laughed shortly. "Did he really say, 'A policeman's lot and all that'? Stunning originality. And you'd rather work with that man than with me?"

"It's not a matter of people, Holland, it's a matter of jobs."

"Are you sure of that?"

Just then the others arrived with John Reddick in tow, all four of them proclaiming a state of near-starvation, and Marian was saved from answering.

Bleary-eyed and fuzzy-headed from insufficient sleep, Marian kept out of Murtaugh's way the next morning. The captain was caught up in the aftermath of a restaurant fire on Ninth Avenue that had been set deliberately. Four people had died, thus taking the case out of the hands of the Bomb and Arson Squad; the investigation was demanding all of Murtaugh's attention for the moment.

It was just as well. Marian felt sure the captain would not have approved of her socializing with what he considered four murder suspects. *DiFalco* would have approved; he'd see it as a chance to worm something incriminating out of them. But Marian had happily ignored police protocol to join her old and new friends for a few hours of relaxation. She was confident they were, mostly, what they appeared to be: decent people who were only too aware that a man had been murdered, a man who was a stranger but whose life had touched briefly upon theirs.

Kelly's suggestion that they go dancing had been unanimously voted down; they'd ended up at Sonderman's again, with its big circular booths that could seat six people. Good food and drink and good company had in time eased away their tensions; even Holland had lost his brooding look, eventually. When he'd dropped her off in the wee hours, he'd merely said to call him when she'd decided. She'd repeated that she would not decide anything until the Nordstrom case was wrapped up. He'd smiled sardonically and driven away.

John Reddick was the only question mark of the bunch. Marian couldn't see John as a murderer; but as long as he had any kind of "collection" at all, she couldn't scratch him off the suspects list. At one point when Kelly and Abby had gone to the Ladies', Marian asked him about his collection. He invited her to come take a look; she accepted. She wanted to see for herself that he didn't collect things such as velvet jackets that had once been worn by theater legends like Sarah Bernhardt.

A reply had arrived from the French Sûreté; Gene Ramsay's receipt for the jacket checked out. The French official had thoughtfully worded his reply in English, apparently aware from past experience that New York cops were not fluent in the language of Racine and Hugo. Marian stepped out of Lieutenant Overbrook's office just as Perlmutter was getting up to leave. She asked if Captain Murtaugh had told him to show pictures to the doorman of Ernie Nordstrom's building, to try to get an identification.

"Yeah, but I'm going to have to *take* some pictures first," he said, holding up a Polaroid. "I got publicity photos of all the actors, and of the director and the producer and . . . who else? Oh yeah, the playwright. But I got no pictures of the backstage crew. I have to track all those people down."

"For the time being, just get Leo Gunn's picture," Marian said. "If the doorman can't identify anyone, then go back for the rest of the crew. But right now, don't waste time on it."

"You think Gunn's the one?"

She shrugged. "He has a 'collection'—of sorts."

Perlmutter scowled. "Sergeant, if one of these people knocked off Nordstrom, he's not going to admit to having a collection. He'd lie about it, keep it hidden."

"Believe it or not, I did think of that," Marian said dryly.

"But you know damn well I'll never get warrants to search all their homes on the chance that they *might* have a secret collection that *might* have something to do with Nordstrom's murder. We'll have to do it this way. Show the doorman the pictures."

"Right." He gathered up his things and left.

Marian called Gene Ramsay's office to check on his alibi for Tuesday night, but the producer wasn't in yet. And Captain Murtaugh wasn't in his office, either, when she went to see him. Marian left a note saying she was going to the Zingones' shop and then to John Reddick's apartment. But she cheated a little; she stopped off on the way and had a big breakfast.

Feeling better, she was prepared when the Zingones didn't want to buzz her in. The voice coming over the crackly intercom was as unintelligible as ever; Marian finally got them to open the door by shouting the word "warrant" several times.

Upstairs, only Matthew and Luke were on store duty. Matthew peered at her over his glasses and demanded to see her warrant.

"I said I'd *get* a warrant if you didn't let me in," Marian told them blandly. "You really should get a new intercom system."

They weren't interested in that. "You lied to us, *Sergeant* Marian," Matthew said. "We read about you in the paper. You never told us you were a cop."

"Yeah, you took the sails right out from under us," Luke added.

"Ernie Nordstrom is dead," Marian said. "Doesn't that mean anything to you?"

The brothers exchanged a look. "Sure, that means something," Matthew said. "It's scary. Ernie wasn't what you'd call a friend, but somebody murdering him . . . that's scary. What's going to happen to his stuff?"

So much for Ernie. "It belongs to the city now. There'll be an auction announced in the legal notices section of the newspapers—I don't know when."

Luke asked, "Do you know who killed him?"

"Not yet. That's where you can help."

"After you put the wool in our eyes? Why should we help you?"

"To avoid being arrested on a charge of receiving stolen goods," Marian said bluntly. "You guys were hot to deal with Ernie for the Broadhurst loot yourselves. I'm willing to bet you can't prove prior ownership of ninety percent of the stuff you've got here. Shall I get a warrant to examine your books?"

They both glared at her. "I don't like threats," Matthew said.

"And I don't like making them. So how about it? Do I get a little cooperation or not?"

Heavy sighs. "What do you want us to do?"

She took the list of missing items out of her bag. "Keep an eye out for any of these things. We recovered everything taken from the Broadhurst except—"

"A jacket once owned by Sarah Bernhardt?" Matthew interrupted, reading the list. "*A jacket once owned by Sarah Bernhardt!*"

Luke's eyes were big. "Wow . . . that has to be worth thousands!"

"Twenty-two of them," Marian told him. "You hadn't heard about the jacket? Kelly Ingram wore it in the play."

They shook their heads in unison. "Sarah Bernhardt!" Matthew exclaimed. "My god, Luke, we've never had anything of hers, have we?"

"Never," Luke agreed.

"Well, I doubt that anyone will waltz in here and offer the

jacket for sale," Marian said dryly. "Or any of the other items, either. The killer's no fool . . . he's not going to peddle something that'll place him at the scene of the crime."

"Then what do you want of us?" Luke asked.

"I want you to get in touch with your contacts. Ask them to get in touch with *their* contacts. Whatever network you belong to, put it to work. Tell them to keep an eye out for all the items on that list. The killer had to unload them somewhere."

"The river, probably," Matthew said.

"Or garbage cans," Luke added. "Dumpsters."

"That's a possibility," his brother said. "We know several people who regularly check the garbage in the neighborhoods where celebrities live."

"Good!" said Marian. "That sounds promising."

The doorbell rang; after some shouting into the intercom, Luke buzzed the customer in. "Matthew, you start calling people—I want to take care of this dude myself. He thinks he's a Sondheim collector, but he doesn't know his ass from a hole-in-one." He moved away to meet the customer.

Marian couldn't stand it; she had to ask. "Why does he do that? Why does Luke talk that way when the rest of you speak perfectly good English?"

Matthew looked puzzled. "Talk what way?"

Arrgh. Not worth trying to explain. "Matthew, call me if you get anything. And the next time you see Augie Silver . . . tell him I'm sorry."

Matthew gave her a wry smile and a thumbs-up.

Marian took the IRT to Times Square and walked to Gene Ramsay's building on West Forty-fourth; a phone call from the lobby revealed he still wasn't in. Then she took the Forty-second Street shuttle to Grand Central; John Reddick lived only a few blocks uptown.

He was up when she got there, and talking on the phone.

"Have a seat, Marian, I'll be with you in a moment." No *Larch-Tree* today. She sat down and looked around. The apartment was comfortably cluttered, as if the inhabitant didn't pay a whole lot of attention to his surroundings. A few unpacked crates stood in corners; evidently he hadn't lived there very long.

John was back on the phone. "It isn't that I don't respect his work—I do," the director said. "He's always got something to say that's worth listening to. But the man has no ear for natural speech. His characters talk in essays, not dialogue. Going from Abby's lines to his . . . it's too big a jump." John listened for a while and then said, "Oh, all right, all right—I'll read the script. But I'm not promising anything, Gene."

"Is that Gene Ramsay?" Marian asked. "I want to speak to him."

"Hold on, Gene—Marian Larch wants a word."

She took the receiver. "Gene—hello. The word is 'alibis' and I'm collecting them. Mind giving me yours for Tuesday night?"

A mild chuckle. "And if I *do* mind?"

"Then I have to go into my tough-cop mode, and it's still too early in the day for that."

"Um, we can't have that. Alibi, let's see. You're in my alibi's apartment right now."

"John?"

"Uh-huh. Some of us went out for a drink after the performance, and John got to moaning over Kelly and had a few too many—well, you've seen what he's like when he's in that state. I had to take him home."

"What time was this?"

"Oh hell, I don't know—well after midnight. One or two."

"Can you pin it down a little more than that?"

"I'm afraid I can't," he said apologetically. "Nobody was paying attention to the time."

"How long did you stay here?"

"In his apartment? Just long enough to get him in bed. Then I went home and tucked myself in."

"Okay, Gene, thanks." She hung up. "He says he was out drinking with you Tuesday after the performance."

John squinted his eyes as an aid to memory. "That's right, he did join us later."

"Later? How much later?"

"Oh, after midnight, I think."

After midnight. "He says he brought you home and put you to bed."

The director grinned sheepishly. "Somebody did."

John had been in Captain Murtaugh's line the night before, so Marian didn't know the details. "Who else was there?"

"Oh, Leo Gunn. Mitchell Tobin. Ned Young, the properties manager." He squinted his eyes again. "That's all—until Gene came along later."

"How'd he know where to find you?"

"Don't know. Maybe I told him earlier, I don't remember. Why?"

She frowned. "You and he both are a bit vague about exactly where you were during the crucial period. Do you remember what time you left the bar?"

"Marian, I don't even remember *leaving* the bar."

How convenient. Marian let it go, thinking there were three other drinkers she could check with. "Now—how about this collection of yours? Are you going to show it to me?"

"Oh, absolutely. Walk this way." He did a John Cleese Ministry-of-Silly-Walks amble that made her laugh. The collection was kept in what was meant to be a small bedroom.

One glance was enough to tell her that John Reddick was a "paper" collector. A few posters and signed photographs on the walls, but everything else was stacked in piles or collected into plastic crates. Old playscripts, notebooks, sketches for scene designs, even musical scores. He showed her programs for plays she'd never heard of, plays with titles like *Hollywoodn't* and *A Blot on Rorschach's Name*. One fire-resistant box was reserved for reviews of shows that had closed after only one performance.

But his pride and joy was his collection of correspondence. "Letters from directors to producers, to playwrights, to scene designers and costumers," John said. "Gossipy letters to friends and family about rehearsal problems." He sighed. "You know, people don't write letters now the way they did in the last century, or even in this century before the Second World War. Now they just pick up a phone and take care of business that way. All those conversations that could tell us so much about the way directors like José Quintero or Joshua Logan worked—they're all gone."

"What a pity."

"Yes, it is. Once in a while you can track down people who were on the other end of the line, but try getting some old codger to remember word-for-word a telephone conversation that took place fifty years ago. It's impossible."

He went on talking, as much to himself as to Marian, rearranging stacks of papers, occasionally going off on a tangent when a note or a *Playbill* reminded him of something. John Reddick clearly loved his collection, the same way he loved his work. There was no sign anywhere in the room of costumes or stage props or actors' personal belongings, none of the sort of thing that had been taken from Ernie Nordstrom's apartment.

As Marian listened to him, she found herself thinking an unprofessional thought: she earnestly hoped that John Reddick was not the killer she was looking for.

16

Perlmutter's news was bad. "The night doorman at Ernie Nordstrom's building is a washout."

Captain Murtaugh glared at him. "Why?"

"He couldn't identify any of the pictures I showed him. At first I thought that just meant the killer was one of the stage crew I didn't have pictures of."

Marian said, "I told him to skip them for the time being, except for Leo Gunn."

Murtaugh nodded. "Go on."

"I thought I might as well check some of the other tenants," Perlmutter said. "Nobody could identify anyone in the photographs, either, but they did tell me the night doorman had a habit of wandering off for a quick snort or two. Sometimes he'd be gone as long as forty-five minutes. Four tenants told me separately that they'd complained to the management about him. But if he was off wetting his whistle Tuesday night, the killer could have come and gone without ever being seen at all."

"Christ," said Marian, disgusted. "That was our best shot."

Murtaugh looked equally disgusted. "So what's our next-best shot?"

"We don't have one. We do have a couple of vague alibis Perlmutter could check out, all right?" Murtaugh said yes.

"Four of the men were out drinking Tuesday night after the play," Marian went on, "John Reddick among them. Gene Ramsay joined them later, and later still took Reddick home when Reddick was sailing three sheets to the wind. Both Ramsay and Reddick claim they don't know the times involved, so check with the other three." She wrote their names down on a piece of paper. "We need to know exactly what time Ramsay got there, exactly what time he and Reddick left, and exactly how much longer the others stayed on in the bar."

Perlmutter took the list. "Leo Gunn again, huh? Who's this Ned Young?"

"Crew. The properties master."

"Who's the third?" Murtaugh asked.

"Mitchell Tobin. If nothing else, we ought to be able to eliminate those three."

"Okay, I'm on it," Perlmutter said, getting up to go.

"Leave the photographs," Murtaugh said.

"I'll get 'em." Perlmutter went out to the squadroom.

Marian looked a question.

"I want you to show them to Vasquez," the captain said. "Wait until Campos gets back from lunch to interpret for you and then have another go at him. Vasquez has to know more than he's telling us. Find out what it is."

"Yes, sir. But I'm pretty sure he doesn't know who the killer is."

"'Pretty' sure isn't good enough, Sergeant. Make *damned* sure."

Marian said she would. She went back to Lieutenant Overbrook's office to wait for Sergeant Campos and spent her time stewing over a couple of details that didn't quite fit. Gene Ramsay hadn't mentioned he'd joined his fellow imbibers at some unspecified later time; he'd merely said they'd gone out drinking—the implication being that he was with the others all along. It was John Reddick who'd told her that Gene hadn't come until later. Was Gene counting on John's alcohol-befuddled memory not to mention that little fact? Unfortunately, it was the kind of sloppiness of detail that characterized most statements made to the police by guilty and innocent alike.

Or had John Reddick got it wrong? If he'd been drinking heavily, he might easily have gotten Tuesday night mixed up with some other postperformance toot he'd been on. Or perhaps John wasn't drunk at all; perhaps he was acting. So instead of Gene using John as an alibi, it was the other way around? John could have feigned intoxication as an excuse to leave the bar and . . . Well, the other three in the bar could clear up those details; Perlmutter would get the answer.

The other detail that bothered her was the fact that the Zingones hadn't known Kelly was wearing Sarah Bernhardt's jacket in *The Apostrophe Thief* when the play first opened. Gene Ramsay said he'd had her wear it for its publicity value; but what kind of publicity was it when even the Zingones hadn't heard about it? The Zingones knew everything going on in the world of collectibles, according to Augie Silver. And they had known about the burglary at the Broadhurst before the story appeared in the papers. But either the Zingones weren't as knowledgeable as they liked to think, or Gene hadn't publicized the jacket after all.

Gene Ramsay. But as Captain Murtaugh had said, why would a man steal his own property? The most obvious reason was for the insurance. But it seemed such a petty scam for a wheeler-dealer like Gene Ramsay.

"You need me?" a voice said from the doorway. Campos was back from lunch.

"I do indeed," Marian said, getting up. "Let's go."

*   *   *

Vasquez was still in the lock-up. Neither he nor Kevin Kirby could make bail, but Kirby had been kicked loose because he had no priors. Vasquez, on the other hand, had a yellow sheet: illegal possession of a firearm, a drugstore hold-up, and a B&E. The charges had all been dropped and Vasquez had done no prison time. But this time around, the kid lawyer from the Public Defender's office had been unlucky enough to draw a hardliner judge; as a result Vasquez still languished in the Pens, officially known as the Court Detention Facilities on Centre Street.

Marian and Campos sat across a table from the prisoner and his young lawyer in an interrogation room. Marian spread out the photographs Perlmutter had collected and watched Vasquez's face carefully as he looked through them. Not a flicker of recognition registered for most of them, but he named Kelly Ingram and Ian Cavanaugh. Nothing there; virtually everyone knew those two faces. To the question of whether he'd ever seen any of the people in the photographs in the company of Ernie Nordstrom, Vasquez answered no.

Through Campos, Marian questioned him again about what Nordstrom had told him of his contact at the Broadhurst. Vasquez repeated that all Ernie had said was that it was an important man. At least they knew it was a man; that was something. But how important? Marian pressed. The producer? The director? The stage manager? Vasquez didn't know. Even when Marian offered to go to the DA's office and put in a good word for him, Vasquez still couldn't come up with anything.

"He just plain doesn't know," Campos put in.

"I think you're right." Marian thought a minute. "Ask him how the loot was to be divided—the stuff from the Broadhurst."

Vasquez said he and Kevin Kirby were paid in cash;

Nordstrom didn't want his two helpers peddling memorabilia before things had had time to cool down. Marian pointed out that Kirby had lifted a hairbrush belonging to one of the play's stars; did Vasquez too, perhaps, filch a little something for himself? Vasquez hesitated; but when his lawyer advised him to cooperate, he admitted he'd managed to slip a notebook computer inside his windbreaker when Ernie wasn't looking. What did he do with the computer? Sold it, at a pawnshop on Canal Street. The name of the pawnshop? Liberty Loans.

Marian said, "Tell him he may just have earned his word in the DA's ear after all."

She and Campos hurried up to Canal Street and took a right; Liberty Loans was only a few blocks along. It looked like a hardware store from outside; inside was long and narrow, two counters separated by an aisle. Among the guns, knives, jewelry, and musical instruments, four notebook computers were for sale; but only one was the same make as Mitchell Tobin's. The Hispanic clerk pretended not to understand when Marian started talking about receiving stolen goods. Campos took care of *that* in a hurry, and the clerk sullenly pushed the computer across the countertop toward them. Marian wrote out a receipt.

Their ride back uptown on the BMT was an exuberant one; finding the computer might not turn out to be the break in the case Marian was looking for, but it had to be a step in the right direction. One way or another, it would tell them *something*.

"*Vasquez* took it?" Captain Murtaugh said in surprise when Marian told him how they'd found it. "Well, well . . . the things you come up with when you ask the right questions. Nice going! I didn't realize the computer would be so small . . . to fit inside a briefcase?"

"I guess," Marian said.

"Do you know how to work it?"

"Not me."

"Uh, I got to get back to my arson case," Campos said and disappeared.

Perlmutter knew how. He had the small computer up and running in seconds and set himself the task of reading all the files. It didn't take long; there were only nine. "Four letters from Mitchell Tobin to his agent," he said, "two to his business manager, one letter each to two different fans, and a letter to momma. That's it."

"Just what he said was there," Marian remarked. "What about hidden files?"

"No, the byte count doesn't leave anything unaccounted for," Perlmutter said.

Neither Marian nor Murtaugh asked him what he meant. "Okay, that just confirms what we already know," the captain said. "Tobin's out of it. So are Leo Gunn and the properties manager."

"Their alibis check?" Marian asked Perlmutter.

"Yep. Ramsay didn't show up until a little after midnight, and he and Reddick left less than an hour later. The other three stayed until two A.M.—which is the latest time the ME set for the murder. So those three are in the clear."

"But Ramsay could have killed Nordstrom at eleven-thirty," Murtaugh said, "and then showed up at the bar in a hasty attempt to establish an alibi—which would indicate an impulse killing. Or Reddick could have been faking inebriation to establish his own alibi and then gone out again after Ramsay dropped him off—which indicates premeditation."

Perlmutter was nodding. "One of those two."

Gene Ramsay or John Reddick. "The shaving mug," Marian said.

"What?"

"Why'd the killer take Ian Cavanaugh's shaving mug? We know now he didn't take the computer, and taking the other costumes makes sense—hide one costume between two others? But why'd he stop to pick up the shaving mug? It doesn't fit."

"Hide one costume between two others," Murtaugh repeated slowly. "Yes, that's exactly what he did . . . he wasn't trying to confuse matters especially, he just didn't want to risk being seen carrying the jacket. As to the shaving mug . . . " He shrugged. "Maybe the killer didn't take that either. Nordstrom or one of the other two could have broken it when they were moving their haul into the van. I don't think it's important. Ramsay or Reddick, Larch. Which one would you say?"

"I'd say Ramsay, except for one minor little point."

"No motive, right. Was the jacket insured?"

"Yes, for twenty-two thousand. But Ramsay's a high roller. Would he kill a man for twenty-two thousand dollars?"

"Depends on how badly he needed the money. I want you to run a financial check on him. Find out how the shows he's backed are doing, see if he's suffered any big losses lately. And check out Reddick too, while you're at it."

"Sure thing, boss," Marian said with a smile. "First thing Monday morning."

Startled, Murtaugh looked at his watch. "Where the hell did Friday go to?"

Marian was wondering the same thing; the day had flashed by like lightning. But she felt good as she drove home. She felt good about finding the notebook computer, and she felt good about narrowing the field to two suspects. She didn't feel *quite* so good about the fact that those two suspects were men she rather liked; it was better when the bad guy was so callous and nasty you couldn't wait to punch him out. *I should have been a television cop*, she thought.

When she got home, the building super had a package for

her. It was a compact disk player, plus a recording of *Don Giovanni.*

She'd fallen asleep to the strains of Mozart, happily thinking of nothing at all. And had a dream about Sarah Bernhardt: the Divine One was berating Marian for failing to find her jacket. Marian couldn't understand the words, because they were in French; but she couldn't mistake the essence. Sarah was furious with her.

Saturday morning Marian awoke slowly, lazily, not feeling the least bit guilty about having two whole days off. She felt totally relaxed, not tied up in knots the way she usually was when a case wasn't breaking. Give it time. After thinking about it a while, she decided to get up. The first thing she did was check the CD player; it had turned itself off sometime after she'd fallen asleep. That was nice. The phone rang, the strident sound jarring her mellow mood.

"So?" the sharp-edged voice demanded imperiously. "How did you like it?"

"Dammit, Holland, I'm not even awake yet!"

"That means you haven't had breakfast. I'll bring it." Click.

Marian banged down the receiver and headed toward the shower, her languid mood completely shattered. *Aren't you supposed to feel happy and excited when your lover is coming to see you?* she thought. Even a twice-only lover who irritates the hell out of you sometimes.

But by the time she'd finished her shower, she'd regained some of her former good mood. *Today is for relaxing,* she thought as she dressed. *Monday I'll find a way to nail Gene Ramsay.*

With a shock, she realized what she'd just thought: sometime during her sleep, she'd eliminated John Reddick as a suspect. She finished tying her sneakers and sat down to figure out why. After a while she thought it must be Ramsay's office, laid out as it was to intimidate anyone approaching the producer. It was the office of a man who enjoyed his power, and power always went hand-in-hand with a certain amount of ruthlessness. But was he ruthless enough to kill? More so than John Reddick, Marian thought. Abby James had said John was more likely to run away from trouble than meet it head on, and Marian respected Abby's judgment. The woman who wrote *The Apostrophe Thief* had to know a great deal about what made people tick.

But none of that was evidence. Monday she'd check into Gene Ramsay's finances and see where that led. Marian went into the kitchen to start the coffee. She'd just taken out the pot when the door buzzer sounded.

Holland breezed in, smelling like a brisk autumn day. "Don't bother with coffee," he said, putting down his packages on the kitchen counter.

"Don't bother with coffee?" What an outrageous suggestion.

"We can have it later, if you like, but with this breakfast, the taste is wrong. Where are the plates? You get the silverware."

Marian set the kitchen table and sat down to Holland's idea of breakfast. Cold lobster. Sliced tomatoes. Champagne.

Five minutes later she was thinking it was the best breakfast she'd ever eaten. And he was right about the coffee; it wouldn't have gone with the rest of the meal. She told him so.

"I know," he said seriously. "I tried it once. Just not right, somehow. Now tell me. How did you like *Don Giovanni?*"

"Mm, I thought it was very nice."

"Nice?" He put down his fork. "Did you say . . . nice?"

"Wrong word? I liked it. But I haven't heard all of it yet." She didn't think it necessary to mention she'd fallen asleep.

"What part did you like best?"

"Uh, I don't know the names of the arias or anything."

Holland picked up his fork and resumed eating, eyeing her suspiciously all the while. "You *did* listen to it."

"Yes, I did," Marian said firmly. "And thank you for sending it. I'm genuinely pleased to have it."

They continued eating, Holland not completely convinced. "How was it compared to that rock band you listened to Tuesday night?"

"Well, Waltzing Brünnhilde is a lot louder."

"And?"

"And more bad-tempered."

"Ah. That's something. What else?"

"I didn't know there was going to be a quiz," she said caustically and speared the last piece of lobster on her plate.

He looked at her a long moment, and then said, "Try this." He whistled two notes.

"Mau fuh."

"Your mouth's full?" He waited until she'd swallowed and whistled the notes again.

Marian whistled back. "What's this all about?"

"Try this." He whistled two more.

She shrugged and whistled. "What's the name of this game?"

"Please. Just once more." Two more notes.

Marian whistled and said, "That's it. Tell me what you're doing."

He was working hard at keeping his face impassive. "How many notes did you hear me whistle?"

"The same one, over and over. Are you going to explain yourself?"

"I whistled six notes. Three different musical intervals. You heard one note, over and over. You're tone deaf."

She felt as if she were being accused of some embarrassing breach of taste. "Oh, I'm so ashamed. Should I apologize?"

He let his feelings show—a disconcerting mix of astonishment, horror, and pity. "Mozart and rock, they're the same to you, aren't they? All you hear is noise."

"Not exactly. I can hear rhythms. And variations in volume. It's just that I'm not always sure whether the notes are going up or going down."

"Good god. Why didn't you tell me?"

Now she was astonished. "Why on earth should I? I didn't tell you about a scar on my knee I got playing softball, either."

"I've seen the scar." Holland's voice softened. "Marian, I'm sorry. When I think of all you'll never be able to hear . . ." He shook his head.

This was ridiculous. "So I've got a tin ear—so what? It's not a handicap, you know." He looked as if he didn't agree. "Holland, you're beginning to annoy me."

A sigh. "Yes, I'm sure I am. I'd be annoyed too, in your place. But try to see what a shock this has been. Music is important to me. I wanted it to be important to you as well."

"So music is important to you, okay. But is that any reason to look at me as if I'm the two-headed beast from twenty thousand fathoms that ate Tokyo?"

He laughed. "Is that what I'm doing?" She nodded. "Grossly unfair of me, I must admit," he said. "I know perfectly well you never ate Tokyo."

"*Holland!*"

He pointed a finger at her. "Gotcha." They were both smiling, the danger point passed. Holland leaned back in his chair and looked at her through half-closed eyes. "We still have a lot to learn about each other, haven't we?"

Lord, yes, Marian thought. Starting with where he lived. But she was damned if she'd ask; when he wanted her to know, he'd tell her. If he wanted her to know. When, if.

When the phone rang, Marian was inclined to let the

answering machine take it. But then she heard a voice identi-fying itself as belonging to Matthew Zingone, and she picked up. "Matthew—I'm here. Got something?"

"I'm not sure. You'd better come take a look."

"What is it?"

"I'd rather not say. It may be nothing."

"Oh, Matthew. Just tell me what it is."

"You want to know what it is? You come look at it." He hung up.

Marian did the same. "I've got to go to the Zingones'," she said to Holland.

He raised an eyebrow. "Will you need a passport?"

"The Zingones are dealers, in the Village—you know about them. Luke's the one who told the hairy-spider story, remember?"

He remembered. "I'll go with you."

"No, you won't. This is police business. Why don't you, ah, listen to *Don Giovanni*? I shouldn't be long."

He didn't like being left out, but it wasn't his case. "That's turning into my primary occupation," he said testily as she went out the door. "Waiting for you."

17

Mark and Janet were there with Matthew, but Janet wasn't speaking to Marian. She turned her back and retreated to the rear of the shop. "She's still mad at you," Mark said unnecessarily.

Because she gave away too much about how you do business. "I know, and I'm sorry," Marian said. "What have you got?"

"This." Matthew reached under the counter and brought up something wrapped in tissue paper. He pulled back the tissue to reveal two amber velvet sleeves.

"The sleeves," Marian said flatly. She'd never expected *that.*

"*The* sleeves?" Matthew asked. "From Sarah Bernhardt's jacket?"

Marian picked one up and looked at it closely. It was stained and wrinkled, but the amber velvet looked like the right color. The trouble was, she'd seen the jacket only once, and that time from the audience. "You fellows are the experts," she said. "How old would you say this material is?"

Matthew fingered the other sleeve. "At least fifty years old."

"Older," said Mark.

"What about seventy?" Marian asked.

"Easily. It's old enough to have belonged to Bernhardt, if that's what you're getting at."

She looked at the part of the sleeve that attached at the

shoulder; it had been ripped away, not cut, with no care taken to preserve the material. Marian brushed away what looked like coffee grounds. "Garbage?"

Both brothers nodded. "One of the scroungers found them," Mark said. "Not in the garbage, although that's where they've been, obviously. But a bag lady working the same garbage cans as the scrounger was wearing them."

"She was wearing them?"

Mark laughed. "Yeah. See how the seams are strained? She pulled them on right over the sweatshirt she was wearing."

"Did your scrounger ask her where she got them?"

"He tried to," Matthew said. "But she just kept mumbling about signs and portents and the price of cheese. He thought she was one of those people who get released from Bellevue too soon."

"But she wasn't completely nuts," Mark added. "She made him pay fifty bucks for the sleeves."

"And he charged *us* seventy-five," Matthew finished.

"Seventy-five, huh?" Marian said. "Okay, I'll see that you're reimbursed."

They both laughed. "No way," said Matthew. "Those sleeves aren't for sale for any seventy-five bucks. We realize you have to take them with you, as evidence. But we want them back when you're through. Write us a receipt."

Marian looked at them in amazement. "Don't you understand? You're not going to get these sleeves back. You don't own them—they don't belong to you. They're *stolen property*. Do you know what stolen property is? I said I'd get you your seventy-five dollars back because you helped us out, not because I'm buying them from you. I *can't* buy them from you, because you can't *sell* them. I will, however, write you a receipt."

She did just that, while the brothers muttered under their

breaths. "Jeez, if I'd known you were going to be such a hardass, I never would have called you," Matthew said.

"And then done time as a fence? That's real smart, Matthew. You guys just aren't plugged in at all, are you? From now on, get written receipts for everything you buy, and I do mean everything. Names, addresses. Dates of purchase and amounts. I'm not going to give you any flak—but sooner or later *somebody* is going to come down on you, and the more documentation you have, the better off you'll be. Do it. Start now. The Zingone family has got to clean up its act or you're all heading for trouble. Am I getting through to you?"

They stared at her sullenly without answering.

Marian sighed. "I'm trying to keep you out of jail," she said. "But I can't make you listen. Where's your phone?" Mark lifted up a telephone from under the counter. "Thank you." She stared at them until they started edging back out of earshot.

Marian didn't know Captain Murtaugh's home number, so she had to call the station first. But her second call caught him just as he was going out the front door, he said. What couldn't wait until Monday?

Marian told him about the sleeves. "I think they're the right ones, but I should be able to get a positive ID at the Broadhurst—Kelly Ingram or the wardrobe mistress would know."

"*Just* the sleeves?" the captain asked.

"That's all. Which pretty much rules out a collector or a dealer as the man we're looking for. Nobody hooked on memorabilia would destroy that jacket."

"No. So that leaves the insurance money. Ramsay. Will he be at the Broadhurst?"

"I doubt it. He rarely comes in."

"What about the director, uh, Reddick?"

"He'll probably be there. But he's not the killer."

"No, I don't think so either," Murtaugh said. "Only one person could collect that insurance."

"I don't think it was the insurance." Marian took a deep breath. "If I'm right that Gene Ramsay wouldn't risk a murder rap for a scam as small as the insurance settlement, then there's only one possible explanation left. Captain, how about putting in a call to the French Sûreté? Find out if there's been a sizable jewel robbery in France recently."

He saw it immediately. "The jewels on the jacket weren't imitations?"

"It's the only explanation I can think of. Replacing the stage fakes with real stones would be a good way to get them past customs. That was probably the only reason he bought the Bernhardt jacket in the first place—everybody knew about it, it was nothing he'd have to conceal. He was hiding the jewels right out in the open."

"It sounds like a long shot to me," Murtaugh said, "but I'll make the call. What made you think of it in the first place?"

"Oh, something Kelly Ingram said. You know replacement costumes were made up right after the burglary? Kelly remarked that the fake gems on her replacement jacket were larger than those on the original. Well, on the stage, small things have to be made bigger than they really are, or else the audience can't see them. The original jacket was designed to be worn on a stage—so why didn't it have large stones as well? I didn't really think about it until we ran out of other possible explanations."

"'Painstaking attention to minutiae is what solves crimes,'" Captain Murtaugh quoted, but Marian didn't know whom.

"Something else," she went on. "Maybe we ought to get Gene Ramsay to come to the Broadhurst. There's a small safe in the office the director uses. The first time I ever talked to John Reddick, he told me only the producer had the combination."

"You think Ramsay may have stashed the jewels there? Doesn't he have a safe in his own office?"

"I don't know. I didn't see one there, but it could have been concealed."

They were both quiet a moment, thinking it over. Then Murtaugh said, "Perhaps he meant to throw suspicion on Reddick, if anything went wrong. All right, see if you can get an ID on the sleeves and I'll call the Sûreté and Gene Ramsay. Wait for me at the Broadhurst."

"Yes, sir. I have to see the stage manager anyway. There's one loose end that still needs tying up."

"Tie it tight," Murtaugh said and hung up.

Marian pressed the phone's plunger and released it, and then tapped out her own number; she wanted to tell Holland she wouldn't be coming right back after all. Busy signal.

She hung up and started to leave; she'd reached the door when she heard her name spoken. Marian turned and saw Janet Zingone standing behind the counter where her brothers had been earlier.

"I heard you," Janet said.

She meant Marian's harangue about the Zingones' cleaning up their act. Marian smiled in relief and waved goodbye. Now if Janet could make her brothers listen, the Zingone family just might be all right after all.

Anne-Marie St. John, née Elsie Greenbaum, ran her hand over the amber velvet. "They're from the Bernhardt jacket, all right." She held up the two disembodied sleeves. "Such a thing! Who would do such a terrible thing?"

"Are you sure?" Marian asked. "Take your time."

"Yeah, I'm sure. Look here." Marian went over to stand beside the wardrobe mistress. "See these pale gold threads in the seams of the lining? I put those in myself. The original threads are even paler—faded, you know. Here's one."

Marian squinted. "You can barely see it."

"Tell me about it. I thought I had all those old threads picked out." She used what to Marian looked like a surgical instrument to lift the offending thread from the jacket. "Used to be that gray thread was used for everything, because stitching doesn't show from the stage. It was a lot easier then."

"What happened?"

The wardrobe mistress shrugged. "Who knows? Everybody's a prima donna, everything has to be just so." She turned one of the sleeves inside out. "These seams are stretched—how'd that happen? This lining's new, you know. Gene Ramsay sat right there in that chair and watched me the entire time I was putting it in." A big laugh. "You'd think that thing had the crown jewels sewn on it. He took the jacket home with him the first few nights, until he got a new lock put on the costume room door." A snort. "Much good it did him."

"Did he select the new lock himself?"

Another laugh. "He sure did. Shows what he knows about locks."

He knew enough to get a cheap one. Marian wrapped the sleeves back up in the tissue paper and put the bundle into her shoulder bag. "That's all I needed to know. Thanks, Elsie." The other woman glared at her. "Er, Anne-Marie."

It was still early, and the cast was just beginning to drift in for the matinee performance. Kelly wasn't there yet. Marian went looking for Leo Gunn, and found him reading the riot act to an electrician. She'd wondered before why the stage manager wore a hook instead of an artificial hand; now she saw one of the hook's side benefits. Gunn spoke softly, but he kept tapping the other man's chest with his hook. For emphasis.

The electrician kept glancing down at the hook tap-tapping his chest; he appeared somewhat uncomfortable.

"Last night Ian Cavanaugh's face was in shadow again when he was standing by the fish tank. He can't step away *into* the spot because he has stage business at the tank. So *you* have to keep the light on *him*. Is that so hard to understand?"

"It, it just slipped again, Leo—I'll fix it."

"That's what you said last time. What are you using on that light, chewing gum and a rubber band? You've got some worn threads there somewhere. This time don't just tighten it, replace it."

"I'll do it right now." The electrician scurried away.

The stage manager saw Marian watching and shook his head. "I should have been born in the last century, when you could still *fire* incompetents."

"Unions?"

"Unions."

"Any danger the light will fall?"

"No, the big clamps are secure. It's just the positioning arm that keeps slipping. Well, Sergeant, can I do something for you?"

"Yes, you can. You told me that when Ernie Nordstrom first approached you to steal props et cetera from the show you were working, you notified the producer and the director, right? Was Gene Ramsay producing that show?"

"No. Why?"

"What about the other times? You said that every new play you worked, Nordstrom would show up, didn't you? Did you notify the producers and directors then as well?"

"Every time." Gunn's eyes narrowed. "And Gene Ramsay was the producer on one of them. *Little Green Apples.*"

"John Reddick?"

"None of them." The stage manager looked incredulous. "Gene Ramsay killed Nordstrom?"

"He's only a suspect at this point," Marian said firmly. "I just wanted to pin down whether he knew about Nordstrom or not."

"He knew. My god! I've known Gene for twenty years!"

"Mr. Gunn, let me repeat he's only a suspect. I don't have evidence." Yet. "Captain Murtaugh will be getting here before long. I'd appreciate it if you'd have someone let me know the minute he shows up."

"Yeah, sure. Gene. My god."

He was so shaken that Marian felt bad for him. She put a hand on his shoulder and said, "Can you keep it to yourself? I'll know today whether he's the one or not."

Gunn said he'd keep it quiet and turned away. Marian let him go.

She went to warn the doorkeeper that Captain Murtaugh was coming. She'd just finished telling him when Ian Cavanaugh made his entrance.

"Ah, Sergeant Marian!" he sang out in booming tones. "I say 'Sergeant Marian' because I never know whether you're here as the police or as yourself. Which is it today?"

"We're the same person," Marian said with a smile. "But I'm afraid it's the official-capacity designation this time. Where's Abby?"

"Abby's at a different matinee today—change of pace, she said. She went to the opera. *Don Giovanni.*"

Oh boy.

"Ian!" exclaimed a young voice. "You got here before me!" Xandria Priest had just come in.

"Hello, Xandria," the actor said. "Yes, I got here before you." His tone said: *So?*

"That's a sign of a true professional, isn't it? Not only out-standing on the stage, but always early to the theater, champ-ing at the bit?" She was gushing.

Ian frowned. "Young woman, I do not *champ* at anything. And I'm early today only because Abby dropped me off on her way to the opera." Then he relented. "But I never mind being early, do you?"

"Oh, no! Abby's not coming?"

"That's what I said. Marian, stop by my dressing room if you have time." He strode away.

The doorkeeper looked amused. But Xandria Priest looked . . . *stricken*. It had been a long time since Marian had seen such naked yearning on someone's face; she'd made a friend-ly overture to her idol and he'd rebuffed her. Was that why Xandria had been flirting with everyone in the company . . . because Ian Cavanaugh was ignoring her? "Let's go to your dressing room," Marian said, leading her away.

Marian had barely got the door shut behind them when Xandria burst into tears. "Why does he do that to me?" the younger woman snuffled. "I never embarrass him in front of other people!"

Are you sure about that? "Where's your Kleenex?"

Xandria pointed a shaky finger toward her dressing table. "Bottom right-hand drawer." Then her eyes grew big and she cried, "Wait! I'll get it!"

But she was too late. Marian had already spotted the shav-ing mug behind the box of Kleenex. Carefully, she took the mug out of the drawer.

Xandria let out a wail and sank down into the chair before the dressing table. She buried her head in her arms and bawled.

Marian went to the sink and wet a washcloth. "Your eyes are going to be red and puffy for the performance. Blow your nose and cover your eyes with this."

The young actor did as she was told. Eventually, she calmed down, sitting with her head thrown back and the washcloth over her eyes. It was easier for her that way, not having to look at Marian.

"It belonged to his grandfather, you know," Marian said at last. "That shaving mug means a lot to Ian."

A moan. "I know. Are you going to tell on me?"

Tell on me—the language of children. "I won't have to. You're going to return it yourself."

"I can't do that! He'll hate me!"

"Xandria, be realistic—he's not exactly falling over himself to get at you right now. What else of Ian's have you stolen?"

Sniffle. "Some of his make-up. One of his shirts. A note he left for Leo Gunn."

"Anything else?"

"That's all, I swear!"

Nothing of real value lost. Lovesick teenaged girls were not high on Marian's list of Interesting Things, but she felt sorry for Xandria. "In case you haven't noticed," she said, "Ian's living with the woman he's chosen. He's taken."

"But they're not *married*! He could—"

"Listen to me. Ian and Abby belong together. Accept that, accept it right now. He's not going to leave her for you. Not ever." Another wail. "I know he's big and beautiful and he carries himself with authority . . . and he's old enough to be your father." Marian took a breath. "Xandria, you're young and pretty and talented. You're better equipped to take care of yourself than most girls your age. So do it. Rely on yourself. Stop looking for Daddy."

She sat up straight in her chair, the washcloth falling from her eyes. "I am *not* looking for Daddy!" she said, horrified.

"Aren't you? You're impressed by an older man who's in control in the adult world that's still new to you. Of course you're attracted to him. But you don't know how lucky you are that Ian's a decent man who'll never take advantage of that starry-eyed innocence you work for all it's worth. Xandria, it's time to grow up." Marian went to the dressing room door. "I'm not going to say anything to him about the shaving mug. You know what's right to do."

She left, closing the door quietly behind her. *Today's my day for giving lectures*, Marian thought.

Something she was supposed to do? Oh, yes. She stopped by Ian's dressing room; he wasn't there, but she saw him coming out of Mitchell Tobin's dressing room.

"I'm out of pancake, so I filched one of Tobin's," he said. "I don't know why I'm using the stuff up so fast."

"Hm. Did you want to see me about something?"

"Not really. I wanted to get a certain message across to Xandria, if you know what I mean, but I didn't want to be rude to you too. Oh—there is something. Abby says call her after you catch the villain. She wants to get better acquainted."

"Good! I will."

"You *are* going to catch the villain, aren't you?"

"Count on it. Maybe even today."

He looked surprised and pleased. "I'm glad to hear that," he said in a quieter voice. "You don't know what it can do to a play, having something like this hanging over our heads." Back to his stage voice. "You didn't happen to see Leo Gunn, did you?"

"Yes, he's on the other side of the stage."

Ian waved goodbye with his eyebrows and went looking for the stage manager.

Marian decided to take a look in the director's office. John Reddick wasn't there, but the door was open. She stepped inside and looked toward the corner; yes, the safe was still there. Dumb: where else would it be? She squatted down in front of it and gave the dial a spin. Were there precious gems inside? She wondered what was taking Murtaugh so long; he should have been able to get through to the Sûreté by now. Maybe he was having trouble locating Gene Ramsay.

This time when she went back to the dressing rooms, Kelly had arrived. She was standing outside her door, watching Ian Cavanaugh, as were a number of other members of the cast. Ian was practically doing a jig, he was so happy. "Sergeant Marian!" he called. "Look!" He held up the shaving mug.

"Your shaving mug?" she asked innocently.

"My grandfather's shaving mug, my father's shaving mug, *my* shaving mug! It walked in all by itself and sat down on my dressing table! Isn't that glorious?"

"Wait a minute—it *walked* in . . . ?"

"It must have. When I got back from talking to Leo, there it was!" He gave the mug a kiss.

The others were laughing, pleased for him. "Congratulations!" Kelly sang.

"Thank you!"

"All that fuss over an old shaving mug," Xandria Priest said with a pout, and went back into her dressing room.

Ah, me. "I'm glad you got it back," Marian told Ian sincerely.

"I am too. Funny how attached you can get to old things. I really missed this mug."

Just then one of Leo Gunn's assistants came up. "Sergeant Larch? There's a police captain here to see you. He's in Mr. Reddick's office."

About time. "Thanks." She turned to Kelly. "I'll be back later." Kelly nodded.

Marian hurried back the way she'd just come. The door to John Reddick's office still stood open. She started to go in . . . but stopped dead when she saw who was sitting there.

"I knew you'd show up sooner or later," Captain DiFalco said. "Come in and shut the door. We have a lot to talk about."

18

"How did you know I was here?"

Captain DiFalco grinned. "I told the stage doorkeeper to call me the next time you showed up. Sit down, Larch. We're going to straighten out a few things."

Her mind racing, Marian took her time closing the door to John Reddick's office. She picked up a stack of file folders from the chair facing the desk and sat down. DiFalco's appearance at the eleventh hour of an investigation always meant one thing: he was getting ready to horn in. How could she stop him? She knew she was broadcasting anxiety, but she couldn't seem to stop it. And that bastard DiFalco was enjoying her discomfort. Where the hell was Murtaugh?

"Vacation's over, Larch," DiFalco said. "You're coming back to the Ninth. And the Nordstrom case is coming with you."

"What!"

"Monday morning your Captain Murtaugh will get a letter from the Chief of Detectives ordering the transfer. Since the detective in charge of the case is a Ninth Precinct cop, the Nordstrom murder is now a Ninth Precinct case. Just the way it should have been all along."

"Monday morning," Marian repeated, trying not to feel panicky. "But until that letter arrives, I'm still under Captain Murtaugh's command."

He smiled ferally. "You're that close to cracking it, are you? Nailing it down this weekend? All right, Larch, fill me in."

She licked suddenly dry lips. "I think we'd better wait until Captain Murtaugh gets here."

He leaned toward her across the desk. "I've had just about all the prima donna behavior from you I'm going to take. *I'm* in charge here, Sergeant. I gave you an order. *Fill me in.*"

Not seeing any immediate way out, Marian started telling him what she'd done and what she'd learned, going into more detail than necessary, stretching it out as long as she could. Where the *hell* was Murtaugh? She told DiFalco how the burglary had been staged to get one specific item out of the Broadhurst, and how Ernie Nordstrom had been killed for that item. How the killer had taken more than one item with him when he left Nordstrom's apartment.

"Uh-huh," said DiFalco. "Muddying the waters?"

"That's what we thought." *At first.*

"Okay, what was missing?"

Marian told him, including the notebook computer and the shaving mug—after all, they were not found in Nordstrom's apartment. The fact that they had never been in Nordstrom's apartment didn't alter that.

"What costumes?" DiFalco wanted to know.

"A jacket, a dress, and a fur coat."

"Real fur?"

"Two people say not." Marian cleared her throat. "Based on the label."

"The label saying it was synthetic? Maybe it was the label that was fake and not the coat. Labels can be changed."

"Captain, I don't *know* that's what happened."

He leaned even closer. "But that's what you think."

"I didn't say that. I have no evidence the labels were switched."

"But if they were . . ." He mused a moment.

She helped him along. "It doesn't seem likely that only one coat would be involved. But I can't prove anything illegal about the coat." Which was true.

"Fur smuggling?" DiFalco said. "With phony labels sewn in to disguise them as fakes? And one coat accidentally gets sold and ends up being paraded on the stage of the Broadhurst. Yeah, I like it. The fur that got away . . . it could blow the whole racket."

Marian said carefully, "Do you understand I am *not* saying a fur-smuggling operation is using New York as either a conduit or an outlet? I have no proof of any such operation."

"Yah, yah, I got it. But there's such a thing as being too careful. More likely an outlet than a conduit—big market here."

"Which brings up the problem of where the contraband furs would be kept—if there are any, I mean. Real fur needs cold storage."

"That's right, it does. Have you checked out all the cold-storage places in town? Sure you haven't missed one or two?"

"Captain, I haven't had a chance to check *any* of them!" Which was also true.

He gave a contemptuous snort. "What kind of chickenshit operation is Murtaugh running? You'll start on that Monday, and you'll have help. Murtaugh's coming here this afternoon?"

"He should be here any time."

"Why? What are you two planning to do here?"

Careful. "He's trying to get some evidence linking the play's producer with the stolen item." There, that was accurate.

"What's the producer's name?"

"Gene Ramsay."

"Ramsay . . . okay. Is he here now?"

"Not unless he came in during the last ten minutes. He's rarely here before the performance." *Or during. Or after.*

DiFalco scowled. "And if Murtaugh does show up with this evidence, you're just going to ask Ramsay politely to tell you where he has the goods stored? Dumb move. He's not going to tell you anything about those furs."

"I agree," Marian said honestly.

A grunt. "At least we see eye to eye on that. You have to locate the goods first."

"No argument there. Without the goods, we've got nothing." She was careful not to look at the safe in the corner.

DiFalco stared at her a long moment. Then he got up and walked around the desk where he could tower over her. "Larch, if you're lying to me, I'll have your ass."

"I've told you the truth, Captain."

"Because if you've been feeding me a line—"

"If you have a polygraph on you, I'll take a test. I haven't told you one single lie."

He grunted again. "Has Murtaugh made any announcement to the news media?"

"No."

"Is he going to?"

"He didn't say. I don't think so."

That's what he wanted to hear. "All right, when Murtaugh gets here, you tell him about the letter from the Chief of Detectives and that you briefed me. I can't give him orders, but I would *prefer* that he didn't talk to this Ramsay today. No point in spooking him and giving the game away. And Larch, I'm counting on you to make sure he understands what my wishes are."

"I'll give him your message," she promised wholeheartedly.

DiFalco indicated they were through and opened the door, to find John Reddick waiting outside. The director placed a finger over his lips and said in a low voice, "The performance has started." DiFalco nodded and walked away softly; Marian ignored the curiosity on the director's face and followed the captain.

They stopped for a moment to watch the scene being played; there was Frieda Armstrong on the stage, resplendent in her fake fur. DiFalco whispered, "That's not a real fur?"

"Don't whisper," Marian said in the same low voice John Reddick had used. "Whispers carry. That's a fake."

"You could have fooled me," DiFalco said softly. "Doesn't that look like real fur to you?"

"I don't know anything about fur," Marian replied truthfully.

Onstage, Ian Cavanaugh turned his back to the other actors and surreptitiously dropped a key into the fish tank. Marian and DiFalco watched for a few more minutes, and then the captain turned to go. Marian followed him to the stage door, and only when she saw him leave the building did she let out the breath she'd been holding. She sank down on the door-keeper's chair and gave in to a moment of trembling. Close. Damned close. And when DiFalco found out about the Bernhardt jacket, he was going to come looking for her with a shotgun. And if he called a news conference and made a fool of himself talking about a nonexistent fur-smuggling ring . . . somehow the thought of that cheered her more than it frightened her.

When she'd calmed herself, she went back and watched the play from the wings, being careful to stay out of Leo Gunn's way. Marian tried to keep the little knot of excitement in her stomach under control; she didn't want to make a mistake this close to winding up the case. Intermission finally arrived, and all the actors came rushing off the stage, adrenaline pumping. Kelly grabbed Marian's hands and did a little dance. "Come on—I have to change."

John Reddick intercepted them before they got to the dressing room. "Ah, Kelly, that was magnificent! Keep up that level for the second act and you'll have the rest of the cast flying with you!"

"Thanks, John," Kelly said, and pushed Marian into the dressing room ahead of her.

"And don't worry about Xandria," John went on. "I think I've got her straightened out."

"Good, good." She closed the door before he could come in. "Whew."

"Problem?" Marian asked.

"No problem." Kelly started taking off her costume. "I just don't want him hanging around, that's all."

"I thought you liked John."

"I do, but not as much as I used to. He drinks too much, for one thing. And he's getting to be a pest. Would you mind hanging this up?"

Marian took the costume from her and put it on a padded hanger. "Be gentle."

"I *was* gentle! Didn't you see me being gentle? I didn't tell him to get lost, did I?" Marian laughed. Abruptly, Kelly asked, "Marian, why are you here? I mean, you had a purpose in coming this afternoon, didn't you?"

Marian could see no reason not to tell her. "We're close to wrapping up the case. If some evidence I think exists comes through, we'll make an arrest before the day's over."

Kelly's eyes were enormous. "You know who killed that man?"

"Yes, I do. I could make the arrest right now, except for that one piece of evidence."

"It's someone I know." Kelly's voice was small. "Someone I work with . . ."

"Kelly—"

"No, I'm not going to ask—I know better than that. But

dammit, Marian, you have to know this is *killing* me!" Then
she thought of something. "You're right on the verge of making an arrest?"

"That's right."

Kelly looked at her oddly. "Then why aren't you depressed?"

With a shock, Marian realized it was true: she wasn't
depressed in the least. That punishing, enervating emptiness
that came over her whenever she arrested a killer—not a sign
of it. Ever since she first won her gold shield, she'd known she
had days of bleakness to look forward to whenever she solved a
case; but she felt none of that now. Now she felt anticipation,
satisfaction.

"It's gone, Kelly," she said wonderingly. "The depression is
gone!"

Kelly let out a whoop and jumped at her, almost knocking
her over. Marian laughed and hugged her friend, and felt better than she had for years. It was gone! It was completely, thoroughly, forever-and-ever-she-hoped gone! That dark,
suffocating tunnel was no longer her "reward" for a successful
investigation.

Marian sat down to think while Kelly finished getting ready.
Looking forward to nailing a killer was a new feeling to
Marian, and she examined it gingerly. If ever there was a time
to feel depressed, it was now, when she was about to arrest a
man she knew personally and had rather liked. But the only
thing that was truly worrying her was the possibility that the
Sûreté would say no major jewel robbery had taken place in
France recently. If that was the case, then they'd just have to
try Antwerp, Amsterdam, London. *Sooner or later we'll find
out where the jewels came from.*

We? We who? She and Murtaugh. She and the NYPD. She
and the whole damned system of law enforcement—*of which
she was a part.* All along she'd considered her unwillingness to

go on enduring depression as part of her reason for wanting to resign; but now it occurred to her that it might be the only reason. It was the same reason that she'd equivocated when Holland asked her to come work with him. It wasn't the job or the people or police politics; it was something *in her* that she had to work her way through, that sense of failure and loss she experienced every time she pointed her finger and said: *You are a killer.* It was a form of private exculpation, she now thought, a way of absolving herself for spending her life in the pursuit of losers, people whose humanity had failed them when the crunch had come. But that was behind her now, that debilitating misgiving. She no longer felt a need to apologize to herself for what she did.

Marian would not resign. She was a cop, not a private investigator or a politician or a short order cook or anything else. Police work was what she did. It was what she knew and, god help her, what she loved.

So what lay ahead? What if she was passed over again for promotion? What if she had to go back to the Ninth Precinct to work for a captain who soon would have reason to hate her guts? What if, god help her, Foley wriggled free of his suspension and ended up her partner again? Well, she'd handle it. She'd wrangle a transfer, she'd challenge Personnel if her promotion didn't come through, she'd do *something.* And if she had to have enemies, she couldn't think of two better ones than Foley and DiFalco.

Yes. She would not quit.

Marian looked up to see Kelly dressed and ready for the next act, quietly watching her. "Are you back?" Kelly asked.

"I'm back," Marian said with a smile.

"You're not going to resign, are you?"

Marian was startled. "My god, am I that transparent?"

"Only sometimes. You aren't going to quit, are you?"

"No. That was a bad decision. I'm going to stay with the police."

Kelly gave her a sweet smile. "I'm glad, Marian," she said simply.

Marian glanced at her watch and stood up. "It must be getting close to time. I know you need to concentrate, so I'll leave you alone now."

"There's no need to go."

"No, I'll just be a distraction. Knock 'em dead, Kel."

Marian's step was buoyant as she left; an enormous weight was off her shoulders and she felt ready to take on the world. In fact, she felt so good that when she saw Holland standing there, she walked over and kissed him. Right in front of everyone.

"I'm glad somebody's having a good time," John Reddick said gloomily. "I might as well have gone to *Don Giovanni*."

"Hel-*lo*," Holland said softly.

"Let's find a quiet place. I have something to tell you."

Elsie/Anne-Marie was not in the costume room, so they went in there. Marian closed the door and told him what she'd decided.

He wasn't surprised. "I've seen this coming. I won't say I'm not disappointed, because I am. But if this is what you want, then I wish you success and satisfaction."

"Thank you." She couldn't tell if he was hurt or not. "I'm sorry, Holland."

"Yes. We would have made good partners."

She didn't care for the implications of that. "That almost sounds like goodbye."

He looked at her a long moment, and then said, "Aren't you saying goodbye to me?"

"No!" That came out more emphatically than she'd meant. "No," she repeated in a more moderate tone.

Slowly, the downturned corners of his mouth lifted. "Well, then. Perhaps this isn't such a devastating day after all." He reached for her.

They broke apart when the door suddenly opened and the wardrobe mistress walked in on them. "Sergeant!" She sounded scandalized.

"Uh, sorry, Anne-Marie." Marian grabbed Holland's arm and dragged him out, trying not to laugh.

They checked with the stage doorkeeper; Murtaugh hadn't arrived yet. "What time is he supposed to get here?" Holland asked.

"We didn't set a time. But he should have been here before now. I can't make an arrest until I get an all-clear from him. One bit of outstanding evidence still to be nailed down."

"Which one is it—the producer or the director?"

"The producer."

"Well, all we can do is wait," he said. "Meanwhile, let's watch the play."

"By the way," Marian said, "how is it you're able to get into this theater any time you like?"

"Kelly. She had the doorkeeper add my name to his list."

"Um. As far as that goes, how did you know I was here?"

His sardonic smile returned. "You're not the only detective here, you know. When you didn't come back, I looked up 'Zingone' in the phone book and went to their place. One of them had eavesdropped on your conversation with Murtaugh and told me where to find you."

So they'd listened in; she wasn't surprised. "I did try calling once. The line was busy."

"That was Gloria Sanchez. She wanted to tell you that Foley has been found guilty of neglect of duty and is being allowed to resign without a pension."

Marian caught her breath; rough justice, of a sort. *One down; one to go.*

They found a place in the wings to watch from. The second act had just started, and the actors were giving such a high-energy performance that Marian soon got caught up again in the action. Several minutes passed before she realized she could see Captain Murtaugh standing on the other side of the stage. When he knew he had her eye, he lifted one hand in an OK signal.

Marian raised both fists above her head and silently shouted *Yeah!* Holland had witnessed the exchange and nodded at her when she turned to go. She borrowed a flashlight from one of Leo Gunn's assistants and followed the dim red beam around behind the set to the other side of the stage.

Murtaugh beckoned to her and said to John Reddick, "May I use your office?"

"Why not? Everyone else does."

Marian followed the captain into John's office and closed the door. "What?"

"Right outside Paris," Murtaugh said, perching on the corner of the desk. "Over four million in diamonds, emeralds, and rubies, coming by armored van from Antwerp. Three men in ski masks shot out the tires and used a laser beam to cut into the van. The guards were roughed up a little, but no one was seriously hurt. The Sûreté has a good idea of who the three are, but without the stones they can't prove anything. I told them about Ramsay and suggested they look for a connection."

"Four million," Marian repeated. "One mil apiece, if they split equally. *Now* we've got a motive."

"We've also got a warrant to open that safe over there. That's what took so long—I had to track down Judge Agostini."

"Where's Ramsay?"

"I sent two uniforms to pick him up. They'll be here in a few minutes."

"Good. That'll give me time to bring you up to date on something that's happened. DiFalco was here." She went on to tell him about the order transferring the case to the Ninth Precinct, and how DiFalco worked it out for himself that a fur-smuggling operation was behind Ernie Nordstrom's murder.

Murtaugh was both amused and aghast. "The letter's coming through Monday? If those gems aren't in that safe, we've got a problem. And you know DiFalco can suspend you for misleading him, don't you?"

"Captain, I didn't tell him anything that wasn't true. I'm not responsible for *his* mistaken assumptions, am I? I told him repeatedly that I didn't have evidence of a fur-smuggling ring."

"But told him in a way that made him suspicious?"

Marian shrugged. "DiFalco's quite good at jumping to the wrong conclusion. He does it all the time."

"Seems to me you're on thin ice there." He sighed. "But I'm grateful to you for diverting him, even though there'll be repercussions later. I'll see what I can do when the time comes. Right now I want you to go wait by the stage door for Ramsay. Leave one of the officers there."

"Yes, sir." She opened the door to go. "There's one other thing. I've decided not to resign."

His face broke into a smile. "A wise decision, Sergeant. I've felt all along you belong on the force. You enjoy the hunt, you know you do."

"I've always enjoyed the hunt. It was the kill that bothered me."

"And now it doesn't?"

"Now it doesn't."

He nodded approval. "You'll have my recommendation for lieutenant on Monday."

"Thank you, Captain." She went out to the stage door to wait for Gene Ramsay.

19

The stage doorkeeper was edgy, sensing that something was up. He didn't feel any better when the two uniformed officers appeared with the play's producer in tow.

"Marian, what the hell's going on?" Gene Ramsay demanded angrily. "These two won't tell me anything."

"We'll tell you all about it now," she said. "In John's office." She told one of the officers to stay by the door.

Captain Murtaugh was sitting behind the desk; Marian pointed to the chair facing the desk. Ramsay sat down and said, "Well?"

The second police officer closed the door and stood with his back to it; with four people in the small room, the office was uncomfortably close. Murtaugh put a folded court paper on the desk. "That's a warrant," he said, "entitling us to examine and recover the contents of that safe in the corner. You have the combination. Open it."

Ramsay turned white as Marian watched. He swallowed and said, "Why on earth do you want to open that safe? I don't think there's anything in it."

"Let's find out, shall we? Open it."

"I don't remember the combination."

"Then get it. Or I'll get a police locksmith in here. That safe is coming open, one way or another."

Ramsay heard the determination in the captain's voice and abandoned that line of resistance. "Oh, very well. I think I have the combination written down here." He made a show of taking out his billfold and looking for it. "What do you expect to find in the safe?"

"Gems. Stolen gems."

"Oh, really?" His hand was shaking when he turned the dial, but he got the safe open.

Marian moved him aside and looked in; a good-sized canvas carryall made up the entire contents of the safe. Her heart beating rapidly, she put the carryall on the desk in front of Murtaugh. At his nod, she opened it; it held a number of small black velvet bags. Marian picked one up, loosened the drawstring, and upended the bag. About two dozen emeralds spilled out on the desk.

"Jesus," exclaimed the uniformed officer.

"Sergeant," Murtaugh said.

She turned to Ramsay. "You have the right to remain silent. You have—"

"Wait a minute, wait a minute!" he cried. "You aren't arresting *me*? I didn't put those stones there!"

"Yes, you did," Marian said. "You're the only one with the combination to the safe, and you're the only one who could have smuggled those stones into the country." She reached into her shoulder bag and pulled out one of the amber velvet sleeves; Ramsay made a choking sound at the sight of it. Marian looked at his stricken face and said gently, "Gene, it will go easier for you if you cooperate. Once these gems are identified as the ones stolen in France, we have an airtight case. Don't you see? It's all over."

He did see. He buried his face in his hands and shuddered. When he raised his face again, he looked ten years older.

"Your confederates who stopped the van wanted to get the

stones out of France," Marian said. "That's where you came in. You bought the Bernhardt jacket, substituted the real gems for the stage fakes, and got them through customs that way. But back home you had a problem. Everyone knew about the jacket and expected you to donate it to the museum. So you gave the jacket to Kelly Ingram to wear for a few performances and recruited Ernie Nordstrom to burglarize the theater for you—that way no blame would be attached to you when the jacket disappeared. But I don't understand why you didn't just replace the real gems with the stage fakes again. Nobody would have known the difference."

Ramsay was taking short breaths; he ran his tongue over his lips before he answered. "I'm not a costumer. I would have had to hire somebody to do it for me. It was too risky."

"Then how was the switch made in the first place? In France."

"One of my confederates, as you call them—he's a *costumier*, a stage costumer."

"Why not bring him over here to do the job, to switch them back?"

"He's under suspicion in France. The police won't let him leave the country."

Marian looked at Murtaugh; the captain gave a satisfied grunt. "Okay, so you staged the burglary," she said to Ramsay. "Then things really went wrong. Ernie Nordstrom figured out why the jacket was so important, and . . . refused to give it back? Held out for a percentage?"

Ramsay sighed tiredly. "He wanted half. I was willing to cut him in for a piece of my share, but that wasn't enough. He wanted half of the total value or he'd try to fence the stones himself."

"So what happened?"

"Oh, so what started as an argument degenerated into a shouting match. I was ready to punch him in the mouth when the little bastard pulled a knife on me. He pulled a *knife* on me!"

"And?"

"And I was wrestling with him, and I got him to drop the knife. He was going for it when I grabbed up something, that Victorian bellpull, and got it around his neck. I just meant to cut off the oxygen to his brain so he'd pass out." Ramsay looked at Marian, then at Murtaugh. "I didn't think he'd *die*."

Murtaugh said, "We found no knife at the scene."

Ramsay gave a bitter laugh. "Do you want to hear something funny? It was a stage knife. One of those with blades that slide up into the handles. He couldn't have hurt me. I wouldn't have had to . . . to do anything."

The room was silent for a moment. Then Murtaugh said, "What did you do with the knife?"

"Tossed it into one of those boxes he had all over the place. It's still there."

"And then you hid the Bernhardt jacket between two other costumes and left."

"Yes. That's all there was to it. A stupid fight that went stupidly wrong. I didn't intend to kill him. I didn't know people could . . . could die so easily."

One corner of Murtaugh's mouth turned down. "Yes, well. A smart lawyer might make a plea of self-defense work, but you'll still have the jewel-robbery charge facing you. We were planning to check your finances anyway—were you having money problems?"

"No, nothing serious. But when the *costumier* approached me with the scheme, it looked like a million dollars falling into my lap with very little risk for me. They were to do the hard part, no one was to get hurt, and all I had to do was get the jacket out of the country. It looked so simple."

"Yes, these little schemes always do," Captain Murtaugh

said sourly. "And upstanding, law-abiding citizens suddenly discover they have a larcenous streak they never before knew existed. You can try that argument in court, too. You'll probably be extradited to France to stand trial there as well as here, but that's up to the District Attorney."

Marian put the velvet sleeve back in her handbag. "Did you have to ruin the jacket getting the jewels off?"

Ramsay snapped, "I told you, I'm not a costumer."

Murtaugh motioned to the uniformed officer standing by the door. "Take him in."

The producer rose slowly and watched as if hypnotized as the officer pulled out a pair of handcuffs. The sight of those cuffs did something to Ramsay: they made him panic. With a strangled cry he drove his fist into the officer's stomach and pushed the man toward Marian. He was out the door before Murtaugh could get around the desk.

"Gene!" Marian called. "Don't be foolish!"

He started toward the stage door but saw the officer stationed there. He turned back to see Marian and Captain Murtaugh closing in on him. The only way out was through the audience, and the only way into the audience was from the stage. He ran out on to the stage, almost colliding with Ian Cavanaugh. A gasp went up from the audience.

Like a cannonball, Holland shot out from the other side of the stage. He tackled Ramsay, hard and low. The two men crashed into the base supporting the fish tank—and the tank tipped over, drenching them both and spilling its contents to the stage floor.

Xandria Priest screamed. "The fish! Save the fish!"

"Curtain!" Leo Gunn yelled. The curtain closed.

Marian slipped and skidded her way to Ramsay, one of the uniformed officers keeping pace with her and Murtaugh and the other officer not far behind. This time the officer slapped the cuffs on the producer before he could try anything else. "Not a brilliant move, Gene," Marian said. "Now we'll have to add resisting arrest to the charges." Ramsay moaned.

"That was an impressive bit of derring-do," Ian Cavanaugh said smoothly, giving Holland a hand up. "But if you want to go on the stage, it's generally best to audition first."

Marian gave Holland a quick once-over: wet, but not hurt. She turned back to Ramsay. "Now I'm going to do this again, and this time don't interrupt." She read him his rights.

"*Why* are you arresting our producer?" Frieda Armstrong demanded imperiously.

No one answered her. When Murtaugh made sure their prisoner was cuffed, Mirandized, and under control, he turned to Holland. "Are you all right?"

Holland shook his arms and head, shedding some of the water. "I'm not about to burst into song," he said resignedly, "but I'll survive."

"I want to thank you. That was quick thinking and quick acting."

"Thinking had nothing to do with it—it was all instinct. That's one thing the FBI teaches you. Act, don't think."

"You're FBI?"

"Former."

Kelly came running up with a towel. "Curt—here." Holland wiped off his face and looked down. His trousers were clinging to him like a second skin. Almost daintily he wrapped the towel around his waist and hips. Kelly laughed.

Stagehands were busy with mops, and one man was going around with a bucket of water picking up fish. John Reddick was trying to calm everyone down; cast and crew alike were looking at Gene Ramsay in horror, once it sank in on them he was being arrested for murder. The two uniformed officers hauled their prisoner to his feet and led him away.

"Yes, we're going to finish the performance," John Reddick was saying. "Just as soon as—"

"You're not asking us to *finish*?" Xandria Priest broke in loudly. "Well, I can't. My concentration's broken. I'm too upset. I can't finish."

John planted himself in front of her, fists on hips, and said in a voice that silenced everybody: "*Yes. You. Can.*"

Xandria blinked. "Yes, I can."

The director grunted. "The rest of you—take deep breaths, compose yourselves. I've got to make an announcement." He stepped out in front of the curtain. Backstage, they could hear him say, "Ladies and gentlemen, our apologies for this totally unexpected interruption. We intend to finish the performance." A smattering of applause. "Just give us a few more minutes to get squared away back here, and thank you for your patience." He stepped back through the curtain.

Ian said to Marian, "Abby will *die* when she hears what she missed."

The stagehands were rolling up a wet carpet from the stage floor, and the now-empty fish tank was upright once again. The water was all mopped up and Leo Gunn was warning the actors that the damp floorboards could be slippery. They were almost ready to go.

Marian felt a hand on her arm. "How're you doing, kiddo?" Kelly asked.

That was an easy one. "I'm doing just fine, Kel," Marian said with a big smile.

Kelly squeezed her arm and went to take her place. Holland seemed to have disappeared; Marian left the stage and went looking for him. She found him still wearing his towel sarong, talking to Captain Murtaugh.

Murtaugh saw her coming and said, "Well, Sergeant, that was a good day's work. I'll expect you at Midtown South

Monday morning, eight o'clock sharp. I still haven't seen any letter ordering you back to the Ninth, and you have a report to write."

"Yes, sir! I'll be there."

"Holland—thanks again."

A sharp nod in response.

Murtaugh smiled goodbye and left. Leo Gunn's assistants were moving swiftly around the backstage area saying *Quiet, please*. The matinee performance of *The Apostrophe Thief* was ready to resume.

And Marian's stomach growled. "Breakfast's wearing off," she said.

Holland looked down at his wet clothes. "Do you mind stopping off at my place while I change? Then we'll go get something to eat."

Did she mind . . . ? "No, I don't mind," Marian said as casually as she could. Did she mind!

They left the theater and walked four blocks to where Holland had left his car. Although it had been bugging Marian that she didn't know his address, she'd never really wondered about how Holland lived. But now she wanted to see the place. She wanted that very much.

In the car, Marian looked at her watch. "Will we make it in time for the early news? DiFalco may be on."

"DiFalco? Is he back in the picture?"

She told him about the captain's showing up at the Broadhurst and what she'd done. Holland burst into laughter. "It's funny now," she said, "but when he finds out—"

"He's going to feel like ten kinds of idiot," Holland said, still laughing. "Fur smuggling! How did that man ever make captain?"

"I've wondered the same thing myself."

"Nice, Marian—nice." He heartily approved of her exercise in misdirection.

"DiFalco's going to want my hide."

"Perhaps. Take it as it comes."

Holland's place turned out to be an apartment on Central Park West. Two bedrooms, two baths, a dining area, and a balcony opening off the living room. The living room itself was dominated by an entertainment center—big-screen TV, VCR, stereo, tape deck, CD player, laser disk player, amplifiers, speakers, mixers, things Marian knew no names for. The center dominated the room simply because it was the only thing *in* the room. No furniture. No pictures on the walls. Not even a lamp. Nothing to sit on.

The dining area was completely empty. One of the bedrooms contained a computer and all its accoutrements, but nothing else. The bedroom Holland slept in did have a bed, Marian was relieved to see. And a bureau. But the only chair in the entire apartment was the one facing the computer screen.

"I see you go for the minimalist styles," she said dryly.

"What?" Holland looked around as if he'd never seen the place before. "Oh . . . yes, I'll need to buy some furniture." He took a pair of trousers out of the closet.

"I want to watch the news."

"Right." He tossed the trousers on the bed and led the way back to the living room, where he produced a remote control from somewhere. The television screen flared to life.

They watched a Zoning Commission report, forty commercials, a report on an upcoming transit workers' strike, forty more commercials, and then DiFalco was on.

"He didn't waste any time, did he?" Holland murmured.

DiFalco didn't mention Marian, Murtaugh, or Midtown South. He told the reporters—only two of them, he must not have had time to contact everybody—that Ernie Nordstrom's murder was connected to the presence of a fur-smuggling ring operating right here in New York City. He dodged questions about names, details, leads.

"The reason I'm making this announcement," he said earnestly to the camera, "is to warn the people of New York. Don't buy a fur coat from someone you don't know. Stick to established, reputable dealers. And especially don't buy a fur that's offered to you at a discount. One other thing—don't believe what you read on a label. I don't want New Yorkers taken in by this gang." Very public-spirited, Captain DiFalco was.

The show went to a commercial. Marian applauded. "I should have asked Murtaugh when he was going to release the news about Ramsay. Oh, I wish I could see DiFalco's face then!"

"It'll have egg on it," Holland said. "I wonder how he'll try to weasel out."

"By blaming me."

"Will he? Is he going to admit his only source of information was the unsupported word of a detective who's supposed to be under his command but who won't come home? Anything he can say will just make him look all the more foolish."

Marian thought about that. And smiled. "Yeah."

"You may get out of this free and clear." He handed her the remote. "I'm going to change." He went into the bedroom.

Marian turned her back to the screen and inspected the otherwise empty room. A place of residence was supposed to reveal something of the person living there; but this apartment was only a resting place for a transient, a man on the move, a sojourner. All the place told Marian was that Holland liked music and high-tech gadgetry—which she already knew—and that he was able to do without certain creature comforts other people took for granted. His origins, his past . . . they remained as much a mystery as ever.

She clicked off the TV and wandered out to the balcony. From there she could look over Central Park, where the lights were just beginning to come on. "God, I hate mysteries," Marian said.